BENDING TO
BREAK

A BEFORE I BREAK NOVEL

A. L. HARTWELL

COPYRIGHT

Bending to Break is a work of fiction. All names, characters, locations, and incidents are the products of the author's imagination or are used fictitiously. Any resemblance to actual events, locales, or persons, living or dead, is entirely coincidental.

TABLE OF CONTENTS

DEDICATION

To my husband, for always believing in me and for refuting
any self-doubt I ever had about myself or this book. Your love
and patience made it possible. Thank you for always being my
guiding star.

To my mum and dad, I love you both so much and I'm
grateful for your undying support with everything that I do.
But please, on this occasion skip the rude bits!

Jessica, Brittany, and Zak you are the best marketing team a
girl could ever need. Thank you for your fierce support.

And to those that will read this story, thank you for taking a
chance on an unknown author.

CHAPTER ONE

Oliva Heart

The inane chatter around the table made my stomach clench, but I fought my urges to push this meeting on. I had no desire to be here, yet I was bound by my boss' demands to make this right. to fix the problems he had caused. Fingernails tapping against the dark oak table helped force my mind to focus on the room, forced my jaw to soften, forced myself not to speak yet. My boss, Jackson Bells, had positioned us to fail right from the get-go when he had taken on this case.

Inconsiderate asshole

Now I'm anxious and dealing with a case that made my skin crawl.

Jessica, to my right, nervously placed the coffee down in front of our very unimpressed client. I had tried to throw her a sympathetic smile, but she barely looked up from her curtain of lovely red hair. Could I blame her? No, not really.

"So, what you're saying, Mr. Bells, is that my son is going to jail?" Archer Caine blistered, spittle flying from his wrinkled lips as he glared over at my boss.

Jackson barely flinched as he crossed his hands on the table, highlighting the new Rolex Submariner he had recently purchased. It was ostentatious just like its new owner, whose blonde hair had been slicked back, his clothes crisp and fitted with designer privilege.

"Only for two weeks, Mr. Caine. Given the circumstances surrounding your son's case, this is really a win for you both."

"A win!? A fucking win?! Are you out of your god damn mind?"

There it was, the anger that I had been waiting for. In this job, you get used to seeing people fall apart, and it was always my job to put them back together.

Clearing my throat, I bought the attention of the room onto me.

"Sir, given your son's accused crime and the evidence stacked against him, it would be in his interest to accept the deal. If the deal isn't accepted within the next twenty-four hours, we're looking at court. We're looking at seven years in jail."

I surveyed his initial reaction of disgust as I, a woman, had interrupted his rage, but he quickly fell apart in my hands. I was holding his precious son's life in front of him with an unforgiving stare.

I was not to be messed with.

My deal's golden.

I hadn't worked my ass off for the past two weeks to let this get away from me.

Leaning in, I swept away my dark hair and pushed my prepared file across the table.

"Take it or leave it," I said boldly. "You won't get anything better."

"Olivia!" Jackson hissed, as he reached to touch my elbow, but I was prepared for this, too. Snatching out of his grip, I leaned back into my chair where he could no longer touch me and surveyed the room.

Jackson was irate with anger, his chin wobbling under his fierce emotions. Jessica was trying her hardest not to shake while she waited to take further notes. Mr. Caine was still blinking away his anger towards me while the clogs in his brain continued to turn.

Scott Caine at his father's side simply glared at me.

Scott Caine was everything I hated about my job. Privileged teenagers with no set of rules or boundaries to live by. Scott had recently been accused of trying to sleep with a drunken teenager at a frat party. The victim had refused to press charges but the cops in charge of the case had pressed on.

Money and power allowed him to step into a corrupt system and come out unscathed.

I felt sick to my stomach every time I sat in a room with the predator, but I kept it locked away and allowed my repulsion to simmer. Even when I had caught him staring down my blouse or licking his lips as he ogled my body – I remained neutral.

"Miss Heart, he'll take it," Mr. Caine said, as he snatched up the paperwork, his stubby hands trembling while he opened the file, ready to force his delinquent son to sign away his freedom for a measly moment in time.

****

A. L. Hartwell

An hour later, I found myself staring at the small square mirrors in the bathrooms after the tense hour Jackson had forced me into. I should not be doing this. I shouldn't be in charge of brokering deals for the evil that stalked New York's streets. At twenty-five-years-old, I was just making my way into a career that I was not certain about, telling myself that once I was qualified, I could put myself to work. To start doing good in the justice system that had done so little for me.

Instead, as I stared into my deep green eyes, all I saw was the wearing down of my soul. All I saw was the fraying of my consciousness while my heart battled with white fingertips to keep the rest of me whole.

I shook away the dread and stood back. I began quickly smoothing down my black pencil skirt, and straightening my white silk blouse while mentally preparing myself for the next meeting.

A banker who had been caught cleaning money for a drug pin.

Taking the lift to my floor, I pulled myself together, ignoring the warm bodies that joined me as we made our way up.

As the door pinged open, I stepped out and found Jessica waiting for me at my desk. Jessica had only been with us for three weeks, even with her nerves she was efficient and eager. Jessica was from Ireland, but her accent had been dulled since she spent the past ten years living in Albany and now New York.

"Jackson's cancelled the next meeting," she told me, with a relieved smile. "Said something's come up with an important client."

An important client probably meant 'off the book client' which did not faze me. I was very aware of Jackson and his black book of clientele that would supply him with a further wage. I was grateful that he had never once involved me with this side of his business. I already dealt with enough heathens; I didn't need the worst of them adding to my list.

"Okay, can you send me tomorrow's meeting list?" I asked, taking my seat at my desk and kicking my heels off as I switched on my computer.

"It's already in your email." She smiled and stood up, no doubt to make me another coffee so that she could keep her nervous energy at bay.

"You really are a godsend Jessica," I muttered, as I entered my password to my computer before groaning aloud. There really weren't enough hours in the day to get through my emails.

CHAPTER TWO

Olivia Heart

B y the time I'd pulled my body from my desk, my skull was already throbbing with pain and exhaustion. Having spent the past five hours working through my caseload, I had forgotten all sense of time and become lost in my computer.

I called my uber and left. I was fortunate enough to live in the Upper East side, thanks to a condition with my job. It was an added sweetener for me to take the position, and at the time, I was thrilled. The old building was deceptive from the street as it sat back slightly from its neighbors with tall windows on each floor. It was the perfect balance between homely and showy.

As I entered the building, my iPhone alarm screamed up at me. I needed to call my Aunt Sarah to catch up. These days, my whole life was scheduled so that I wouldn't forget a thing. Pulling up her contact details, I shimmied my bag up my arm and waited for the ring.

"About bloody time," she chided, after she picked up on the third ring.

"I'm sorry," I apologized. I truly was, I hadn't called her in weeks and knew she would be worrying sick about me.

"I know you are, Love," she breathed in her perfect English accent, that reminded me so much of home and what I was missing. "Just coming in from work?"

I pressed the number four on the elevator and sank back into the wall. "Yes, it's been a long day."

In the background, I could hear the tv was on and someone was snoring softly. It was no doubt Sarah's dog, Otto. I smiled at the thought of the little terrier tucked in at her side, protecting her.

"Want to talk about it?" she asked softly, no doubt ready for me to tell her it wasn't anything important. Like I always did.

Today, however, I wanted to tell her.

"I had this kid accused of rape on my caseload. I know he did it, hell I could see it in his eyes."

Sarah sucked in a deep breath and the phone buzzed in my ear.

"You were just doing your job."

I leaned my head back against the cool metal as I continued to climb in the metal box and closed my eyes. If only that would stem the guilt, I felt for the poor girl that he had tried to molest.

"I'm not sure I can do this anymore," I whispered suddenly, my barrier falling and the floodwater rushing in. "I'm not sure it's worth it Aunt Sarah, the people that I deal with, these men with money don't care for the damage they're doing..."

"Oh Love," she whispered softly. "You can't take it all on your shoulders like this, it's not healthy."

Suddenly, I wasn't a twenty-five-year-old woman that had a budding career and stability. I was a teenager who needed her aunt to console her against the evil that lurked in every corner

15

of the earth. Maybe it was the sound of her accent or her pet name for me, but I never felt more homesick.

"You can always come home and finish up here. I know it's not ideal, but if you're unhappy...."

I felt my throat constrict at the last word I heard but was saved by the beep of the elevators opening. A gentle reminder not to dwell.

"I'm just tired. I'm sorry, I shouldn't have unloaded on you like that. How's things at home?"

"We're good here. Alice is coming to pick me up to go wedding dress shopping tomorrow. Isn't that exciting?"

I felt a pang of guilt as I stuck my key into my apartment door. I had been invited to my cousin Alice's wedding that was in a few weeks, but there had been no move from me to book the time off yet. A subject I did not want to bring up yet.

As I stepped into my welcoming apartment, I searched for the light that led into my hallway, my fingers pressing down on the switch.

Click.

Nothing.

"Er, Aunt Sarah, can I call you back? The power's out in my apartment."

All I could see was a faint outline of my hallway from the light my phone provided.

"Of course! Ring me as soon as you can."

"I won't be long."

I ended the call and used the phone light to guide me down the hall. All I needed was a glass of wine and a long hot shower, not the possibility of being without power while I waited for maintenance. Especially, given that the maintenance manager was a pervy sixty-year-old man who smelled of cheap liquor and cigarettes.

Huffing to myself, I dropped my bag on the side table before entering the kitchen. All I needed to do was find the damn fuse box, which I was pretty certain was here somewhere.

Kicking off my heels, I squinted into the darkness as I tried to remember where I had seen the fuse box. Just as my eyes landed on the small white cupboard, I felt my body react to the darkness.

I paused and listened for any unusual sounds, but shook my head. The darkness had many ways of playing with fears and I wasn't going to let that get to me. I pushed away the shiver that rippled down my spine and opened the cupboard to find all the switches had been pulled out.

"What the-"

Freezing cold shivers shot back up my spine as I stepped back. Goosebumps decorated my body as my eyes fixed themselves to the missing fuses. Teetering on the balls of my feet, I landed into a firm body.

I tried to turn, but arms snaked around my chest and pulled me back. My airways snapped shut as they gave in to fear; my hands desperately fought to push my attacker away, but my strength was no match.

"It's okay," I heard the rough grumble of a voice I didn't know while their hands snaked up to my throat. "Don't fight it."

I felt a scream bubble up into my throat as my useless body was pulled further back and out of the kitchen into the living room. Away from the knives, I had subconsciously tried to grab. My ankle gave way and I dropped, but that didn't matter.

My captor was strong and hoisted me back up to his chest with one hand.

"This will help," he uttered, stabbing me in the neck with something sharp. The only noise to have slipped out of my mouth was the yelp from the pain I felt as I tried to free my hand to pull away the needle still there.

It was too late. I could feel the burning liquid searing underneath my skin as it began to dull my senses. The liquid was whispering for me to give in and remain still. It was now two against one.

I began to tumble down into strong arms as the liquid fought my nervous system. Even as I tried desperately to stay in the moment, I knew it wouldn't be long before I was rendered useless.

My last-ditch of desperation was to turn my head so that I could see my intruder. It was my last hope. My intruder wore all black, blending into the darkness.

I tried to open my mouth to scream for help, but instead, my voice box shut down. A gargle of shock trickled out of my lips as my arms twitched for escape. My body was no longer under my control.

"In a few minutes, you will fall asleep," he whispered, while he stroked my hair away from my face, his warm fingers lulling me closer to the subconscious. "You're safe, Miss Heart. I promise."

The darkness around us laughed.

CHAPTER THREE

Luca Caruso

M y eyes betrayed me as they stared out of the small circular window, looking down the dark private runway that was half-hidden with darkness. I hated impatience more than anything on this earth. It was infection to the brain that could make you indecisive and weak. I was not weak. My whole life was structured around controlling myself and those around me. A king that sat on his throne while he took what he wanted.

But the impatience seeped from my fingertips as they tapped on my armrest. I needed to pull myself together before it was too late.

A cloud of desperation hung over my shoulders while I waited for what was mine. It had been hours, and yet, we were still stuck on the cold tarmac of New York City.

"How long?" I demanded. "You said it would take an hour, Chen. We've been here for three."

"Two minutes, sir," Chen Zil, my security advisor said, as he swept past my seat to prepare the doors. Chen was of mixed ethnicities. Pitch black hair that was immaculately slicked to the side, matching perfectly with his even darker eyes and contrasted against his tanned skin. I had chosen him personally due to his impeccable record of keeping people like me safe.

Two minutes and Chen's team would bring on the most precious cargo to have ever graced this private jet. In two minutes, my whole life was going to change. In that short fraction of time, I was going to get my reward for being so fucking patient. Eight years I had waited for this moment, a moment that was not all of what I had hoped for, but I was an opportunist.

It was supposed to be me who had gone to that apartment, me who would have coaxed my target to come willingly, but that had been snatched from me due to incompetence beyond my control.

"Sir, they're on the runway now."

A shot of adrenalin punched my heart as I looked out of the window to see a black Mercedes making its way towards us. In the back of that car was eight million dollars' worth of what I wanted.

What I needed.

I smoothed down my trousers and stood up to meet Chen at the door. The plane doors were now open, allowing the ice-cold weather of New York to seep into my body. It couldn't deter me from catching this moment as the back door of the car opened and one of Chen's men slipped out.

A quick nod up to us, he leaned back into the car, his legs tensing as he picked up my precious gift and pulled her out.

My knees locked into place as I finally saw her sleeping peacefully in his arms. Peering down the darkened steps, I saw the soft glint of her skin from the runway lights, her long flowing hair as it poured over his arm, she was beautiful and safe.

Mine.

As they ascended the stairs, I felt a rush like no other. My body zinged with purpose and excitement, while I stared down at the face that had haunted me for eight years. All the agony and frustration had disappeared so suddenly that I was almost breathless.

Olivia Heart was everything I remembered. The closer she got, the stronger my pull to her was. I couldn't *control* myself as I stepped forward to get a better look at her. Even in sleep, she was a picture of perfection with her face pressed to a man she didn't know.

I glared.

"Give her to me!" I demanded, with cold authority. *"Presto!"*

Olivia's weight was distributed into my waiting arms and I wasted no time in pulling us both back into my world. As I moved down the plane, I looked down at her, my eye's not quite believing that she was here.

In the short walk to my chair, I studied her face. The thick dark lashes were the same, her plump lips, a delicious pink that contrasted against her pale skin. The only thing different about her was the perfume, gone was the soft vanilla, replaced with sensual woody tones of a woman that had blossomed in eight years.

Softly placing her down on the chair across from me, I efficiently strapped her in and gently leaned her head to rest against the window. It was only when she was bathed in the plane's warm light, did I really see her, truly see her.

"Why the fuck are her lips blue!?" I hissed, turning around in my seat to glare at Chen.

Chen's face remained frozen as he regarded me cautiously. "Nothing more than the cold air, sir." He nodded to end the conversation. I snapped my fingers for the air hostess who was making her way towards us and demanded a blanket.

As I waited, I let myself look at her once again, to drink her in before both our lives changed. Olivia's small frame was hidden mostly by her mahogany hair that cascaded down her chest, she was thinner than I expected, but it suited her frame. Allowing my eyes to travel, I admired that she was all legs in a skirt that highlighted her tiny waist.

All business. Olivia's attire told me everything I needed to know; she had only been home minutes before she was snatched away. A hard worker with a need to complete her tasks before she permitted rest. Was she as controlling as I was?

A few of the recent reports had suggested she was not into socializing with people from work, or those that had tried to befriend her in her apartment complex, an outsider whose drive outweighed her needs for relationships.

My eyes continued to scan her and rested on the black heels that had miraculously stayed on her small feet.

Fuck.

"Sir," the blonde air hostess whose name I had already forgotten, interrupted my thoughts as she placed a blanket on my sleeping guest, as if this was an everyday occurrence.

I watched cautiously while the blanket was pressed into the crooks of her elbows to ensure it stayed on during our trip.

I wanted to touch her again, but denied myself the pleasure until she was awake, until she was aware of who I was and my role in her new future.

Leaning back in my chair, I turned away to meet the eyes of Chen who was buckling up in the seat behind my new guest. Only Chen and I had travelled together, but we were leaving with a team of men who took their seats around me. These men had lived in the shadows of Olivia's life for the past four years to serve me, to protect her.

Now, they were returning with me to carry on their one task.

"The doctor will meet us once we land, sir," Chen interrupted, as he eyed me over Olivia's sleeping head.

I nodded stiffly before I let my eyes wander back to Olivia. Under that curtain of luscious hair, would be a small needle prick where the necessary had to be done. I wasn't thrilled with the idea, but it was the safest extraction plan that Chen and his team had.

In the next few hours, there would be another dose to keep her sedated while we travelled home, to my home in Sicily. It wasn't wise to allow her to meet me for the second time in a space that I couldn't control if she lashed out, so Chen would be the one to administer the prepared dose that sat on the table in between us.

Letting my eyes slide back to her, I tried to swallow the raging emotions coursing through my body as she sat perfectly still, like a royal statue ready to wake and wreak havoc on my life.

"We're good to go," Dante, my cousin said, whilst he took the seat to my left, his shirt crumpled, and tie shoved in his pocket. Dante had weaponized his good looks on some poor air hostess who would have to spend the next seven hours attending to him.

"She good?" he asked me, his eye's trying to get a good look at her.

Shifting in my chair, I thought about the weighted question as I let my eyes rest on her peaceful face.

"She's fine now."

Now that she was sedated, stolen, and placed in my hold, she would be fine. Safe.

Protected.

"Is she everything you remembered?" Dante asked cautiously, knowing that my temper tends to strike hot around the subject of her.

Was she everything I remembered? No, she wasn't.

Olivia was more.

It had always been easier to forget that in our time apart, we were both changing. My eyes were greedy as they continued to search for the small changes I had missed through my weekly reports.

"I'm sure I'll find out when she's awake. Did Mr. Bells send the signed paperwork?"

Dante smirked at me, letting me know that he had done what I had asked. "Yes, it's in your email. Do you want me to start closing the banks and leases?"

My cousin had the knack of ensuring that whatever strange business I dragged us both in, he would act as though it was the most normal thing in the world. Nothing fazed Dante, he was not locked in with control like me, but he also provided me with intermittent reprieves when I needed to let go. Simply an ear to borrow, to listen, or to do as I ask.

"Yes, close them down. We need to clear this up as quickly as possible."

Just as I finished, I felt the familiar whir of the plane's engines kick into life, and I felt my chest expel a small fraction of air that I had been holding.

We had been on this runway far too long and I was grateful to get moving. In seven hours, I would be back where I belong with the woman that belonged to me.

CHAPTER FOUR

Olivia Heart

I felt hungover. My stomach was tense, my head throbbed and my mouth, God my mouth felt thick with fluff. If I opened my eyes too quickly, I was certain that I would throw up, so I stayed on my back, taking in small bits of air while I tried to ignore the throbbing in my skull.

Testing my body, I stretched out, my eyes still firmly closed, and let my bare legs glide over the silk sheets.

Silk sheets? I didn't have silk sheets.

Snapping my eyes open, I was hit with a severe wave of nausea that forced me to close them again with a groan. How much had I drunk last night? I don't even remember having plans.

The pain in my skull snapped its fingers at me for attention.

Slowly retesting the waters, I lifted my body up by using my elbows and took in a steady breath. Cracking one eye open, I let my fuzzy gaze blur out before my eye refocused, alerting me to the sudden change in environment.

In seconds, my hangover worsened with added panic as I stared around a bedroom that wasn't mine.

The bed that held my body was not mine.

My bed was soft and cream, this bed was a large ornate four-poster bed with soft white drapes and white silk sheets. I whipped my head and groaned as my stomach rolled from the swift action. The whole room was the same size as my apartment with so many stark differences.

Had I gone out last night?

Was I in some one-night stands house?

Was I in *Simon's* house?

I can't be. That wasn't me.

My eyes were sluggish to respond as they tried to focus on the room, importing every new detail into my brain. The floor was tiled with a beautiful white and grey slate that looked expensive. The furnishings were soft and feminine, but with all modern clean lines. To the right of the bed, there was an open door to what looked to be a walk-in wardrobe. In front of me, across the vast room, there was a large door that held an open plan bathroom.

I didn't understand.

Scrambling up the bed only made me focus on my body. I wasn't wearing my clothes. I was wearing someone else's. Gone was my white blouse and black skirt, replacing them was a blush baby doll dress.

The sickness rolled around in my stomach as I peered down at my body. This was an item of clothing that I would never wear, ever. Grabbing the hem of the dress, I peeked to check that I was wearing my *own* underwear. A small sigh of relief fell past my lips when I saw that I was.

A second wave of panic hit me when I noticed that my bag and shoes were not by the side of the bed. Swinging my legs over the edge of the mattress, I fought back another urge to wretch and rubbed my neck that had decided to join the party of confusing pain.

Where's my phone?

I felt my spine tense when my fingers touched a tiny scab on the side of my neck.

Then I remembered.

I could feel it happening once again as I fell into the dark memory of my blind panic as I fought off an attacker in my kitchen. I remember the hard body of a chest against my back as I was pinned into submission. It must have happened in seconds.

I remembered the pain in my neck.

My hands scratching up to remove the needle.

I propelled myself away from the bed and towards the bathroom as I felt my stomach betray me. Retching over the toilet, I felt my stomach roll and my chest burn as I began to purge the drugs that had kept me from fighting.

Hot tears stung my eyes when I pulled away, my body already struggling to contain itself. My heart was seized with fright, but my brain refused to give in. As I struggled to catch my breath, I recounted all the moments leading up to this. I had left the safety of an uber, only to have walked into the danger of my own home. The power had been out, and I was so worried about having to wait around for the maintenance man that I hadn't realized there was someone lurking in the darkness.

My body began to shake as I pushed away from the toilet. I needed to get out of here before it was too late. The average time to escape a kidnapping had shortened dramatically now that I had been moved to a secondary place. Even if I could push myself up, I was certain I wouldn't remain upright for long – but I would try.

What the hell had they given me?

Get up Olivia. Now!

My lungs burned wickedly and painfully in panic. My chest heaved with terror, but my brain was sluggishly still trying to catch up, to clear the grey fog. Just as I was about to wretch again, I felt cool fingers hook on my shoulders and pull me back from the toilet.

"Pick her up Red," I heard a deep voice hiss from behind me.

I froze.

My eyes were now ringing with the sounds of shoes squeaking on the perfectly polished floor. Lashing away from the intruders, I began to scramble my useless limbs to the corner of the room.

A cold hand returned to my body, gripping my ankle and yanking me back. I turned quickly, my head searing with pressure as I looked up to find four men dressed in black suits staring down at me.

"Don't fucking touch me," I hissed, before kicking my attacker with my left foot, only for it to bounce pathetically off his ankle. "Get away!"

I tried desperately to see his face, to memorize something about him so I could squirrel it away in my brain for when I would escape. Instead, all I saw was a darker grey silhouette that gripped tighter and slid me across the floor.

"Don't fight it, Miss Heart," I heard from the corner of the room, as my attacker yanked me up into his hard chest, pinning both my hands in one of his.

I could smell him, he smelled of fresh soap and cigarettes, but it was not enough to identify him. As I squinted up, I was thrust forward before my eyes could reach his.

The pressure in my skull was unbearable while I was dragged helplessly from the bathroom, into the bedroom, and then what I believed to be a hallway. I felt curses fall away from my mouth and my legs desperately fighting to keep me upright.

"The harder you fight, the worse it will get," I heard in front of me. It wasn't a voice I recognized. There wasn't a hint of emotion in the gruff voice which made my fear peak to disastrous levels.

My head fell forward as the sickness rolled once again.

"Where are you taking me?" I cried, when I felt a soft carpet underneath my bare feet. The light was brighter in this room, I knew this from the grey silhouettes brightening and their shapes suddenly becoming more defined.

"The sickness hasn't stopped in twenty minutes. You need to do something and now," I heard someone bark from the corner of the new room, but again, I couldn't identify the voice. All I knew was that their voice was different from those I had already heard. It was rich, dark, and held a thick accent.

I was thrust into what felt like a soft chair. It was so quick, that my loose hair covered most of my face. Yanking away my hand, I quickly pushed my hair away and squinted into the room. I needed to see something. I needed to give my brain something to latch onto before I lost it completely.

"Has she eaten?" I heard the soft melodic voice of a woman that had an English accent and cried.

"No."

"Okay, hold her down."

A bubble of panic squeezed my chest when I tried to run, but once again, I was captured by large hands, more than one set as I was gripped and pinned down. The bubble of panic popped and suddenly my eyes were clear, torturously clear as I saw many dark eyes staring down at me.

Before my brain could speak to my tongue, to articulate the fear it felt from being pinned by several men with guns held to their hips, I was jabbed in my left arm. I flinched away at the sharp invasion.

"That's for the sickness," the female's voice cooed in my ear, as her perfectly polished fingernails pulled away.

Red nails.

"You'll start to feel better soon."

"Please," I begged, my voice suddenly hoarse. "Let me go, please just let me go – I can't breathe!"

I was trying with all my might to free myself, but I barely made my captors move. I was weak and weightless, a feather that they had pinned underneath their pinky fingers.

Hot tears sprung to my eyes as their hands began to paint bruises against my skin. I was suffocating under their touch, desperate to break free for just one moment. Even in my terror, I was aware that the thin straps of my barely their nightgown were slipping down my shoulders, ready to reveal my chest.

"Why are you doing this to me?" I cried, as I tried to hit out at the guy who had pinned my right leg. "What do you want from me?"

"*Merda*," I heard hiss from the corner, the rich tones of an Italian accent travelling to my ears like someone had screamed right next to me. "Put her out."

"No!" I screamed, my own shrill scream wiping away all noise in the room. "Don't you touch me! Don't you dare touch me with that-"

My scream was interrupted by a set of cold hands leaning into the pile of men pinning me down and grabbed my jaw, lifting me to meet a pair of hazel eyes that brandished honey hues.

My brain fuzzed and misfired. It was trying to warn me about these dark eyes that pinned my soul back into my body, controlling every breath that I took. I knew by the way this person's possessive hands held my face that this was my captor. I watched as his lips curled, ready to speak to me once again.

Instead, my brain fought when my body couldn't.

I spat at him, my saliva slipping down his face, which forced him to painfully release me in disgust.

A vicious hand slipped from my shoulder and pinned itself over my mouth, preventing me from fighting any further. It didn't matter, this was one small victory that I had over them all.

I sank my teeth into the hand over my mouth.

"Fuck!"

Before I could bask in my small victory, another needle stabbed into my arm, unlike the first needle, I began to feel the effects instantly. My fired blood was suddenly turning to a soft burn, my strength was faltering alongside it and my eyes were returning to the grey haze.

"No," I mumbled, as I felt hands slowly release me and a cozy warmth spread over my body. My muscles had no choice but to obey as the liquid invader infiltrated, wrapping me up in warm hands.

"Don't hurt me, please, please don't hurt me."

My eye lids fluttered closed even as I screamed at myself to stay awake. The noises around me sounded so far away once again and I knew I had seconds left.

"Why?" I whispered, hoping that someone would hear me and answer before the darkness ripped me away.

"We can't keep dosing her up like this," I heard the woman again, her voice cold and distant. "If we do, we risk it affecting her heart muscles which could cause her further issues down the line."

"This will be the last time," the thick Italian accent was back again, hissing in my ears.

"I need to put her on an intravenous drip."

No, no more needles.

"That wasn't in your plan, Miss Williams," he growled back, his voice dangerously low.

The warm hands hugged me tighter.

"Plans change, Mr. Caruso. Miss Heart will be incredibly weak and sick when she wakes up if we don't implement this now."

It couldn't get any worse than this. Let the drugs kill me.

"I don't like this. I don't fucking like this," he hissed back, before I heard the slam of his hand against a solid surface.

"We'll take her back to her room, sir," this voice was louder than the rest, it was right next to my head.

I felt warm hands pick me up, holding me to their chest as they distributed my weight and supported my back. I felt weightless now that the drugs had taken over, pulling me further into the abyss.

"Fine, but I want a fucking report when you're done. Do you understand?"

"Yes, sir."

I felt my limbs sway as we began to move, the soft rocking was pushing me further and further into sleep and the helplessness was being phased out by the drug teeming in my system. I wished I had been stronger to fight it, to fight them, but I was simply no match. Not at all.

CHAPTER FIVE

Olivia Heart

I don't remember the exact moment when my brain sparked back to life, but I'll always remember the lack of fear I had when I opened my eyes to a familiar dark room. Sitting up in a daze, with my fingertips gripping the top of the sheets, I glanced at my hand that was covered with a small band-aid.

A rush of memories spiraled, screaming at me that I was under threat and tried to force me to move. As I hazily sorted through them, I realized that my terror was dulling, my heart spluttered before returning to its gentle drum in my chest. I couldn't *force* myself to be scared, couldn't conjure the feeling to blaze action back into my body. I was weak, frighteningly weak, as I remembered the men that had dragged me to a separate room to drug me once again.

Goosebumps raised up on my arms, but my brain barely twitched at the fear I should have felt. My lungs didn't squeeze painfully, my toes didn't tense, and my hands barely moved. My emotions were frozen either in shock or from the drugs – either way, I was screwed.

"Don't worry, it will wear off soon," I heard from the corner of the room. Perfect English with a clipped Italian accent alerted me to him. I was certain whoever had spoken was the man I had seen before I was knocked back out.

A flash of large hands grabbing me over the pile of men pinning me down blazed through my head. I could feel his fingers tightly grabbing my chin as he tried to speak.

A gasp fell from my lips as I scrambled the sheets around my body, desperately looking to see the invader of my room and thoughts.

From the shadow in the corner of the room, he stepped forward, the moonlight spilling from the crack in the blinds lighting across his face.

I still couldn't force my body to react to the fear, but my soul knew that my life was in danger, it began to stretch and pull away from my core.

As I looked up, I remembered seeing him before I was drugged. I remember his dark eyes haunting and cold as he tried to force me to submit. Even in the poor lighting, I knew he was teeming with anger. I could feel it rolling from him as his eyes drank me in, waiting to see how much fight I had left in me.

Formidable and cold, he stood broadly before me with honey tanned skin, pitch-black hair that was tailored to his look of youth. To match his perfect jaw, he had full lips and a straight nose. Masculine and young, he was a model fresh from an Armani campaign but with broad shoulders and muscles.

"Who are you?" I croaked, my throat sore from screaming and lack of water.

"Luca Caruso," he told me carelessly, as he moved back into the darkness, his fingers flicking on a lamp. As the light sparked into the room, he took a seat in a large cream chair that sat by the window. Leaning back, he surveyed me calmly while waiting for me to speak again.

"You drugged me," I tried to scream, to be forceful but all that came from my dry lips was a soft whisper.

We were cocooned in the warm light of the lamp, making it harder for me to concentrate. I needed to force my brain and limbs into action. My life depended on it, but all I wanted to do was place my head back on the pillow and drown in sleep.

"You were… upset," he announced, the hint of an Italian accent returning on the last word that rolled from his tongue. "So upset, that you spat in my face," he growled, as we both remembered at the same time.

I pulled the sheets further around me and saw my hands shaking, at least my stupid body knew I was under immense threat.

"Why am I here?"

Sighing, he leaned forward and rubbed his face, trying to expel some of his anger, but he didn't succeed. The shoulders of my captor only wound tighter as he looked up at me, his nostrils narrowing as he sucked in air.

"That's a loaded question, Miss Heart, and not one I'm willing to answer now. Just know that you're safe."

Safe?

I ignored him. I knew I wasn't safe; I was far from anything remotely safe. If that were true, I wouldn't have been kidnapped and drugged, I would be on the phone with my Aunt Sarah, talking about weddings. My stomach dropped as I remembered the last conversation I had with her, promising her that I would call her back. Was she worrying? Was anyone worrying?

"Where am I?" my voice was climbing to the top of desperation as the fog in my brain shifted slightly.

Hidden in his emotionless stare, he cleared his throat to answer me. "Sicily."

I finally felt the squeeze of death as my fear kicked in. Sickness rolled in my stomach when I looked towards the curtains. I wanted to propel myself towards the window, to rip away the curtains and see for myself. Betrayed once again by my body, I simply sat still with my building anxiety.

All I needed was a breakthrough in the fog so I could pull myself out.

Get it together Olivia.

"How long have I been here?" I whispered, as I pulled my eyes away from his face. I couldn't stomach to look at him any longer. I focused on the artwork across the room that sat proudly on the wall. A single-painted Strelitzia with its purple and orange hues taunting me. A flower that represented freedom and the irony was not lost on me.

"Four days," he replied. There was no emotion in his voice to help me deem whether he was telling the truth. The man watching me, carefully leaned back into his chair, preying on me from his throne.

I flinched. "How did you get me here?" I asked. I returned my eyes back to his, willing my brain to remember all the smaller details about him. Enough to build a case.

Luca moved slightly to straighten out his cuffs, showing me two tattoos across his wrists. If my head were clear, I would have stored them in my memory, but I simply glazed over them.

"We took you from your apartment to a private runway. It took them a total of fifteen minutes."

Was he pleased with himself?

Fifteen minutes was all that it took to infiltrate my life. In fifteen minutes, I could walk to work, have a shower, eat breakfast, but also be kidnapped, stolen, and moved without knowing it.

"The men that pinned me down?" I whispered, my voice trembling as I remembered the possibility of four of them. "They took me, on your orders?"

Luca nodded before sitting back, his face was only half bathed in warm light now. In this lighting, he looked dangerous as he watched me.

"We had to move quickly. They're a team that have been hired by me to protect you."

I closed my eyes to block him out, to concentrate on feeling anything but exhaustion. I knew the moment I laid eyes on him that I had been given something else. I was subdued and delayed. Would he keep plying me with these drugs, numbing me up so that he could hurt me without me being able to fight?

Had he already taken from me?

"What are you going to do to me?"

Standing up, he shoved his hands into his pockets and glanced at me once before shaking his head. As he moved, the warm shadows bounced across his skin, highlighting his collar bone where another tattoo sat proudly on his skin. I tried to force my eyes to evaluate the dark lines but couldn't. I was sinking into unconsciousness as my hands let go of the sheets and my body began to slip back down onto the bed.

My brain screamed at him to demand an answer. Wild thoughts of drug rings, prostitution, and sex slaves ran through my mind. I wanted desperately to claw at him, to run away back to my normal life, but my body had other plans.

"Tomorrow," I heard him start, his rich accent luring me deeper into the shadows. "I'll explain this all to you tomorrow Olivia. You need to rest now, don't fight it any longer. Your new life can wait a few more hours."

I knew he had gotten up by the faint sound of the chair squeaking. As he moved through the room, I noticed his smell, expensive and clean, not like I had expected. Somewhere faint in the background, I heard the turn of a handle and then nothing. I was enveloped once again in silence.

CHAPTER SIX

Luca Caruso

I shouldn't have gone to see her, but *fuck*. I was supposed to wait and allow her to adapt to her new beginnings, but instead, I had found myself sat staring at her as she slept. My fingers had twitched to smudge away the faint line of mascara under her right eye, to smooth away her damp hair, to place the sheets over her, but I forced myself to remain statue still.

Two hours had slipped by as I watched the rise and fall of her milky chest. There haven't been many moments where I have sat for that long with just my thoughts, but I found it a difficult but satisfying task. Difficult because of the situation, but satisfying because only my eyes guarded her tonight.

Originally, I had gone to bathe her in my anger from her obnoxious treatment towards me, the moment she spat in my face, I almost lost all sense of who I was. I felt vitriol spill into my veins quicker than any man-made poison. Instead, I found myself quietly observing her – forgiving her, wanting her to wake up.

"Shit."

This wasn't what I wanted. Years ago, I had made a promise to myself not to interfere, to let the universe take control, but now, I found myself in a rare position that I hadn't been prepared for. I made a choice within five minutes. In those five minutes, I had set a motion of pure destruction in the hopes that I could fight off the universe's plan to take away my only source of happiness.

It was still up for debate whether I had it in me to fight further.

Slipping into my office, I wasn't so surprised to see Dante with his feet up on my desk as he chugged back whiskey that had been a gift from his mother.

"How's it going Lucie?" he said, with a smirk that he reserved for his teasing. Only Dante knew when he could push my buttons, after spending his life glued to my side, he was the only person I let piss me off without consequences.

"Fine," I lied, as I snatched up the bottle of whiskey from the table and poured myself a glass.

Dante had the grace to give me a moment to take a sip before calling me out on my shit.

"You're out of your depth," he breathed, as he noisily placed his glass down on my desk. "What's your plan now?"

I felt my jaw clench at the insult but decided to let it slide. I couldn't deny his view of the situation was correct, but it didn't make it any easier to tolerate.

"I'll speak to her tomorrow," I bristled. "She'll have no choice but to submit to her new life here."

Dante didn't miss a beat. "Choice, no, but she will fight cousin. Women like her won't just accept a situation like this. You need to be smart moving forward, you need to-"

I slammed my glass down on the table which made him flinch. Brittle was my temper right now and I didn't need him telling me how fucked the situation was or how to handle it. In thirty-two years of being alive, I had fought through far more dangerous situations than this one.

"I know what I'm doing," I glowered at him, but he barely flinched, instead, he shrugged carelessly and picked his glass back up.

"I hope you do." He smirked. "Because she's an *ardente* force that will either bring you to your knees or keep you warm at night."

"What do you know about her?" I snapped with a dismissive hand, as I tapped my computer back to life.

"I know everything that you do, remember? I have been with you for the past eight years as we kept watch."

This isn't what I needed to hear, and he knew it. Dante couldn't leave well enough alone with his misplaced worry. It was me that was doing this and not him. I didn't need him to burden himself with the same guilt.

Why should we both sink for my mistake?

"This will be on me Dante. I don't need you wrapped up in this."

Dante scoffed before grabbing at his leather jacket that hung over the side of his chair, signaling that our conversation was ending.

"Too late, Luca," he sighed, "I made a promise to your mother that I would look out for you. I'll continue to do this but don't expect me to lie to you. If this starts getting out of control, I will speak my mind."

"I expect no less of you."

****

Ever since she had arrived in my home, I hadn't been able to sleep. Instead, I worked until my eyes ached for anything but the bright light of my computer screen. When that did nothing to help, I turned to exercising in a private gym situated beneath the house.

Four days and my routines were destroyed.

Four days and I was second-guessing myself.

Tonight, was no different. After pushing myself in the gym, I retired to my room in hopes that I had done enough to force my body to submit to sleep.

Tomorrow we would start our lives together. For eight years, I had practiced the perfect patience and never stepped a foot over the boundaries I had set. Now I was steaming headfirst, feet barely registering the ground as I catapulted over the faint white line I had placed there many years ago.

I suddenly felt desperate.

****

The land that I owned the following morning was bathed in bright sun, warming the grounds around me. In the quiet, I sat beside the pool, covered in the shade as I waited.

Waiting was never my strong point. Being used to a strict schedule, my body struggled to remain still – to ignore the urge in my feet to pace. That urge only increased when I peered at my watch to see they were now five minutes late.

Before I could demand that the maid hovering around the table go find them, my ears were alerted to the sound of shoes clipping against the stone tiles.

"Don't fucking touch me, asshole."

Good morning, Miss Heart.

"Keep moving, Miss Heart," Chen spoke clearly, no doubt heading her up from the back to avoid her slipping out of his grasp.

A mere second later, they were approaching me from across the pool.

Olivia Heart was surrounded by four of the best mercenaries' money could hire. Dwarfed by their large muscles and weapons, she was huddled in the middle, her willowy figure wearing a black shift dress with bare feet.

Looking over my sunglasses, I saw that her hair was damp, drying naturally in the heat as she moved slowly while her eyes scanned the grounds.

There wasn't a doubt in my mind that she was gauging her surroundings for an escape.

You won't find one.

I stood to greet her, ignoring the tension building in the base of my skull.

Held back by Chris, formally known as Rum by his colleagues, she snatched her arm away from him, no fear present on her tear-stained face.

This was interesting.

It was my turn to face her wrath as her eyes found me beneath the canopy, simmering with rage, and terror glinting back at me.

"I said don't touch me," she hissed, as she looked at Rum with all the distaste in the world.

I wanted her attention. They were not worthy of it, even if it was to be on the other end of her venom.

I couldn't control it, my mouth opened. "Good morning, Olivia."

Stopping abruptly, Chen had to pull back quickly before he ran into her from the back. Olivia's glower quickly receded, leaving only terror on her pretty face. Chen moved to bring her closer, but she recoiled from his touch, wrapping her arms around herself.

"You have questions, and you want answers – sit," I demanded, while motioning for her to take the seat next to me. Ignoring my gesture, she squinted across the pool to the other side, looking at the wall that span around the front of the house.

It gave me the perfect opportunity to gauge her emotional status. From the shake of her hands and the quick rise and fall of her chest, I knew she was struggling to contain her fear.

"Are you going to drug me again?" she whispered, as she took one step towards the table.

Towards her fear.

Brave and bold.

A strange tingle swept down my spine when our eyes connected. This behavior wasn't expected and given the sudden calmness, I knew she was silently plotting, hoping for a way out.

Brave little thing.

Would I need to drug her if she didn't accept the new terms of her life?

"Only if you don't behave," I said, as I took my seat, ignoring my body's urge to touch her.

Looking around her, all four men faced forward, their eyes going over my head, but I knew they were on edge as much as I was – I sensed as much from Chen who kept his gaze pinned on the back of Olivia's head.

They had expected a fight, violence, and for her to scream like she had when she first woke up.

Sitting hesitantly at the table, she forced her eyes on me, unblinking green eyes full of questions penetrating my human shell before I could prepare my defense.

Miss Heart took me by surprise when she began to control her rage and fear, letting it sit with her while she observed me.

Suddenly, I was on the back foot and she was in control.

"Sir?" Chen butted in, as he stepped forward, his eyes down on Olivia's head.

"Thanks, Chen, you can go."

Olivia glared over at them all, her wet hair swishing in the gentle breeze as she looked them all over one more time. Inputting them into her brain in case she got away. It was obvious by her calculating stares that she would have made a good lawyer, she knew how to read people without them realizing it.

However, I did, I knew when I was being read and I knew how to stop it.

Chen's team moved with swift precision as they left us to it, but she was no longer interested in them. Turning her attention back to me, she unapologetically eyed the tattoos across my wrist that weren't protected by my usual black shirt.

"You can take in as much as you want, Olivia. It won't help," I mused, as I held out my wrists to her.

"Why the hell are you doing this?" she flared, finally.

Urges to touch her spawned down to my fingers, but I didn't give in. Instead, I focused on her face, her perfect lips while she waited for my answer. Those lips were made by God's hands himself – I was certain of it.

"Doing what?" my voice was void, giving nothing away.

"Keeping me here?"

If it wasn't for her voice breaking, I would have assumed she was handling this situation far too well, but I knew she was close to her breaking point, I knew a lot about her breaking points. If I was a kinder man, I wouldn't use this knowledge to my advantage – but I was far from kind.

"Because I can."

A pained noise echoed in her throat as she bit down on her bottom lip, trying not to cry. Trying to be strong.

As I drank her beauty in, my eyes resting on her skin that had been untouched by the sun, I thought about what she would look like with a tan, would the sun honey her skin just like mine?

"I don't understand," she whispered, her hand going to her stomach.

Was she going to throw up?

Shit.

I sipped my espresso to give myself a break from the tortured look on her face. "I decided I wanted you here, so I made it a reality. You'll see from your few days here that I have everything in my possession to get what I need."

"Is this some sort of sick joke?" She stood up, her hips hitting the table, forcing her untouched drink to spill across the glass top table.

"You need to let me go, now."

I stayed put in my seat. "No. Now, sit down so I can tell you how this is going to go," I growled, as I slammed my cup down onto the table, cracking the glass beneath it.

"Go to hell!" she snapped, as she turned to leave.

Had she not realized her options were at zero? Could she not already see that there was no way out of this?

I was quick as I jumped from my seat to snatch up her hand, clamping it with my long fingers as I dragged her back. Oliva fought me by trying to claw at my wrists with her free hands, but I pinned it with the other. Dragging her into my chest, I flared, my jaw clenching as she fought me.

Looking up at me, I had a front-row seat to her terror as she realized this was the first time that I was this close, but it didn't deter me.

"I said sit *down,* Olivia. We're not done here."

Before she could try to break free or spit in my face, I slammed her into the chair next to mine and let go of her wrists. Taking my seat, I saw Chen hovering across the yard, but I dismissed him with my hand, letting him know I had this under control.

"If you touch me one more time, I swear I will-"

"You'll what!?" I hissed her way. "Last time I checked; you were all out of options."

Sniffing, she turned her nose up while she rubbed her wrists where I had left pink marks.

Already I was out of control.

"Just let me go. I won't breathe a word to anyone about this. I'll go back to my life in New York," she begged, which only made it worse. I didn't want her to beg, the sound alone threw fuel onto my simmering temper.

"You have no life there anymore," I said, as I pushed my hair back. "I made sure of it."

Olivia gasped as she jolted forward, her eyes swimming with panic. "What do you mean? There are people that are going to worry, people will know I'm missing."

I couldn't talk, I was still dealing with my temper, so I pushed a file that was sitting on the table to her. It would give me a reprieve to collect myself, but also deal with some of her questions that would no doubt lead to further volatile behavior.

I couldn't win.

Slowly, she took the folder, and with trembling hands, she opened it, her beautiful moss-colored eyes widening with terror as she read through my book of sins.

"This- this is my..." she blustered, as she flicked through more pages.

I remained cool and passive on the outside, but my soul was itching for a release. In four days, I had opened eight years' worth of secrets and let them ooze out with no care for the stain they would leave on her life.

My selfishness was already winning.

My legs pushed me up to a standing position and I clicked my fingers for her guards to collect her. Cowardly, I moved away from the table without a glance in her direction, too afraid of what I would see across her tear-stained face.

CHAPTER SEVEN

Olivia Heart

My head spun while I raced back into my prison. This was far too important to wait. I slammed the heavy door in Chen's face, and raced over to the rug that lay at the bottom of the large bed.

Slipping down to my knees, I ripped open the folder and began pawing at the sheets of paper. Frantic for more information and for the real reason I was here with a psychopath, I didn't take a minute to prepare myself.

The first sheet of paper was a recent visa that had been signed by Jackson Bells for my move to Italy which was witnessed by Jessica, his assistant.

I gulped in air, desperately trying to push away the anxiety attack steamrolling its way into my chest and picked up another sheet.

Olivia, breathe.

This sheet was a lease agreement which had been signed by me, the property owner at the bottom was stamped with 'Caruso Property Management.'

The third was a signed job contract with my scrawl of a signature which was stamped by LC And Law, the sister company to Slater Law.

I scrunched the sheet in my hands as bile rose to my throat, burning me for being so blind to the overtaking of my life. As I stared down at the next sheet, I realized it was only going to get worse.

A medical form from last year when I was given iron tablets for anemia.

My bank statements and the closure of my personal account.

Phone records from the past eight years

My travel records and vaccinations

My hands shook that much that the letters on the sheets became blurred, but I had to see how deep this went. Had to know how much of my life had been his to voyeur into.

I slid the sheets across and cried.

A picture of me leaving my apartment in my running gear, my face masked by the hat that I always wore when I went for a run.

Another photo, but this time it was me leaving work with Simon from accounts, the one and only time I had accepted his offer for a drink. Two years ago.

Even with my lips gulping for air and my eyes burning from my tears, I pushed on, willing myself to get through this.

Screenshots of private messages between my Aunt Sarah and I, discussing my cousin's up-and-coming wedding. More private messages of flirty messages from Simon who struggled to take no for an answer.

A picture of my apartment, the sun shining through the open blinds.

I paused, staring down at the one place I thought of as my sanctuary after a hard day's work. Was I now a woman without a home?

Laying onto the rug, I brought my knees up to my chest and cried as quietly as I could. Surrounded by what I thought was my life, I began to realize that I had not an ounce of control and I never did. My whole adult life had been orchestrated and watched for what I only assumed was for Luca to bide his time and snatch me away.

Retching out painful sobs, I didn't care to know the reason why he had done all this. Instead, I wished that I would sink into the floor and become nothing but dust in this beautiful house.

****

It may have been mere minutes or several hours that I lay on the floor, but I didn't care. Even as the sun moved through the room, I couldn't bring myself to follow its light. My heart sat in darkness as the severity of the situation began to sink in.

I, Olivia Heart, was being erased with every second that I lay stranded on the floor. The woman that had been as free as a butterfly only days ago was being caged in by the lies that were her life. My blame would lay on her and Luca, both as evil as each other.

I should have been smarter, should have felt, realized that my life was under a microscope, but I was too busy trying to succeed in my career. Why couldn't I have opened my eyes to see the monsters lurking in the dark?

"Oh merda!" I heard the faint sound of a man hissing in Italian, but I wasn't sure if it was real. "Miss Heart, are you okay?"

Warm hands touched my cold shoulder, breaking me from the box I had locked myself away in. I looked up to see a man around the same age as Luca staring down at me with all the worry in the world. Like Luca, he wore all black, but his hair was longer, his eyebrows thicker and he had a warm aura around him.

I quickly sat up and scrambled to rest against the bottom of the bed, my eyes never leaving his outstretched hand.

Would he hurt me?

Are they going to *share* me?

"My name's Dante," he breathed, as he took a seat on the floor with me, his eyes never leaving mine, regarding me cautiously. "Don't be scared, Miss Heart. I won't hurt you. I'm just here to check on you."

"Let me go," I whispered.

Maybe it was his soft brown eyes that made me trust him or the way he held no pity, but I knew I was safe with him. There was no suffocating darkness in his eyes.

"I can't," he told me, without emotion to his voice. "But I can make this easier for you," he said. He held out his hands to show me, he wasn't going to hurt me. I saw a tattoo across his right wrist, but he moved too quickly for me to see it.

Scoffing, I wiped at my sore eyes. "The only way you can make this easier for me is to let me go."

Sighing, he gave me a soft smile. "These papers," he pointed to the scrunched-up paperwork we were sat on, "Is not what you think. None of this is done to hurt you, to rip away your pride...it was done for your protection."

"Protect me? What kind of bullshit is that?" I spat, as I pulled the shift dress over my knees, trying to distance myself from the files. "There's pictures of my apartment in there, private messages and-"

Dante laughed before shoving his hair back. "Luca was right, you do have a lot of spark in you, Miss Heart. All I can do is promise you that you're safe with us and when he's ready, he'll tell you everything. It will all make sense; I can promise you that."

"When will that be?" I demanded, as I sat up straighter, my body reeling for more answers even if my brain was still hiding behind a curtain of grief.

"When he can trust you." He shrugged like it was the easiest thing to understand.

Speechless, I stared dumbfounded at the strange man across from me. If this were in a normal situation, we were in the same bar, I probably would have thought him cute, but all I could see was a guard to my freedom and there was nothing *cute* about that.

"Instead of dwelling in this room, why don't I show you around? Get some sun on that pale skin of yours," he laughed, as he stood up and held out his hand to me.

Ignoring his hand, I stood up and crossed my arms over my chest. If I had to, I would infiltrate his kindness until I could find out more. Nodding, I motioned for him to lead the way. I would use this time to devour my surroundings and build a plan to find my freedom.

Dante grinned at me as he linked his arm in mine, he was even polite enough to ignore my flinch. We left the bright space of my room to the corridor that was lined with the guards in charge of keeping me hostage.

"We're going for a walk Chen, so we won't need you all."

"Dante, Mr. Caruso was specific that we are not to leave-"

Dante waved Chen off. "I've confirmed with him, so stand down." He fixed Chen with a glare that gave me a small insight into the power the stranger holding me had.

Chen had tried to introduce me to his colleagues earlier that morning, but I had hit out at him only to be forced into a barricade, the niceties ceasing as they walked me to Luca. All I knew about them was that they were possible ex-military and had worked together before.

Dante tugged us along silently while my eyes scanned the clean white walls that looked to have been recently painted. The hallway was rich with modern artwork and ornaments that looked like they belonged in a museum somewhere. The whole building breathed wealth and power as we moved down the white marbled stairs and into the belly of the house.

"This is the dining room," he said, as we poked our heads into a room that was bigger than my apartment in New York. Decorated in rich gold, creams, and whites. "Not that it's ever used. How do you say it, pompous?" He grinned at me, showing his perfectly white teeth.

"Something like that," I mumbled, as we returned to the hallway where a maid was passing through, pushing a trolley with fresh sheets on. I tried to catch her eye, but she stared straight ahead, as if we weren't there.

Merely ghosts.

"Luca has twenty staff members which are here to help with anything that you need," he told me, when we came to another room which was an open planned living space that held four large couches. "They won't help you escape, but they will make your stay here comfortable."

"Lovely," I hissed under my breath, as I looked out the living room window and saw the pool that I had seen this morning. The sun shone brilliantly on the body of water, creating a mirage of hovering diamonds.

"Where's Luca's room?" I asked cautiously, as we began to step outside, his arm never leaving mine while we walked through the wide doorway together.

The mid-day heat hit me first before Dante's answer. "Three rooms down from yours."

My heart seized in my chest before spluttering alive once again. We walked across the tiled floor while my mind began processing the new information. Three rooms down? That meant he was keeping me close, possibly worried that I would get by my guards.

Signs of a weakness?

"A house this size and he's three doors down," I mumbled, and I let go of Dante, looking across the outside area that was immaculately designed to invite you to sit and look out across the expansive land.

Dante stepped to my side and looked across the house with me. "Beautiful, isn't it? Luca designed this and had it built eight years ago. It took three years to complete, but it was all worth it."

"A prison is a prison no matter how pretty it is."

Dante ignored me as he pointed out towards the grounds behind the house, the only part that didn't have a sixteen-foot wall hiding it. "Over there is the vineyard. Do you want to go see?"

I wanted to see it. The vineyard was on the outside of the house which meant I would get a better look at what was close by and how long it would take me to escape.

****

The vineyard was not what I had expected. On the expansive land sat one hundred rows of vines with the deepest shade of purple grapes I had ever seen. Each post held a plaque that explained the type of wine the grapes would become.

Was this what Luca did, wine?

We had to travel here by a small golf buggy which gave me plenty of time to realize that we were nowhere near a main road or dirt track. All my eyes captured were rich greens and well-manicured land.

"This is looked after by Henry Tailor," Dante said and smiled, his English perfect if not made better with the Italian accent that covered his words gracefully. "Luca flew him in from France."

"Why didn't he use someone local?" I asked, as I turned to look back to the house, wondering what my captor was doing as I stood outside the grounds of my prison. Were the four guards he employed watching from afar? Were there cameras watching us?

Dante shook his head. "Here in Italy, Luca and his family are well known. It's hard for him to trust people."

"What is he known for?"

A small smirk graced his lips as he popped a grape off the nearest vine and popped it into his mouth. "A bit of everything, Miss Heart. There isn't a business that the Caruso's aren't involved with."

"Drugs? Kidnap? Trafficking?" I spat, moving closer to him, wanting to pull as much information as I could from him.

Dante's eyes widened which gave me more information than his words did. My few years working for LC and Law had taught me how to read people and Dante had just admitted that Luca Caruso was involved in the dark aspects of business.

"Not all of those," he bumbled. "Ah diavolo." His hands wound tightly into his dark hair, yanking at the strands.

Crossing my arms over my chest, I ignored the sweat building at the back of my neck. "Then which ones Dante?"

"You're an exception, Miss Heart," he tried to reason, as he grabbed me by my elbow and began dragging me back to the buggy.

"You're not being honest with me," I told him, as I climbed into the buggy. "Is it drugs?"

Dante blanched before waving me off dramatically, turning the key, the buggy purred to life. "He's trying to get out of that market, but it's not as easy as just stopping."

I closed my eyes and felt the sun burning my lids, nose, and collar bone, but I didn't care. Today had just sunk to another low, the more information I sought, the worse it got, and I had to deal with it somehow. Luca Caruso was dangerous, his grip on my life had gotten tighter, cutting blood from the limbs of my freedom one by one.

"Is that what I'm here for? To help him get out of that business legally?"

Dante paused and looked away. "No nothing like that. You're here because you're important to him Olivia, that's all I can say right now."

"Important how?"

"I've already said too much, come on, we better get back before Chen releases the dogs."

CHAPTER EIGHT

Olivia Heart

D ante had forced me to eat only hours after our visit to the vineyard which I was grateful for. It had been a while since I had last eaten, and I was feeling the repercussion of cutting my stomach off. As soon as I had eaten the small meal, I had felt the pull of sleep, my body collapsing onto the bed before I could stop it.

Whether it was a full stomach or the sun on my skin, I had slipped into a dream that I hadn't visited in years. I watched from the outside as an eight-year-old me sat outside of the headmaster's office in England. Even my innocent mind knew that something bad was coming. I watched as she looked up from her seat with tears pooling at the bottom of her bright eyes.

Fear prickled down my arms as I tried to move from my dark corner to comfort her, but I remained statue still. The door opened and out came my Aunt Sarah who was trying her best to keep it together, but the shakes of her hands gave her away.

"I'm here," I cried from the corner of the room, but nobody heard me. They never did.

All I could do was watch my Aunt Sarah fall to her knees in front of me as she grabbed eight-year-old me's hands.

Snapping awake, I felt my hand snake up to my neck to feel my pulse racing under the skin. It had been years since I had dreamt about the moment, I had lost my parents, but now it's all I could think about.

I needed to get out, to feel the cool air on my skin. Pushing away the sheets of my bed, I tip-toed towards the door and gently opened it. Just down the hall was one of my guards, Rum who had made it his mission to manhandle me that morning.

It was possible I had bitten him when they sedated me the second time.

I remembered Dante's words when he said that I was free to walk around so I decided to put his words to the test. Slipping on a pair of sandals, I stepped out of the door.

Rum looked up and greeted me with a cautious nod. "Can I help, Miss Heart?"

"No. I'm going to get some fresh air," I mumbled, as I tried to pass him, but he pushed off the wall and fell into step with me. Glaring at him, I stopped dead in my tracks. "I don't need you to follow. I'm very aware I cannot get out of here, so your company isn't required."

Rum remained emotionless as he viewed me from his baby blue eyes. "I'm following orders from Mr. Caruso. Until he tells me that himself, you're stuck with me."

I sighed angrily before turning on my heels and heading towards the outside of the house, to the open yard where the pool was. Ignoring the brute that was babysitting me, I kicked off my sandals and took a seat around the pool edge, gently slipping my feet into the cold water.

"How long have you been watching me?" I asked, without bothering to look back at him.

Rum cleared his throat, a verbal cue that he was nervous by my question. I heard him shuffling his feet against the tiled flooring as he contemplated answering me. "That's not for me to say."

I scoffed as I looked up at the warm lighting that covered the grounds, even at night this place was beautiful. "Let me guess, only Mr. Caruso will allow you to inform me of how long you've been stalking me for?"

"That's right, Miss Heart."

Closing my eyes to the sound of Luca's terse voice, I realized how stupid I had been. How had I not heard his footsteps? My plan to get answers had failed before it had gotten off the ground. Given this foresight, I should have questioned Rum in a controlled setting where I wouldn't be blindsided.

The next sound I heard was a chair scraping behind me before it stopped, no doubt just behind my back so I either had to choose the deep water or him. Luckily for me, I could swim.

"Well, will you answer?" I asked, as I looked down into the water, my hands gripping the edge to keep me from turning around. My knuckles were quickly turning white as I fought the rage I felt whenever he was around me.

"They've been with you for four years," his voice was lower, quieter as he answered, purging some of his secrets once and for all. A small flicker of hope bloomed in my chest before I could stop it, but I needed this more than I could explain so I let it.

"Rum, Red, and Bones have been with you a while. Chen is my personal guard who oversees them."

"Why?" I tried to keep my voice neutral, but my breathing began to speed up when I felt his body heat against my back.

I had an urge to turn to face him, but this was stopped by his fingers grazing the side of my neck as he pushed my hair over my shoulder. I flinched, suddenly aware of my hammering pulse, I tried to move away but his knees pinned me into him.

"It was a necessity to ensure you were safe from outside…interests," he breathed, as he dipped his hand into the pool, his head coming close to me before he sat back and let his wet fingers return to my neck.

Deftly, he allowed the water to drip across my bare skin before using his index finger to trace the dripping water to the top of my shoulder.

I closed my eyes in disgust as a foreign warmth spread underneath my skin like wildfire. There was no longer an opportunity to turn my head to face him now, instead, I remained tense between his legs as he forced his touch upon me.

Worry began to spread through my chest as the possibility of the man pinning me to him was going to hurt me, going to take the last bit of pride I had.

"What will you do with me now?" I whispered, silently pleading that he would finally answer me, to give me a small ounce of relief.

I needed to see the end.

Luca's fingertips paused along the arch of my neck. "I'll protect you, give you everything…" he breathed, before returning to his task of stunning me into submission with his hands.

I gulped subconsciously. "The only person I need protecting from is you."

My back began to burn as he hissed beside my ear. Luca's pressure on my back and neck increased, touching on the painful side, but I scrunched my eyes closed.

I needed an answer. The little voice in my head was begging, screaming at him to give her something, anything.

Suddenly, his fingers were removed from my skin and grabbing at the back of my hair, gently tugging me back to him.

"That's not true," he whispered close to my ear, his bottom lip grazing the bottom of my ear lobe. "I can give you everything Olivia, anything you want in this world, I can give that to you."

Certain that he could hear my heart thumping in my chest, I tried to pull away from him but his grip in my hair remained firm. It wasn't uncomfortable or painful, but I knew he was exerting his control over me, forcing me into submission so that he could hold all the power once again.

Without my eyes on him, he was free to hide his dark secrets. I had underestimated him greatly. My brain had created a profile for him, labelling him every dark sin on this earth without realizing that he knew this is what I did, knew that I worked people out with my eyes.

Looking down at my legs in the water, I hoped to see his reflection, but he tugged my head back, preventing me once again. A terrifying thought popped into my head before I could stop it; would he drown me if I pushed any further?

"Let me go," I merely whispered.

"No," he breathed, his double meaning into my ear, but his fingers loosened in my hair and trailed down my right shoulder. "We need to talk."

"Then talk," I hissed, as I tried to turn, but he grabbed my shoulders and forced me forward. I gasped as I nearly fell into the water, my hair falling forward with long strands dipping into the cool water.

"Patience Olivia," he snapped back, as he kept me forward.

Being told to be patient when my life was being shredded to pieces forced my terror aside, rage replacing it. The man with his fingertips holding me forward had no shame, no guilt in his dark heart.

Repulsion burst across my skin.

"How long have you been controlling my life?"

"Eight years," he snapped back, his fingers digging into my soft skin again, painting me with vicious bruises.

"Why?"

"Because I had to."

I ignored his evasive answer and tried to wiggle away from him as a fire began to burn in my belly. "Fuck you," I hissed. "You're not letting me see you so you can hide. Be a man and let me go."

Quickly he leaned into me, his mouth next to my ear as he whispered, "As you wish, *bella*."

I felt his fingers leave my skin, giving me no option but to fall forward, slipping from the pool edge and into the cold water. I gasped as the cold water hit my warm skin, forcing me to freeze against the new element. Even in the quick rush, I had managed to keep my head above the water, so I could turn around to face him before he could do anything else.

My dress slicked itself to my body, making it difficult to turn in the water, but I managed, just. Blinking away the chlorinated water that had splashed into my eyes, I looked up to find myself all alone with the only sign of him having been there was the chair that had been pushed away.

Rum walked towards me from the side of the house with a smirk across his arrogant face. Pulling up his trousers, he crouched down and offered me a hand. "Time for bed, Miss Heart?"

CHAPTER NINE

Luca Caruso

My evasive approach was not only wearing thin with her but myself. There was not a chance in hell that I could prolong the inevitable, but I had to try. Last night had proven that around her, I was weak with urges I couldn't trust.

Space – that's what I had tried to give her, to calm down, but mostly for me to place some distance between what I wanted and what she needed right now. If my control snapped and I pushed, she would never be able to trust me.

Olivia's trust was all that I craved.

I waited by my car the following morning with the sun beating down on my head, while scrolling through my emails. Dante was by my side, scrolling down his own phone, huffing every now and then as he argued with the latest conquest.

Shoving my phone into my pocket, I looked up towards the front of the house. Chen was the first to walk through the door and then Olivia as they took the short steps onto the drive. Once again, she was barricaded in by her bodyguards, their bodies in unison as they kept up with Chen's lead. I would never get used to how small she looked in the middle of them all, as they protected her.

Today, she was dressed in an emerald, green summer dress that was tied at her small waist. As my eyes trailed her body, I froze when I saw the black heels. I made a mental note to thank the personal shopper for the shoes that highlighted Olivia's long legs perfectly.

Returning my eyes back to her face, I saw she was glaring at me through the arms of Chen's men, she was letting me know she didn't like being told what to wear and when to wear it.

Tough.

I noticed her hair had been plaited down her back and smirked; she was trying to pull back the control, to let me know that what happened beside the pool last night wouldn't happen again.

Chen nodded, passing a simple message that his team was ready to escort us and headed to the first car. Before I could open my mouth to greet Olivia, Dante had pushed off the car and scooped up her hand.

"Good morning, Olivia." He smiled and placed a quick kiss on her hand. "You're looking just divine this morning."

Careful with her expression, she didn't flinch away, but by the way her eyes narrowed to me, I knew she didn't appreciate the gesture.

Neither did I, Olivia.

"Hello Dante," she replied, while looking over his shoulder at the three cars lined up and ready to go. It gave me plenty of time to look at her face, to watch as the sun brightened her green eyes so much, they were almost see-through.

"I'll be in the car in front," he told her, as he let go of her hand. "See you in an hour."

Regarding him carefully, she replied with a simple curt nod before returning her eyes back onto me. I moved quickly and opened the door. "Let's go."

"Where?" she asked, as she crossed her arms over her chest, her eyes alive with trepidation.

I gritted my teeth while willing myself patience, but it didn't make a damned bit of difference when her eyes were on me.

Nodding at her team to get into the cars, I waited until they had walked away before answering her.

"I need to oversee some business."

"Why do I need to go?"

"Do you want to stay here?" I hissed, as the last drop of patience ran out. Running a hand through my hair, I took in a deep breath and told myself to give her time. It wasn't as though I had stolen her life away from her and was forcing her to live by my side.

Regarding me with cool eyes, she moved around me before getting into the car, no doubt only doing so in hopes there would be more options for the escape. As I followed, I was careful not to touch her and made sure I kept my eyes ahead. Being in a small space with her was going to prove difficult and I needed to exercise control so she could at least be comfortable in my presence.

The only comfort to be welcomed in my life came from my many successes in my work life. I was comfortable in difficult situations, calm and controlled as I mastered the ups and downs of my complicated need for success. It wasn't family, love, or friends that pushed me forward. It was my own personal drive to be better, to succeed where nobody else could.

It had made me many enemies, but most had the sense to stay away. Even a few had honor and would show me respect by sticking to the rules of fraught business.

Those that didn't share the same sentiment very rarely lasted. How long would I last now that there was something I wanted more in this world other than success? Somewhere down the obscure lines I had drawn, I had broken my own rules and ignored the warning signs.

Looking to my left, I watched as she stared out of the window, admiring my homeland with her soft eyes framed with thick lashes. Biting down on her lip, she was lost in her own thoughts and I knew by the way she was twisting her fingers that they were about the complicated situation she was in.

My hands itched for her to stop.

As we moved further towards the city, she furrowed her brow, a small v forming between her eyebrows as she leaned closer to the window, drinking in the beauty around us.

"Do you like it?" I asked her, as I leaned towards her, both of us looking out the window as we passed through beautiful fields blooming with wheat, their beige branches swaying in the breeze.

In seconds, her body went from relaxed to frozen with fear, the body's natural reaction to when it senses danger. "Like what?" she asked me, her voice tight as she looked down at my hand next to her thigh.

I leaned back slightly to allow her to feel some relief from my presence but to also remove myself from her smell, her sweet smell that made me do stupid things. "Sicily."

Olivia continued to stare out of the window. "I've seen a few fields. I can hardly say if I like a place or not based on-"

"You're wound very tight Miss Heart," I mused, as I leaned back into my seat with a small smirk on my face. "Are you always like this?"

"Yes."

Olivia turned to face me; her eyes alive with frustration as she regarded me with a cool stare. When she was like this, I almost felt smug, smug that she would have to look at me, but that I could invoke the most passionate emotions from her.

"Where are we going?" she asked me, as she looked towards the front of the car, her eyes trailing the driver's waistband where a gun sat.

Even with all the rage teeming through her blood, I knew she wasn't brave enough to reach forward and grab the gun. Olivia was a woman of words, not action.

"I have a meeting," I told her, as I smoothed down my black trousers, eager for a distraction from her glare.

Her anger did things to my body. It whispered into the darkest corners of my soul, bringing out the man who wanted more – *now*.

"This friend happens to be involved in narcotics?"

Snapping my head up, I glared right back, my jaw flexing with irritation. "I'm assuming your question comes from your conversation with Dante?"

Olivia's eyes left mine briefly, but she had given me my answer in the simplest way, Dante had been running his mouth.

Fuck.

I shook my head, trying to ignore the tension building in my shoulders. "I know you think low of me Olivia, but I would never bring you to one of those meetings."

Rolling her eyes at me, she turned back to the window – shutting me out. All I could see now was the sun shining down on her hair and shoulders, revealing the soft slight pink skin from her time in the sun.

"You have no idea what I think. Those files you have on me are nothing but useless facts, not enough to give you an inkling into my head."

Stunned. The first time in my life I was perfectly still with shock as I traced the tense muscles at the top of her spine with my eyes. Did she really think them as useless? Was she really that naive?

Before I could control my hands, they were back on her hair, wrapping around her loose plait as I pulled her back into my chest.

This time she expected it, silencing her own gasp as she bit down on her lip.

"You're being naive," I mumbled against her soft neck, my lips chastely touching the skin I wanted to devour. "They're only half of what I know about you Olivia."

"You're bluffing," she hissed, so that only we could hear, but I didn't give a fuck about the driver who was trying his hardest to keep his eyes on the road or Chen who was glaring at the side of his face.

"Oh si?" I whispered to the soft spot below her ear lobe, and smirked when she shivered in my hands. "I know about the hours you would spend running to get away from the sexual frustration humming in your body. You've spent years denying yourself pleasure…"

My free hand brushed across the top of her bare thigh, relishing in the smooth skin, it glided higher.

Olivia shrugged violently out of my hands and then turned around to slap me across the chest, but I was quick. I scooped her forward and pinned her close so that her smacks barely had momentum.

"You need to get help," she growled into my chest. "What you're doing to me isn't normal – you're sick!"

To the outside, we looked as though we were embracing as lovers, but given the opportunity, I knew she would claw out my eyes if she had the chance. The unmistakable feeling of rage coursing through her body and her frustration unravelling, made it harder for me to concentrate.

My hands held her tighter, cutting off the circulation to her wrists while I waited for her to calm down.

"The sooner you accept this, the better. I won't let you continue in this way. Do you understand me?"

Patience worn thin, I squeezed her wrists harder, demanding an answer.

My answer quickly came as she slumped against my chest, finally giving in. Slowly releasing her wrists, I allowed her to scoot away from me, returning to her seat.

Naive – that I was not. I knew she would not just give in like that.

Leaning back, I closed my eyes and took in a deep breath through my nose. When I was around her, all sense of calm disappeared, sucked out by the raging fire emitting off her skin. Olivia would suffocate me if I didn't find a way to make her understand that she was mine.

It had to be this way.

CHAPTER TEN

Olivia Heart

We had been travelling for exactly thirty minutes. I knew this from the quick glances at Luca's Patek Philippe watch that glinted at me from the sunlight streaming in my window. I made a mental note that in thirty minutes, we had gone from the countryside to the city. Carefully, I watched as we slipped through Palermo, avoiding the tourists that crossed the streets without a care in the world.

My eyes drank in the beautiful city, its architecture so rich in wealth and appeal as we moved through narrow streets. The city oozed romance with its warm colors and beautiful mix of agriculture, so much so, that I forgot I was sat beside the devil and allowed myself to feel like a tourist – if only for a few moments.

I wanted to open the door and fling myself into the streets, to be free with all the moving people who were so keen to get on with their day. Instead, I sat in a blacked-out range rover as we drove on, no one aware that I was being held against my will.

"What?!" I heard Luca bark from my side as he thrust his iPhone to his ear, his lips turning up into a snarl. "It's going... fine."

I turned back to the window, trying to ignore the conversation going on beside me.

"Did they say when?" he uttered quietly, trying to keep the next part of the conversation away from my ears. "Scopri se sono nel paese."

****

We arrived at a small industrial estate at the far end of the city only minutes later. Without the dusting of cars, I would have assumed the place was abandoned until we pulled up to the last building with only one entrance, a single grey door.

The hairs on my arms stood up as I looked to Luca who was already leaving the vehicle. Pushing open my door, I ignored Chen's outstretched hands and looked for one set of eyes I could read in the crowd.

Dante sought me out just as I had him, but the difference was he held a boyish grin on his face while mine was no doubt was covered with fear. Grabbing my arm, he pulled me toward Luca who was making his way through the grey door.

I was so easily forgotten by Luca as he sauntered into the building, but it didn't matter. While he wasn't around, I could think rationally and begin to plot a way out of the mess he had dragged me into.

As soon as I stepped over the threshold, I felt Chen shadowing me, his body inches from mine. Ignoring him, I focused on the back of Luca's shirt, his wide shoulders relaxed as he stepped to a man who was waiting by the bottom of steel stairs that led to the second floor of the building.

The mysterious man took Luca's hand with enthusiasm, greeting him in a way an old friend would as they shook. Luca responded with grace, but didn't return the enthusiasm – instead, he was cold and reserved.

I let my eye's focus on Luca's business associate who was dressed in a well-fitted navy suit with expensive brown Italian shoes. While observing his wardrobe, hoping to find clues, they started to converse, a familiar British accent floating to my ears, a gruff cockney accent to be exact. An overwhelming feeling of home warmed my body but before I could bask in the brief relief, Dante was pulling me forward.

"Nice to meet ya, Miss Heart."

My hand was pulled from my side by him, forcing a handshake I wouldn't have willingly given.

"Nice to meet you, too," I lied, it wasn't nice to meet him, especially by the way he was looking at me, with piercing blue eyes that shone with perverse thoughts.

"The name's Jeff Greene, been doing business with Luca ere for years," he said cheerily, as he let go of my hand and shoved them into his pockets.

I could have scoffed at the fake name he used, but decided against it, given that Luca was glaring holes into the side of my face, telling me to behave or things would get worse. Dante on the other hand was growing bored with the slow introductions and had took to his iPhone for a distraction. What I wouldn't give to have my phone back, to make the one phone call I so desperately needed.

"And what business is it that you do, Mr. Greene?" I asked, only to have Luca move forward, his hands burning my hip as he pulled me into his side, his fingers pinching me to stop.

I had asked the wrong question and he wanted me to stop.

"Mr. Green, shall we go upstairs?" Luca butted in; his smile tight with irritation.

Ignoring the awkward display, Jeff nodded with a small nervous smile, his eyes finally resting on the guards who towered over me. It was obvious that they weren't expected but he wouldn't make a fuss about it – too afraid, so instead, he moved to the stairs.

"Greene imports specialist vehicles," Dante whispered, as he took my hand, helping me up the stairs.

"Why the secrecy?" I whispered back, as we came to a landing space that spanned across the whole building. On the edges of the landing sat numerous glass-fronted offices that had people working at computers. In the middle was a large glass table with four men hunched over, their Italian whispers rushed while they conversed over a large blueprint.

"These vehicles are military-grade and expensive, not exactly legal here in Italy for private entrepreneurs," he said, as he pulled me aside, his eyes fixed on mine. "Don't ask any more questions here, okay? I'll tell you when we get back to the house."

"Why?" I whispered, looking over his shoulder where Luca and Greene had slipped off into one of the glass offices. Luca's tall frame towered over Greene until he took a seat, but he didn't relax – his shoulders remained firm as he leaned forward to look at something Greene was showing him.

Pulling my eyes away, I focused on Dante who was being careful with his words. "I've already pissed him off once by saying too much."

"Military-grade vehicles..." I muttered, as my eyes gauged the room, to the walls that held samples of metal. My thoughts began to run wild, tripping to conclusions, and images of war-torn countries came to mind.

Before I could demand further answers from Dante, Chen interrupted by thrusting an iPhone in front of my face. It was the phone Luca had used on our way here and now it was dangling in front of me.

"Mr. Caruso has authorized you calling your aunt in England," he told me, in his usual clipped tone. From the way he was looking at me, he didn't think this was a good idea, but I didn't care.

"You're to speak to her for five minutes. If at any time you tell her anything about your situation, we will take it away. Do you understand?" he asked, as he moved me away from his men and to the side of the room.

"Why is he letting me speak to her?" I questioned. A cold shiver ran down my spine. Luca knew about my aunt, knew that she became nervous when I didn't reach out.

My stomach rolled.

Did he think this extension of a somewhat olive branch would make me succumb to him? Panic seized in my heart at the thought of continuing this way, with no way out.

"Do you want to speak to her or not?" he asked, breaking me from the dark thoughts I was tumbling headfirst into. Chen was already bored by me.

"Yes, yes please." I grabbed at the phone and saw my hands were shaking as I dialed her number.

As soon as the phone was up to my ear, Chen's men barricaded me in once again, but I didn't care. Dante moved away with a curt nod towards Chen before joining Luca.

"Hello?"

I felt my heart explode in my chest when I heard my aunt's skeptical voice. Hot tears sprang to my eyes and I gripped the phone tighter – wanting to reach in and hug her.

"Aunt Sarah, it's me, it's Olivia," I breathed, trying to force my throat to act normal as it threatened to crack under the enormous emotions I was feeling.

"Oh, Olivia! I've been calling your phone for days," she chided, "I've been going out of my mind. Ever since I got your email about you moving to Italy for work-"

Ice cold water filled my veins as my body turned to look over at Luca who was smirking my way – no doubt sensing that another one of his victories had slipped to my ears.

"I know," I told her, "I'm so sorry, it all happened so fast-"

"And you couldn't tell me first?" she hissed with frustration, which made my heart sink. This would be a lot harder if she was mad with me.

"I couldn't."

Chen was circling us, nervous by my sudden change in body language, but I chose to ignore him. One of his men, Bones, pulled a seat from a near table and placed it behind me, hoping to settle me.

"I lost my phone on the way over here and it's taken me a few days to get settled. I'm using my colleague's," I muttered quietly, as I took my seat. "I'm so sorry for worrying you."

My Aunt Sarah sighed with relief down the phone with sweet forgiveness. "You'll be the death of me girl. I was thinking all sorts of bad things."

If only she knew the real reason why there had been no contact between us, I thought as I looked through Rum and Bone's bodies to where Luca was sat. My Aunt Sarah was a natural-born worrier who spent more time fretting over her loved ones than living. Guilt and anger swelled in my chest when I thought about the pain Luca had caused her.

"You know I would never intentionally worry you. It's just-"

Chen's hand touched my shoulder warning me, forcing me to pause mid-sentence. Gritting my teeth at his invasive touch, I settled myself with the knowledge that once I was out of this mess, everyone involved would pay.

"Look, once I have WI-FI in my new apartment, I'll skype you and we can catch up. I'm sure there's lots of wedding prep that I've missed out on."

"Like you wouldn't believe," Aunt Sarah's girlish laugh tickled my ear. "I'll also need your address, Olivia; I'll need to send your dress so you can check if it fits – you can still make it right?"

More hot tears sprang to my eyes, so I dropped my head, refusing anyone access to my fresh pain.

"Of course, I can," the lie flew effortlessly through my lips. "I'll text you the address once I get my new phone."

That was enough for Chen as he signaled for me to wrap up the phone call by touching my shoulder, his fingers firmly gripping me in place. It was no doubt for the best, as my emotions were swelling, threatening to push over the rickety wall I had built in my mind.

"I have to go now," fake cheeriness wrapped my words, so that she would know I was okay. "I'll call you again real soon."

"You better," she replied. "Don't forget to send me your address. Speak soon love."

"I will, bye, Aunt Sarah."

Before I could end the call myself, Chen snatched away the phone and hit the screen with his thumb, ending the conversation. Turning from him, I let my eyes make their way over towards the man that had caused me nothing but pain these past few days.

Sensing my eyes on him, he looked at me through the glass wall that separated us. There was a moment when I had first met him that I thought he was familiar, like we had met before and maybe we had. Why else would he had spent years stalking me from afar?

Had I been on his legal counsel? Had I met him briefly in a bar when I went for drinks with the girls from work? Could a moment, a glance across a table, have caused this type of chain reaction from him?

Looking away from his intense gaze, I realized that there had been no moment across a table, no legal counsel… it was more. Much more. I had been blind to see it, but Luca's grip on my life was about obsession and control, but he had resisted until now.

I stood up and ignored the tense muscles of my guards as I came to head height with their chests. As I paced, they began to widen their circle around me, keeping a watch in case I suddenly bolted.

There was a change that caused him to reach in and pluck me away from my life – something to force him to go to extreme lengths of wiping out my existence in New York. I knew it. I could feel it.

Obsession made people do crazy things, hurt people with a warped sense of justice, but this wasn't happening here. I was safe, cared for, my every need taken care of, but I was without freedom.

Luca was controlling his obsession around me by keeping me in the dark. I had felt it every time he touched me, felt his hesitancy around me while he denied himself what he wanted the most.

How long until he pulled me into the darkness with him?

CHAPTER ELEVEN

Olivia Heart

We had stayed in Jeff Greene's workshop for a short while after my phone call. Once Luca was finished, he sought me out first and grabbed at my elbow as he led me out of the building before Dante could. Teetering in heels was no small feat when you had to match the long strides of a man who was brimming with frustration.

Whatever happened in his meeting was following us as we ushered back into the cars. My mouth threatened to open and to ask him what had happened, but I decided against it – decided against showing him any compassion at all.

"Sir, back to the house?" his driver asked, slipping on a pair of sunglasses.

"Yes," Luca snapped through gritted teeth, as he leaned back into his seat, closing his eyes.

The dark shirt he was wearing opened, allowing the sun to cast light across a tattoo just below his collarbone. It was a small feather that was wrapped with chain links, the life being strangled out of the symbol of freedom.

Sensing my eyes on him, he closed his shirt and looked down at me, pinning me with his eyes – demanding that I keep my mouth shut.

Flushing under his stare, I turned to look out the window – we were setting off, no doubt returning to my prison in the middle of the Sicilian countryside.

"Did you speak to your aunt?" he asked me coolly, his temper not evident in his tone but I could feel it.

"I did."

"See, this is what happens when you behave, Olivia."

I turned so quickly in my seat that my hair whipped him across the shoulder, but he didn't acknowledge it nor waver under my sneer. My mouth opened to protest, to scream, and hurl dirty insults his way, but instead, I snapped it shut and turned my back on him.

Gone was the lawyer in training, the woman that spent her days searching for the truth, only to be replaced with a fraction of herself – weak and pathetic. Why was it so difficult to verbally spar with him? To shred him down until he was nothing more than a man rather than a king sat on his throne of power.

"You're not talking to me now?"

Not if I can help it.

"I thought you would be happy to speak to her."

"Your arrogance knows no bounds," I'd already given in as I snarled back and for good measure turned to look at him. "Happy that I get to speak to my family that you're purposely keeping me from? Oh, how charitable of you."

Luca should have snapped back at me or pinned me against him, but he just smirked, with eyes that came alive with fascination.

It only made things worse for my temper as he enjoyed the show of my life unravelling.

"You're very attractive when you're mad," he told me, leaning forward, gripping a strand of my hair and twirling it between his fingers. "Your cheeks flush a lovely shade of pink…"

I watched him carefully as his fingertips dropped the loose strand of my hair, only to touch my face, searing my skin as he traced his index finger down my cheek.

Pulling myself together, I chose to ignore the strange spread of heat across my chest and focus on his face – his eyes as they scanned my face. Luca's eyes were the perfect mix of browns and honey hues, but their softness in color was nothing but a ruse.

"Why me?" I whispered.

Luca removed his fingers from my face and placed them on his lap, his careful mask slipping back onto his face. This happened every time I asked, which meant he was either scared to tell me or keeping this from me for control.

If I didn't know his motive, then I couldn't make a plan.

I needed an answer.

"I've told you, Olivia," he breathed, as he leaned away from me, cutting off my view of his face. "Because I get what I want."

"And that's me?"

I felt brave for the first time in days, strong enough to face this head-on once and for all.

"Yes."

"But you don't know me, and I certainly don't know you. Don't you see this for what it is?" desperately I tried to appeal to the human side of him.

Please, show me something. Give me something.

Shaking his head, he turned to look out the window, but I could tell by the way his right hand flexed against his thigh that he was struggling – struggling to deny me.

I continued to look at his beautiful hands and more specifically the small tattoo on his left hand, the ring finger. There was a small circle just below the knuckle that was pitch black against his tanned skin. An odd choice for a tattoo.

"I see exactly what this is, and I see what you're trying to do. It won't work."

Stretching back, he relaxed his body, the threat ceasing to exist almost instantly, but he didn't return his eyes to mine, instead he looked straight ahead, over the driver's shoulder, and to the car in front.

"How old are you?"

"Thirty-two."

"When did we meet?"

It was a bluff – a sheer bit of hope that he would react to my question, enough so that he would slip a little more. It worked as he cautiously regarded me, the corners of his soft-looking lips turning up with interest.

"Eight years ago."

The evasive answer was enough for me to start wracking my brain, forcing it to go back eight years, to find him lurking in my subconscious and destroy his secrets once and for all.

I'd have been seventeen-years-old…living in England with my aunt.

For eight years, the man who was sat, elbow touching mine, had known everything about me as I went on my fickle way. The question was how could I have forgotten him so easily?

Luca was beautiful, terrifying, but so beautiful that anyone in his company would feel insignificant against his high cheekbones and charm. I wouldn't have forgotten him.

No.

I wouldn't have.

"No more questions?" he asked me, after a pregnant pause, his arrogance filling the car.

I faced the window, willing away the building headache so I could focus on finding him in my memories.

Neither of us said a word for the remainder of the journey, both grateful for the silence as we pondered on our individual questions.

****

Once we were back at the house, there was a few seconds of peace before Red and Bones moved me throughout the house, back to my bedroom with militant expertise. As soon as the door closed behind me, I darted to the walk-in closet, kicking off my heels as I did.

Many things bothered me about this room. The bathroom was stocked with necessities that I always purchased back home, right down to the flavor of toothpaste I preferred. The bedroom itself was decorated to my tastes – it had taken me a few days to realize it was similar to that of my apartment, right down to the style of rug that lay at the bottom of the bed.

But the worst of them all was the closet. It was a spacious room adjacent to the bedroom with luscious cream walls that spanned racks of clothes across each side. On the right side, it was every type of expensive dresses from all varied designers with no cost spared.

The left had blouses, skirts, and lingerie all on small hangers with tags still attached. My fingers traced the lingerie to discover that these were to my size.

Even with all this glorious material, I felt destroyed by the cups of pure silk and lace sets that glared at me under the warm lighting. Everything in this room was picked for me, my body, and probably to wear for him.

I felt sick as I took a seat on the floor, ignoring the stands of heels that sat proudly on their shelves. This felt like a doll's house and I was being forced to play dress up for an unhinged man.

Absorbing all the stimuli in the room, I bowed my head and focused on dragging air through my nose. There was no time to allow the anxiety to creep back up and pull me back down – I needed to be strong so I could focus on what I knew and what I still needed to know.

Eight years ago, we met.

Eight years he has kept watch of my life.

In eight years, he controlled my job prospects and my security.

The change came when he told me that my guards had kept watch of me from four years ago. Why then?

Had something changed so much that he needed to up his control using four mercenaries? Four shadows to protect me from what? Him?

Terror found me once again as I looked across the closet to the white mirror on the wall and found myself in the reflection. My skin had a soft glow from the recent sun, showing a young woman enjoying the sun, but my eyes were wide with fear as I slowly began to realize that there may not be any hope left.

"What are you doing in here?" Dante asked, as he stepped into the closest with big wide eyes full of confusion.

It was starting to become a pattern — him finding me on the floor.

"Trying to figure this out."

Dante took off his black suit jacket and tossed it to the side, taking a seat across from me, careful to give me my space.

"Did he answer your questions?"

Dante was a kind soul; I knew that much from my many years of being able to read people. But he had a flicker of darkness in his eyes that I would have to watch.

"A few, nothing that helped."

The sound of my voice irritated me - weak and pitiful.

Dante's sigh reflected how I felt perfectly. "Well, I'm happy to answer some if you're up for it?"

A cynical laugh passed my lips before I could stop it. "You mean, you'll answer what he allows you to?"

"That's right."

I shifted on the floor so that I sat with my legs in front of me, stretching my legs. "Okay, what was today about?"

"Luca has commissioned four armored vehicles. Today was about finalizing his requirements."

"What does he need with armored cars?"

Dante shifted so slightly that to the untrained eye, it would have seemed normal, but to me, I knew he was uncomfortable with the question, biding time to come up with a lie.

"Well..." he started, rubbing his large hands down his trousers. "They're an insurance policy, so that we can move freely if a threat ever presents itself."

"Fuck," the hiss slipped from my lips, as I began to undo my hair, twisting my fingers through the braid and letting the tendrils fall around my shoulders.

"Not only is he absolutely crazy but he has people who want to get to him that bad?"

Dante quickly pushed up from his knees and stood up so that he towered over me. "You don't need to worry about that, Olivia."

His smile was tight and insincere, but I knew not to push him. "But I will Dante, you know I will."

Running a hand through his hair, he looked up at the ceiling and took in a deep breath. "I suppose you will. Anyway, there's a new phone and laptop on your bed – a gift from Luca."

I scrambled up so quickly with excitement at the possibility of having an ounce of freedom, that I forgot myself for a second.

"Don't get your hopes up, Olivia. Everything that you do on those devices is monitored."

Gritting my teeth, I tried to ignore the last words that came from his beautiful mouth and focused on this ray of light. Forcing my way out of the closet, I found the two boxes sat on my bed as promised.

Dante followed behind. "Like I said, you're being monitored, so be careful what you do with those," he muttered. "It's a test, Olivia."

Did he think that I would be so naive to not see this for what it was? Of course, it was a test – but I didn't care. If this was my only avenue to the outside world, well I would take it.

"I'm aware of what this is, Dante, but it isn't anything different is it? At least I know now."

Dante was growing uneasy with every moment he stood lost in the middle of the room. There were questions looming between us, but we both knew he wasn't willing to answer them – actually, he was afraid to answer them.

Luca kept everyone so tightly controlled, especially Dante, who was no doubt his closest ally, but what Luca failed to realize was that everyone has their limit. Dante would show me his sooner or later. I just needed to exercise patience.

"I should go," he finally said as he made his way across the room, his hesitancy lingering behind him. "Just listen to what I said, Olivia, okay? Be smart about this."

"I won't do anything stupid. I promise"

Chapter Twelve

Luca Caruso

Eight years ago, I had been a very different person compared to the man that I am now. There were no issues of control, no empires to watch over, nobody trying to take what was mine at any given moment. I was free and young with room to be stupid and to live a fortunate life.

In the faint distance, while I was locked away in my head, I could hear Dante leaving Olivia's room and conversing with Chen about the new devices that I had allowed. Neither men could understand why I was willing to take such a huge risk by allowing her access to the outside world, but I did. The longer I kept her locked away, the further her resentment for me would spread.

Moving away from their hushed conversations, I made my way to my office where I could think without distractions. Still not used to the sound of people moving about my home, I used my office as a sanctuary for peace and quiet.

As soon as the door clicked behind me, my phone buzzed alerting me to a text message.

Chen: *Sir, extra security is in place for Wellesby Drive. They will provide updates via your email.*

A headache was looming from the day's events – threatening to ruin my evening. Moving to my desk, I placed the phone down so that I could fire up my laptop. This mess was stretching, morphing out of control, and the more security that was thrown at it, the better. Even if it was costing thousands every day.

Waiting for me were a dozen emails from all types of business – screaming at me for answers. Everyone needed fucking answers – including her.

I need a drink.

Instead, I ignored the bottle of scotch on my desk and poured myself over my computer. Answering ridiculous questions from attending events to investment opportunities was easy, but the emails from my IT consultant weren't. Jack Veen was rapid with his emails, showing me every click of her mouse from numerous screenshots to internet searches.

Olivia Heart was upstairs treading dangerous waters on the new laptop I trusted her with. Bright screenshots of her old cases slid across my screen once I was granted remote access. My temper was fraying and the pain behind my eyes was increasing.

Why couldn't she just leave that life behind? It hadn't offered her a damn thing other than seedy criminals, teenage delinquents, and rich businessmen trying to protect their assets from scorned wives. A woman like her, with her mind, didn't need to be dragged to the depths of depravity – even if it was through my company.

Slamming the laptop shut, I grabbed the in-house phone. In three seconds, my housemaid, Maria Constinti, answered in her clipped voice, her Italian quick and smooth. Ten seconds later, she was prepped and prepared with no questions – this is why I took care of her and her family. Silence really was golden.

****

Hours later after a debrief with Chen and his team, I made my way to Olivia's room alone. I didn't need an audience and neither did she. Knocking gently on the door, I waited, giving her the option to have this other form of normality in her life.

I expected her to answer but she didn't, so I opened the door myself – relieved that she hadn't locked it from the inside. My eyes adjusted to the dark space, the blinds closing off the sun that was setting over the house. I found her sat at the vanity table in front of the window.

The only light in the room was from the laptop screen where the familiar email app was open, her fingers furiously working across the keyboard.

"Olivia?" I called, only to watch her body seize with fear at my voice, her small shoulders turning stiff as her head came up. "I'm going to turn on the light."

The light did nothing to ease her fear as she turned around on the small cream seat to face me, giving me a perfect view of the black silk shorts she was wearing. Olivia's long, smooth legs distracted me briefly, until I had the nerve to look up to see that she was wearing a white shirt with no bra.

Fuck.

"What do you want?" she hissed, her eyes narrowing in on me as she caught me staring at her, drinking in her beauty.

Even her anger couldn't piss me off now that I had seen what she was wearing. The woman across from me could wear a rag and I'd still want her, still want to consume her until she was nothing but weak limbs between my sheets.

"To invite you to dinner."

"No thank you."

I couldn't help it – I smirked, which only fueled the fire more. Olivia crossed her arms over her chest, blocking me from appreciating her further.

"It's not a request – lets go," I demanded while moving into her room, holding out my hand to her.

"You get off on this don't you?" she hissed, as looked down at my outstretched hand.

A dark laugh threatened my lips, but it was pushed down by my irritability that was building every time she defied me. Get off on this? She really had no idea.

"I'm not feeling very patient tonight, Olivia, so go get changed. You can scowl and throw your accusations at me over dinner."

Olivia didn't like to lose nor did she like being told what to do. Every moment we had spent together, she had placed distance between us, protecting herself from scenarios she had conjured in her head – I could see it, after all, I had plenty of time to learn everything about her.

Surprising me, she slipped on the heels that she had worn earlier today, highlighting her glorious legs, and held out her open hands. There was to be no argument by her strange choice of dinner attire, which was obvious by the eyebrow she raised my way.

I could go along with this.

Opening my own hand again, I motioned for her to lead, but she remained perfectly still, her expression blank except for the flicker of fury burning in her big green eyes.

I'm trying here, really trying to give you more.

Ignoring the voice in my head, I walked out of the room, listening carefully as she fell into step with my shadow. Cautious she always kept a foot apart from me as we walked down the corridor, down the stairs to the dining room that had been set up for just us.

"Where are they?" she demanded, as she paused in the doorway, her eyes lingering on the table, the table that had been dressed to perfection by Maria. It was perfect. Red and white roses sat in the middle in crystal vases surrounded by candles. All I could hope was that she would see this for what it was – that I was trying not to be a monster.

"They're around here somewhere."

Shrugging out of my jacket gave me something to do with my hands as I felt her eyes burning holes into my back.

"Take a seat," I hissed, my temper slipping through my lips when she made no effort from the doorway. Always keeping her eyes on me, she walked towards the end of the table, the furthest away from me, and took her seat.

Finally, she was listening.

As soon as she sat down, Maria and Laurel, her right hand, stepped into the room like ghosts, hovering with wine. I nodded to Maria to begin and without fuss, she moved to Olivia first.

"No thank you," she breathed, her skeptical eyes firmly on me. "I'll stick to the water."

Maria was smart enough to not react to the rejection of wine as she made her way to me, pouring the 2015 Bordeaux that had been ordered in specifically for Olivia.

"You don't like the wine?" I asked, breaking the deafening silence.

"I like the wine; I just don't trust that it isn't laced."

Laurel froze mid placing my starter, her eyes catching Maria's who was at the side of Olivia. Rubbing my face, I took in a deep breath and bit back my retort. A reaction is what Olivia wanted and it's what she would get. Picking up my glass, I took a small sip of the wine.

Our plates were placed in front of us and both Laurel and Maria moved quickly and quietly out of the room – most likely to shelter from the storm that was brewing between Olivia and me.

Under her hateful glare, I realized that this was a mistake, it was too early to try and get through to her. I was rushing the process for selfish reasons, for wanting her to understand that I was more than her kidnapper.

"I told you that I wouldn't hurt you. Under any circumstance so please, just relax."

"Don't tell me what to do!" she snapped as she hit the table with her hand, the water from her glass sloshing out of the top and landing on the table. I watched as her chest heaved, her breathing erratic as she trembled with fury.

Picking up my fork, I ignored her outburst and watched her, paying careful attention to her chest – more specifically her nipples that were straining against her top.

"I can't do this anymore, Luca. I want to go home. Let me go home."

My name sounded strange from her lips, empty with no signs of affection.

"Like I said, it isn't a possibility anymore. I closed your position, closed your bank accounts down, and moved you out of your apartment. This is your home now."

The food that I placed in my mouth had no taste, my senses giving leave as they powered my eyes and ears to focus solely on her. Specifically, the way she closed her eyes, her mouth drawn down in disgust as she sunk back against the chair.

"This will never be my home."

I saw it and almost dropped my fork. The one lone tear that slipped down her cheek, stopping at the corner of her mouth. My stomach clenched with pain as I watched her open her eyes and roughly wipe away the tear.

If she wouldn't reject me, I would have gone to her, forced her to look at me as I implored her to just listen, but she wasn't ready for that.

"New York wasn't your home. You lived there for four years and didn't find a shred of happiness."

My hand was gripping my wine glass so hard that I was starting to feel the glass give way. Anger and fear swelled in my chest as the secrets threatened to spill once and for all. The thought of her alone in the big city had bothered me for years until I purchased everything around her so that we would both have the security we needed.

I looked at her to find her eyes watching me, judging me from her side of the table.

"Do you know how many times you were nearly taken on the street?" my voice was cold with venom, as I remembered Chen's briefings over the years. "Do you!?"

Olivia jumped as my voice boomed across the table, but she made no move to answer me.

"Those nights when you would stupidly go running alone in the dark. Three fucking times we saved you from being dragged into a dark alley where no doubt you would have been raped or worse."

Downing the wine didn't help dull the vitriol that was spilling from my lips, it only added fuel to the fire. Even the shock on her face couldn't settle me now. The monster wrapped around my soul was urging me on, whispering for me to carry on.

Laurel stepped into the room at the wrong time, and I growled at her to leave. Olivia made a move to follow her, but I slammed my hand on the table. Even the gasp that fell from her lips couldn't save us now.

"Don't fucking move."

I had tried. Tried to keep my composure and to give her control but she was testing me – pushing me beyond the comfortable boundaries I was used to. Before I could reign myself in, I swiped my hand across the table, clearing the contents and letting them smash on the floor.

Olivia jumped up from her chair and stood back, her hands shaking by her sides as she watched me.

"I'm fucking trying," I hissed. "Sit back down, Olivia."

"Please just-"

"SIT THE FUCK DOWN!"

Without missing a beat, she was back in her chair, her eyes begging me to calm down.

"Did I get my job because of you?"

A. L. Hartwell

The question would have been random to anyone else, but I knew that she was trying to distract me, to pull me away from the sinking fury that we were bathing in.

Shaking my head, I ran my hands through my hair as I dragged air through my nose. "No, you got that job on your own. I just made sure that the deal they offered you was fair. I bought the business after."

Olivia nodded quickly. "When did you have me followed?"

Closing my eyes to her was easier, her beauty couldn't distract me as I let the answers spill from my loose lips.

"Four years ago."

I felt my heart sinking deeper into my chest.

"But you've been keeping watch for eight?"

"Yes," I spat, through gritted teeth.

It sounded perverse when she said it, but it was far from it. This was more than simply lusting for her.

"Something changed in my circumstances for you to send a team to watch me. Luca, what was it?"

"Nothing changed. I just grew impatient," I lied, as I opened my eyes.

Olivia was biting her lip while she contemplated her next question. The action alone had the fury in my veins turning to lust. What I wouldn't give to go over there and bite that lip myself. Bite her so hard that she would bleed.

"Eight years is a long time. So, you just decided one day that you couldn't wait any longer?"

Olivia moved slowly out of her seat; her heels long gone as she padded her way over to me. I'd have thought she was stupid by coming to me when I was this way, but I could see her ulterior motive glinting in her eyes. Stopping in the middle

100

of our seats, she touched the part of the table that was untouched by me and stood where no glass could cut her.

"You can tell me, Luca."

No! No, I couldn't. As much as she thought she could handle the truth, I knew better for the both of us. This whole dinner was a mistake, forcing her to leave her room to spend the evening with me was a mistake.

I was an idiot.

A fool.

"Sir?" Chen was full of tense energy as he poked his head into the room, his eyes narrowing on the state of the floor.

"Take Olivia to her room," I muttered, while I pushed out of my seat, ignoring her wide eyes.

"No!" she called, as she made a move towards me, her feet touching broken bits of plates and glass.

"Chen," I growled, as I moved out of her grasp, denying her fingers when they reached out to touch my arm. If she touched me, I wouldn't be able to stop myself.

Chen moved with quick precision and he scooped her up, his hands under her legs as he moved her away from the destruction. Olivia tried to force him to put her down, but he was quick as he moved them out of the room.

Standing on the edge of the room, I looked down at the destruction of the dinner I had planned in hopes of showing her that she could trust me, that I wasn't the monster that she thought I was.

Instead, the devil in me had decided that I didn't deserve this evening after all. Just like I didn't deserve her.

CHAPTER THIRTEEN

Olivia Heart

Hours had slipped by as my brain agonized over the events at dinner with Luca. In the early hours of the morning, I had turned over every moment of the disastrous dinner in my head, just trying to find an answer in all his mess.

There he was, behind my eyes when I tried to sleep. There he was when I sat on the floor of the shower, sobbing quietly to myself in hope of finding relief. Now even buried under silk sheets, I could still feel his aggression wrapping its way around my limbs, pulling me down into the mattress – suffocating me.

Before I knew it, the sun was rising, pouring through the blinds that I had forgotten to close. Another day, another day of being in this prison without a reason. Another day, where I found myself sitting on the edge of the bed pondering my mere existence.

"Miss?" There was a faint knock at the door of the maid bringing me my breakfast. Slipping out of the bed, I padded gently over to the door to let her in. Maria's bright face surprised me as she beamed my way.

"Breakfast Miss Heart," she breathed as she pushed by with her tray.

"I'm not hungry," I replied sullenly, as she placed the tray down on the desk and began removing last night's tray, the untouched dinner back in her hands.

"You must eat!" she told me sharply, surveying the room with interest, noting the clothes that I had ripped from hangers and piled up in the closet with surprise. "You will get sick if you don't eat."

"Thank you, Maria," I replied curtly, as I stepped towards the tray and looked down at the arrangements of pastries, willing myself to feel hungry. In the few days that I had been here, my appetite had left, and my body didn't appreciate it.

"Sit!" she chided me with her limited English.

Today there was no energy to push back, so I took the seat and picked up a croissant, nibbling on the delicate pastry while watching the sun rise over the vineyard.

"Is Luca awake?"

"Yes, Miss," she replied, while thumping a pillow before carefully placing it against the headboard. "But he's gone."

"Gone?" I repeated, turning my whole body to look at her she was now tucking the sheets in with military precision.

"Yes, with Dante."

Embarrassment flushed my face when she moved towards the clothes piled up, no judgment on her small face as she began pulling the expensive gowns up, inspecting them for damage before she slipped into the closet.

In a few minutes, she had completed her task of putting the room back together while I managed to eat a few morsels of

A. L. Hartwell

breakfast. Bidding me goodbye with a polite smile, she left me once again to the quiet space of my room.

I was ready twenty minutes later, wearing a pale pink sundress with a white bikini underneath. Slipping out of my door, at the bottom of the corridor, was Bones who greeted me with a curt nod.

Bones was a tall blonde man with a wispy moustache and a gnarly scar from the end of his left eyebrow to the corner of his mouth. In his bright blue eyes were untold stories of suffering and pain that he tried to mask with a blank stare. All of Chen's team had the same look.

As soon as the heat hit my face, I felt relief for being in the fresh air and the smell of roses comforted me somehow. Slipping off my shoes, I investigated the pristine water of the football-field-sized pool – what would it be like to slip under the water and stay there? Would I find complete silence?

"Miss Heart?" Bones called to me, as if sensing my dark thoughts.

Ignoring him I, grabbed the hem of my dress and began pulling it up over my body. There was no hesitancy from me as I walked to the steps into the pool. I just walked right in, ignoring the cold on my legs and stomach as I wade further in.

Gone was my timid attitude towards being in skimpy clothes. They had probably seen me in less.

The thought alone made me want to heave.

"It was you that night in my apartment, wasn't it?" I asked, once I pushed myself back to the edge of the pool, gripping the marble tiles to keep myself there.

Bones was uncomfortable – I could tell as much by the way he shifted his gaze from me to the wall that spanned around this side of the house.

"Yes, it was me."

"How long were you waiting?"

The small flex of his jaw was enough to tell me he was uncomfortable with my questions, but it didn't stop me. It was his turn to feel my invasion into his privacy.

"Two hours."

Bones moved and took a seat at one of the tables around the pool, his body stiff as a board as he perched on the edge of his seat.

"But you were with me for four years before that night?"

The water swelled around my body as I moved down the edge of the pool to be right in front of him. Bones looked me in the eye once before looking over my head – trapped just like I was.

Satisfaction bloomed in my chest.

"Yes, Miss Heart. I was assigned to your security detail four years ago at the request of Mr. Caruso."

"How did you stay hidden all that time?"

There was no judgment in my tone, I was careful with that so I could gain more access to the information needed, to build a picture of the events leading to my kidnap.

Bones let out a small nervous laugh before rubbing a large hand across his chin. "Let's just say, we had many inventive options at our disposal. My main post was outside of your apartment building."

"Must have been boring. I didn't exactly lead an exciting life," I said. Looking down, I saw how the water reflected against my skin which was tanner than it had been a week ago.

"My job is never boring Miss Heart." He gave me a small smile that made the scar on his left side scrunch up, ageing him.

"I've seen the photos Bones and some of them are...very personal. Was it you that took the pictures of my apartment and me running at night?"

Leaning out of the pool, I tried to get him to look back down at me, to look me in the eye and tell me the truth. Pathetically, I wanted him to look at me, to see the bikini slicked to my body to lure the answers from him, but he remained stoic - a perfect soldier.

"They were taken by me." He rubbed his jaw again before finally looking down at me. "It was my job to give Mr. Caruso the information he needed. None of those files were used for anything other than security."

I scoffed and I pushed away from the ledge, wanting to place distance between us after he mentioned Luca. The sour taste returned to my mouth at the thought of Luca using the man in front of me to voyeur into my privacy - all while he sat on his throne of power in another country.

Bones touched his earpiece and paused before shaking his head, no doubt listening to the other person on the other end - telling him what to say and what to do. The honesty of our conversation disappearing.

"Look, Miss Heart, whatever you want to believe is just fine with me, but I just want you to know that we're here to protect you. That's all."

I paused in the water as I watched him stand up, his face covered in sweat from the sun that was now directly over us.

"Does that security include protecting me from Luca?"

Bones didn't need to say a word, it was written all over his face as his expression turned from blank to worried. Of course, they wouldn't protect me from him, they were bound to him and only him. If their job was to protect me like he was saying, I would have been placed on the first flight home.

****

Later, that evening, I was back in my bed, wrapped in silk sheets as I tried to will my brain to sleep. In sleep, I could find a way out, find a fraction of peace in all the noise coming from my thoughts.

Before the depths of my depravity could consume me further there was a loud knock against my door

"Olivia!" Dante called, before he knocked again. "Are you awake?"

There was a scuffle outside the door and another bang.

"Cazzo!" he hissed, as I opened the door to a disheveled Dante who was struggling to stand up. His usual scent of wood and leather replaced with booze and smoke.

"Ah bellisama!" He grinned, flashing me pearly white teeth before barging his way into my room.

"Dante what are you doing?"

Whirling around to face me, he threw his leather jacket to the bottom of my bed and looked me up and down.

"I'm taking you out! That's what I'm doing," he replied. Grabbing my hand, he yanked me forward and dragged me into the closet. "Get a dress on, and let's go."

"Go where?" I mumbled, thinking this was some sort of sick trick.

"I'm taking you to a club," he told me, as if we did this every weekend.

"Dante, I don't think Luca-"

"I've confirmed it with him," Dante waved me away, sobering slightly at the mention of his cousin's name. "He will be there too so why not join us eh?"

A club? With hundreds of people as witnesses. Suddenly, my blood flamed with fire as all my options poured out in front of me. This was what I had been waiting for, and there wasn't a chance in hell I would let this slip through my hands.

****

Dante quickly sobered when I stepped out of the bathroom, his eye's traveling down my body before he noisily gulped. The reaction was perfect as he eyed the little black dress with thin straps and a cinched waist. I had paired the outfit with black and gold Giuseppe Zanotti heels, slipping into them as Dante nervously paced around me. Not having much time to finish my hair, I let it hang loose, smoothing the tendrils framing my face while eyeing up Dante.

"Is there something wrong?"

By every second he looked at me, I could see him sobering, his eyes becoming alert, and his relaxed stare being replaced with one of dread.

"Entro la mattina sarò morto," he mumbled, grabbing my elbow and began pulling me out of the room.

Waiting for us was Rum, Bones, and Red who also didn't seem to appreciate my outfit choice either. Smug with power, I sauntered past them all, allowing my heels to be the only noise as we slipped down the stairs and out of the house.

Slipping into the air-conditioned car, I waited for Dante to get in, but he was whispering into Bones' ear – his body tense as they conversed secretly. Looking down at my outfit choice, I regarded it with indifference, it wasn't something that you would find in my wardrobe, but it couldn't be underestimated. It was the perfect distraction for what I needed.

"So, what's the club called?" I asked Dante, when he slipped into the back seat with me, a little more relaxed than five minutes ago.

Dante kept his eyes ahead, cautiously aware of himself in my presence. I would be a liar if I didn't admit that having this ounce of power over the men in this car was satisfying. After all, it was the only control I had.

"Energy," he said, while fiddling in his leather jacket for his phone.

Rum and Bones were in the front, pulling us away from the beautifully lit house while Red was in the car behind. There was a certain feeling when they were all together that of a pack mentality, fierce and protective.

"Is that where you've just come from?" I asked him, hoping that it was located in the city far away from the house.

Dante nodded while steeling a quick look my way. "Luca's there on business and I had the bright idea to come get you," a small groan escaped his lips – his idea turning to ash in between us. "You'll give him a heart attack wearing that."

My eye's widened before I could control my face. "Why?"

In the front, Rum and Bones shared a look that made me blush. Was the dress really that short? Should I ask to go back and change? There hadn't been many evenings where I had chosen to wear such an outfit but needs must.

Dante let out a small laugh before pushing a hand through his hair. "Because, Miss Heart, you look.... well, you look sorprendente!"

I didn't need to be fluent in Italian to know he was paying me a compliment. That was just the way Dante was, he was light and carefree. The opposite of his cousin who could suck the light out of any room.

"It's just he won't want anyone staring at you wearing that. Luca is very protective over you."

I glared at Dante as soon as Luca's name was mentioned before turning away to look out the window. So, Luca bought these clothes for me but only for his eyes? Pig.

"Luca purchased this dress. I didn't realize it was for decoration only."

****

It wasn't long until we were pulling up to a narrow street filled with revelers enjoying their evening. There were people lining down the street to get into the club that we had just pulled up to, desperate to get to the music buzzing out of the doorway. Dressed in the country's latest fashions, they chatted freely, some dancing with others as they waited and some taking pictures with their phones.

The door opened and Bones stuck his hand in to help me out, his eyes full of caution as we slipped into the street. In seconds Rum, Bones, and Red flanked behind me and Dante, creating quite the show as people in line paused to watch.

Dante grabbed my hand and tugged me forward, his fingers squeezing mine offering some comfort. As we stepped closer to the door, two large security guards nodded at Dante before parting, allowing us all the slip through without having to pause.

My ears were infiltrated with the sultry song of "Crazy in Love" by Beyonce that had been slowed down, the usual upbeat vocals replaced with vulnerable notes that sent shivers down my spine.

The darkness enveloped us as we made our way down a long hallway, the walls lit up by small purple lights. Nerves began to build in my stomach while my heartbeat began to pick up, thumping against my ribcage as we moved further into the club.

Dante led us around a sharp corner, and I was deafened instantly by a shrill scream of a woman before she drunkenly jumped into his arms, her pink drink sloshing down his jacket arm.

I stood back, my eyes on the girl's face who looked to be the same age as me, but she was a blonde with very little on. Girlishly giggling, she let him whisper sweet nothings into her ear, completely forgetting that I was there.

Red touched the back of my arm and I turned to face him.

"We need to keep moving," he told me, his eye's alive with excitement but his face was dripping with sweat – giving away his nerves for the tight situation he was in with his colleagues.

It wouldn't be easy to keep watch of me when I was surrounded by a sea of blending bodies under the dark lights. Dante finally let go of his blonde friend with a kiss on the cheek before ushering her away.

"Let's get a drink, shall we?" he told me, as he grabbed my hand once again and pulled us into the main part of the building.

My eyes found it difficult to concentrate on all of the stimuli at once, but I didn't have to worry about where to go next because Dante pulled me to the bar on the far left of the room.

Turning my back against the bar, I watched while my guards created a circle around me, disguising me from the crowds of people dancing and drinking their worries away.

A glass of pink Cristal champagne was thrust into my hand, but quickly taken away by Bones who glared over at Dante, his bear-like grip nearly crushing the dainty glass.

"Sir, we've had direct orders not to supply Miss Heart with alcohol."

Dante didn't like this information one bit and neither did I. Snatching the glass back, I placed the cool glass to my lips and tipped the liquid into my mouth, allowing the bubbles to tickle my tongue before taking a sip.

"Like I said, Luca doesn't control what I do with my own body. If he has a problem with it, he can tell me himself."

Dante grinned wildly at my act of defiance before clicking his fingers for another. Shrugging the annoyed look of the three men around me, I let my eyes travel around the room, enjoying the beautiful structure of the place with its white ornate pillars that were surrounded by soft seating areas. Above the dance floor, was a balcony full of people, some chatting while most of them danced to the sultry music.

Standing in the middle of the balcony looking down on us, was Chen and Luca, neither one of them taking their eyes off me for a second. Luca was dressed in his usual smart attire, but gone were the dark suits and were replaced with a navy blue suit and crisp white shirt. Luca was positively furious as his dark smoldering eyes radiated a fierce disapproval of what I assumed was my outfit choice. Turning smugly, I accepted the second glass of champagne from Dante who was currently under Luca's fierce stare.

"Shit," he hissed loudly over the music, before knocking back a glass of whiskey.

"Dante!" another girl screamed, her American accent catching me off guard as she slid down the bar to us. Rum grabbed the back of my dress and pulled me back so that I was closer to them all, shielding me from the 5ft 2' girl whose voice was bigger than she was.

"Ellie!" he called back, as he kissed her cheek. "What are you doing here? I thought you were heading home?"

Ellie with her flaming bottle red hair looked over to her friends stood in the corner with a smile. "We decided to stay another week. It's hard to say bye to this place."

Dante turned to face me and panicked when I wasn't at his side. Just as he saw me, his eyes went behind my head, bulging wide before he gulped. I didn't need to turn to know that Luca and Chen had joined us – Luca's blazing energy burning my back. It was as though someone had turned the music off because all I could hear was his loud, aggressive thoughts behind me.

"Olivia, come with me," he whispered into my ear, as his hand snaked around my wrist, pinning it to my side – telling me to behave. "**Now.**"

The bravery that had guarded me at the start of the evening faded as he tugged me away from the safety of Dante and a hundred eyewitnesses. All I could do was follow, trying to keep up with his strides as we slipped out of the main room into another darkened hallway.

Chen and his men tried to follow but with one look from Luca, they retreated down the hallway and out of sight. The unpredictability I felt made my mouth dry and my hands tremble as I watched them go.

A. L. Hartwell

Taking a step back, I watched while he wordlessly took off his suit jacket before holding it out to me.

"Take it," he demanded, his eye's not leaving mine as he controlled himself, controlled the urge to appreciate the dress he had bought.

A flicker of pride fluttered freely in my chest before he pinned me with an ice-cold stare, killing the caterpillar before it could blossom into a butterfly.

Crossing my arms with an eyebrow raised, I looked down at his offending jacket, his musky scent enveloping my senses. "I'm good, thank you," I replied. Moving, I side-stepped him and headed towards the corridor where there were people, where there was safety.

It took two steps before his skin returned to mine, his large hands gripping the back of my arm, before he turned me around and pinned me against the cool tile of the walls.

A gasp shot from my lips when my shoulders connected with the cold wall. The jacket that had been offered now lay abandoned at our feet as our eyes connected. There was no softness nor light in his eyes as he glowered down at me, his lips turned up in a snarl.

I was prey and he was predator.

Completely and utterly at his mercy.

"I said, take the damn jacket," he growled. His hand moved up the wall and rested at the side of my head, close enough to stop me from moving if I tried.

"Why?" I whispered, finding myself shrinking away from him.

"That fucking dress is why," he snarled next to my ear, while he looked down my body, burning my skin with his eyes as he went. "The fuck was Dante thinking letting you out like this?"

"Dante isn't the controlling type—I doubt he was thinking about it at all," the words should have left my lips coated in venom, but I was meek and softly spoken.

Luca laughed sarcastically before pulling back, giving me room to breathe but not enough that I could escape his towering frame.

"You don't know a thing about Dante. You don't know the danger he's put you in by bringing you here."

This is what he wanted, he wanted to get into my head, spurt his lies and infect me with his jealousy so that I wouldn't trust Dante. Fire blossomed in my chest as I stepped away from the wall.

"Because of all these witnesses that could possibly recognize the sick bastard that you are?"

A flash of hurt shadowed his face before he could hide from me. I grabbed at the one strand of control I had in this and took a step closer to him, crossing my arms over my chest.

"You can't keep me like this forever. I'll never give in to you no matter how much you force yourself upon my life, so you might as well let me go."

"Everybody breaks, Olivia," he sighed, as he ran a hand through his hair.

"You'll break before I do," I snapped, my voice finally raising enough that I didn't sound like a victim anymore.

Shaking his head, he looked down the corridor, his jaw clenching as he tried to claw back his control, but there was no stopping me now. I moved closer to him, demanding that he look at me and he did.

"What do you think's going to happen here? Do you think I'll just give in and let you ruin me?"

"Ruin you?" he repeated, genuine surprise swept his face before he recovered, masking it with his usual ice-cold stare.

I wanted to scream, to hit him, to throw every insult my brain knew, but I just glared seven bells of hell his way. I opened my mouth, willing the anger to burst at the surface but nothing happened. Floundering under his dark stare, he was winning once again.

"You need help," was all I could squeeze from my lips. Those three words, even though they were harsh, they weren't enough.

"I do," he told me honestly, as he lifted his hand, his index finger suddenly touching my bottom lip, forcing my muscles to lock into place. My eyes never left his as he slipped his fingers from my mouth to tilt my chin up.

Completely breathless, I felt my body react and shame filled me to the brim.

"But not as much as I need you."

My body had reacted to his words with pleasure, humming with bright lust while he stared into my eyes. The feeling was foreign and misplaced. I had never felt anything like this in my life.

Chen's shoes clicking across the floor forced both of us to look his way, Luca dropped my chin as he composed himself, his mask slipping perfectly into place. Turning, we both glared over at Chen, a normal person would have cowered under us, but he remained stoic as he stopped in front of Luca.

"Sir, they're growing impatient."

Chen let his eyes slide to me, checking me over once before deeming me 'calm' enough to relax slightly. Luca, however, hadn't relaxed at all; he was still tense and aggressive by my side.

This was the perfect time to move now that there was a witness, even if this witness would choose Luca's side if push came to shove. Quickly, I moved around them both and rushed down the corridor where I could try and shake off the strange feelings crawling its way into my heart.

CHAPTER FOURTEEN

Olivia Heart

The music had changed in the short time I was in the corridor, the sultry music now replaced with an upbeat tempo that had the crowd of people grinding on each other. Gone was any good mood that I had, and it was replaced with blind fury. Sidestepping my guards, I headed straight across the room to where the lady's restroom was, ignoring them as they followed me the whole way.

"Don't even think about it," I growled at Rum, who tried to follow me in. "Don't be a complete idiot."

Before he could answer me, I slipped through the door into a bright lit area. The bathroom was full of giggling girls taking pictures on their iPhone, some sitting on a chaise lounge in the corner, crying over stupid ex-boyfriends while I stood there like an outsider. This was far too normal.

"Oh my God!" the screech caught me off guard, as a beautiful woman with striking black hair rushed to me, her big green eyes drinking in my dress with amazement. "Is that a vintage Chanel?"

"I-I think so," I stuttered, as her group of friends joined her, one even touching me so that I would turn around like a prized mannequin.

"It is! Fuck, Jessica just look at it!" the green-eyed girl grinned while she turned to her friend who happened to be looking me up and down with appreciation.

"It looks like it was made for your body. What's your name?" she asked, pulling me over towards the mirrors where I caught sight of myself. I was far from the woman who spent her evenings locked in her office.

I looked sexy, sultry – like I had stepped off a magazine page in this dress. It almost looked as though it had been tailored to my body, especially to my feminine hips.

I'd never dressed up like this before. Hell, I avoided anything that would gather male attention.

"Olivia."

"Where did you get this from? I've had my sugar daddy searching the country for it."

Their eyes barely met my eyes as they ogled the prized dress that clung to my body. Back at Luca's house, I had simply picked it because of the short hem not because it was designer. Before I could stop myself from thinking the impossible, I let the plan seed in my head, letting it grow as their excitement for this piece of fashion overwhelmed me.

"Do you want it?"

****

In ten minutes, I found myself trapped in a dark purple cubicle, sliding my hands down a gold waterfall beaded dress that I had swapped a priceless Chanel for. In five minutes, I had persuaded a drunken Jessica that the dress should go to someone that would appreciate it. Even managed to swap my heels for her friends who were the same size as me. I needed a total change.

All her friends screamed in delight when we swapped dresses, like best friends would, but as soon as the dress clung to her body, I was allowed to slink back to the shadows and prepare.

Moving out of the cubicle, my heart thudded with anticipation while my brain steadied me, preparing me for my one shot at freedom.

Sucking in a deep breath, my hands ripped open the door while a group of girls left, shielding myself behind them, I moved quickly, keeping my eyes on Rum who was checking his iPhone at the bottom of the stairs.

Once we stepped onto the dance floor, I slipped into the crowd of people dancing close, their drinks up in the air providing extra cover while I began to make my way through them.

If I wasn't desperate, I'd have allowed the sickness in my stomach to consume me, the fear to make me shake, and my paranoia to force me to look around, but I didn't. Pushing further through the crowd, I ignored the drink that poured down my arm.

At the first exit, Red and Bones stood talking on either side of the door. Pausing, I felt the hand of panic wrap around my throat at having to walk through them both, knowing that I would be spotted.

Stranded, I felt the adrenalin drain from my body until a drunken girl bumped into Bones, her hands scrambling up his chest as she tried to grip him. Red jumped to his aid and tried to grab the girl back.

I surged forward and slipped behind Red's back and back into the purple-lit corridor. The cool air from the doorway lured me out, pulling me to my freedom as my feet rushed me forward.

The relief of my heels touching the pavement was immense. The pressure around my heart was easing with every step away from the club that held my captor and guards. Glee and adrenalin combusted in my chest forcing my legs to move faster as I rounded the corner onto a narrow street.

The street was empty except for one small pastel blue car with the words POLIZIA down the side. Tears sprang to my eyes as I raced across the street until my hands were thumping desperately on the glass of the car, begging, crying for them to help me before it was too late.

****

I was safe.

Safe.

Free.

Sitting in a small room with fluorescent lighting over my head, the only sound was the pipes running above me, creaking and groaning while I waited for them to return.

My arrival here was calm as they guided me with kindness. The officer who didn't speak much English, took me into his car and had given me his spare jacket from the boot. He had bought me an herbal tea while I waited, promising a detective would be in soon.

Had it been hours since he promised a detective would come?

Or, simply minutes?

Trying to stay positive was hard when my face was swollen from tears and knowing that I wasn't home yet, that the feeling of safety wouldn't come until my body and soul was in England with my Aunt Sarah.

Before I could dwell any further into the darkness the old steel door creaked opened, revealing a short gentleman with pitch-black eyebrows, receding hair, and wrinkled skin from spending too much time in the sun. However, unlike the men I had met from this country so far, he was friendly and kind.

"Miss Heart?" he asked me, as he took a seat across the table with a soft smile, trying to offer me some comfort as I sunk further into my jacket.

"My name is Detective Enrico Russe, I'll be looking after your case. You're safe here with us now," he told me, his English better than I had expected. "Do you need anything?"

A sob escaped my throat before I could control it, but he was right there with a handkerchief, well-practiced in comforting those that walked through this police station.

Grateful, I took the small gift and dabbed my eyes. "I just want to go home."

Home. Where was my home? I thought it had been in New York but now all I could think about was the cold weather of England, walking across the countryside with my aunt and her small dog Otto.

"I understand Miss Heart. My colleague has er - filled me in on your – case," he began, flicking through the statement I had given on my arrival, his eyes widening at the details of my account.

Try living it.

"I need to get out of the country!" I blurted. "This man, he has immense power and I'm not sure how safe I am here."

"We're in contact with the embassy to get you an emergency passport, Miss Heart, and rest assured, nobody comes through these doors unless we say so."

A sigh of relief from me fell into the room. "Thank you. Do you have a phone I can use? I'd like to speak to my family."

"Yes, yes," he told me, as he stood up. "I just need you to answer a few questions before I can leave you alone."

I could do this. I could be brave enough.

Nodding towards him while wiping my eyes, I motioned for him to start so I could spend the next few seconds gathering myself.

"How long have you been a prisoner?"

"I think a week...I'm not sure, sorry I know that's no help."

Again, his small smile of comfort settled me once again.

"Do you need to go to the er...hospital?"

I balked at his question, my eyes widening at what he was asking me. Thankfully, I didn't, and it had never got that far. It was one small mercy that I could hold on to.

I shook my head, losing my voice as memories of Luca's hands drifting down my neck overwhelmed me. Remembering the mix of fear and lust at his burning touch.

The door suddenly opened, and a female officer stepped in, regarding me carefully before she leaned over to Detective Russe, whispering into his ear. Russe's face never changed from impassive but his shoulders tensed, sending me into high alert.

Looking up at him, he smiled. "It's okay," he muttered, after sensing my fears. "The embassy is preparing your passport, but they need my signature. Are you okay to wait here?"

"Yes, of course, thank you, thank you so much."

As they left the room, my body sank further into the chair with some stranger's jacket around my shoulders, shielding me from the overwhelming bright lights of this room.

In the complete silence, my thoughts began to tread dangerous water, going back to the moment when Luca demanded I wear his jacket, wanted to brand me so others wouldn't stare at me, his property.

The room in his house that had been purposed for me, with all the things he thought a woman would want to be his, right down to the size of underwear I wore and the shampoo I used.

Then, as if these memories weren't enough, I remembered his face the night he invited me to dinner. The look of terror that slipped across his face when he lost control of his emotions — with it came more of his truths that had singed against my soul.

Sickness rolled through my body, forcing me to bow my head as my brain flexed against the memories. Fear for my future blasted cold air down my arms, forcing me to face the possibility of a life without trust for those around me.

Shaking away the fear with halfhearted courage, I decided that once I was free, out of Sicily, I would permit myself to face what had happened to me.

Breaking me from my thoughts, was the sound of shoes clipping against the floor outside of the room I was placed in. Swells of relief washed over me at the thought of this dreadful process moving on.

Sitting up straighter, I waited as the door swung open, in came Detective Russe first with a solemn look across his old, weathered face. Too focused on him, I hadn't seen his colleague slip in until she was moving behind me.

"What's going on?" I asked. flinching away from the woman behind me, I looked up at the detective for an answer.

"Miss Heart, you're free to go," he told me.

"What!?" I jumped up, my hips hitting the small table as my wild eyes regarded him with shock.

Free to go where? From here? To the airport!?

Before he could open his mouth, we were interrupted by Luca Caruso walking into the room, his cold eyes finding mine with a smirk across his smug face.

At some point during my escape, he had changed, his light clothing replaced for an all-black suit that reflected the darkness that followed him.

He looked like an assassin.

This betrayal burned, searing away at the last bits of hope that I had clung to since I entered the police station. Trapped like a bird in a cage, I was barricaded in by all three of them with no option but to submit to Luca.

Destruction. That's the only word I could use to describe what was happening as he stepped into the room, bringing in ice-cold temperatures with him.

Luca composed himself enough to look me over, checking to see if I was still in one piece before he turned to the detective.

"Grazie per averla tenuta qui. La porto a casa adesso," his tone was firm, business like as he held out his hand to the detective.

As they shook, so did my legs, my whole body shutting back down while I watched my handover happen right in front of me. Luca had control over the police, over me and there wasn't a single thing I could do about it.

"No," I whispered, as the detective left, refusing to look at me as he swept out of the room.

"Let's go, Olivia." He stepped towards me and I shattered. My unblinking eyes watched as he lifted his hand to me, demanding all of me once again.

"Do you understand the trouble your little stunt has caused?" he hissed, lurching forward and wrapped his hand around my arm, pulling me close to his face.

My body and mind were heavy with grief, so it was impossible to speak. My eyes just blinked up at him, trying to force away the scalding tears pooling within them.

"Answer me," he snapped, before roughly shaking me.

I didn't.

I couldn't.

Body heat, the scent of vanilla, whiskey, and musk overwhelmed me, forcing my senses to retreat with my voice. Even my heartbeat decided to thump quietly, afraid to make noise in case it made this worse for me.

Luca's eyes were wild with punishment possibilities when I didn't speak – shutting him off from my thoughts only pissed him off more.

"Fuck," he snapped, as he began to drag me out of the room, pulling me so close to his side that I was under his arm, hiding me once again. The tears that had pooled in my eyes began to fall, leaving tracks down my face as we passed through people going about their business.

Nobody paid any more attention to us as we were buzzed out of a set of steel doors, heading towards the stairs.

"We've spent fucking hours looking for you," he hissed, against the top of my head. "What do you have to say for yourself Olivia?"

Nothing. I had nothing to say.

"You thought you could just slip away, in my country, without me knowing?" he laughed coldly as we descended the stairs. My feet were clumsy, forgetting how to walk which only pissed him off more. Snaking his arm around my waist, he pinned me to him, keeping me upright.

"I own the police Olivia just like I own you," he carried on, lashing me with his venom as we came to a gate at the bottom of the stairs. We were buzzed through without a single look by the guard and Luca forced us onto the street.

There wasn't a single soul loitering around the quiet street, not a single person who would see me for possibly the final time. In front of us was a black two-seater Lamborghini Huracan, dazzling under the moonlight without Luca's usual security.

Were they still looking for me?

"Get in," he snapped, as he pushed me forward towards the passenger door, but my body stiffened, hunkering down.

I couldn't go back.

My answer tumbled from my mouth before I could stop myself. "No."

Cringing at the sound of my broken voice, I stepped away from him and pulled my jacket around me, creating a flimsy shield from his spitting rage. Nothing could have prepared me for the look he gave me as he stepped towards me, his hands shaking at my disobedience.

Lunging forward, he grabbed at my jacket, and in one quick motion, he stripped me of it, tossing it across the street before returning to me.

"You'll wear some stranger's disgusting clothes, but not mine!"

The cool air hit my arms and legs, stripping me of the only comfort I had while I stood in someone else's dress and shoes. Before my bravery could get me into more trouble, he opened the car door and pushed me down into the leather seat, not caring that his constant grip on my arms was painting me with bruises.

CHAPTER FIFTEEN

Olivia Heart

Wild and erratic was the only way to describe his energy as he slipped the automatic car into reverse and pulled away from the police station. Trying to focus on anything but him was difficult, not even the overwhelming new car smell could distract me from his building fury.

Luca's knuckles were turning white around the staring wheel as he expertly sped through the sleeping city. The only sound in the small space was my heartbeat in my ears as I stole nervous glances his way, silently praying he wouldn't crash.

"Very smart of you to swap clothes with a stranger Olivia," he hissed, into the small space.

"It didn't work," I muttered to myself, clinging to the leather seat by my nails. Looking at him from the corner of my eye, I flinched at his side profile, completely wild as he navigated the car down the tight streets of the city.

"No, it didn't. We realized what you had done when the woman you swapped with walked by my table."

I pictured the beautiful girl wearing the dress, reveling in her luck as she twirled around in a vintage Chanel dress without a care in the world. The only positive to come from this unravelling situation was that there was a young woman out there with a huge smile on her face. Luca on the other hand continued to burn scorching hot beside me, his eyes wildly darting to the side of my face as I remained silent.

"What!? No attitude?" he yelled into the small space, my ears ringing as I grabbed the door.

"No fucking questions for me Olivia!?"

Closing my eyes didn't stop the overwhelming urge to cry, it only made it worse as I faced further darkness behind my lids. Sobs threatened to spill from my lips as the car roared forward, his temper now being taken out in means of speed.

"Just stop this," I whispered desperately.

"Stop!? Stop!" he laughed, "I wish I could fucking stop, but I can't. Do you not get it yet Olivia?"

No, I didn't get anything anymore.

Opening my eyes, I found all that surrounded the car was darkness while we sped down a lone road with only fields surrounding either side.

"I told you I wouldn't break."

"And I told you that you would eventually," he sneered at me, but I didn't look, I didn't need to. I could picture his face clear as day in my mind as he pushed the car past its speed limits.

In the faint distance, the familiar glow of light surrounding his house filled the skyline, the sun slowly rising behind the large property. It taunted me, luring at my failed escape as we moved closer.

Maybe if I broke, he would go easy on me.

Maybe if I accepted my new fate, this would be easier on me.

I turned to look at him and knew there was no way out of this. Luca Caruso was barely keeping it together, his hair no longer neat but tousled, his shirt creased from fighting his self-restraint... the full wrath of hell was coming my way.

In one minute, I would be trapped again.

The car lurched forward, burning fuel quickly as it snarled at the road surface.

My mind began to slowly shut down and cut a deal with my heart that whatever happened, I had least tried. That I could live with – if I lived.

Luca barely slowed as the wrought iron gates swung open, taking us from the darkness and spilling us to the front of the house where Chen, his men, and Dante were waiting for us.

Barely registering their presence, I was ripped out of the car by Luca within seconds of the car stopping. My right arm burned against his grip, but I swallowed the pain and let him drag me.

"Luca!" Dante called, appalled as he rushed towards us with wild eyes full of apologies. Chen stepped forward, preventing him from reaching us and I realized with my whole heart that I hated everything about Chen.

"Vaffanculo Dante, prima che ti strappi la gola," Luca growled, as he began dragging me up the steps, away from them all.

Finally, a cry slipped by my lips, but it didn't stop him.

Dante pushed Chen away and lunged towards us, but he was stopped once again, being pinned back with Rum and Bones who had refused to meet my eye.

"You're hurting me," pathetically I cried, "Luca, please stop."

"Luca listen to her! Look what you're doing," Dante cried, as Luca pulled me up the final steps, growling at me to move.

"Don't hurt her, Luca, please!"

The last thing I saw, was the look of horror on Dante's face before being pushed into the foyer. My gasps for air echoed across the space and met with the sound of my heels dragging across the perfectly polished floor.

My skin scorched under his grip. I could feel the horror that was coming my way as he wordlessly dragged me up the long curving stairs. Stumbling, my ankle rolled in my heels and I fell into him with a yelp, clinging to his suit jacket as I scrambled to stay upright.

"Move," he snapped down at me, his anger only consuming him, turning his eyes from brown to black, the darkness winning.

I moved along with him, biting my lip as I tried to force away the pain throbbing in my ankle, tried desperately not to push him any further.

That was until my eyes locked on the corridor leading towards our rooms.

NO!

Light as a feather, he pulled me forward towards his room with a vice-like grip. Wild with panic, my body twisted away, to try and run back down the stairs, but he yanked me forward into his chest and pinned me close.

"Don't even try it," he hissed, and pushed me through the door. Darkness suffocated my eyes as I fell onto what felt like a soft carpet. My ankle seared with pain, my palms were burning, and my wrists bruised from trying to free myself.

Terror climbed onto my back and kept me down.

Hysterical sobs were climbing up my throat until a switch was flicked, illuminating the corners of the room with soft warm light. Before I could take in my surroundings, I was yanked back up by my shoulders to face him.

My soul flinched in my body as he peered down at me. Luca was frighteningly calm now, his face cold and void of any emotion but his eyes were the opposite – wild and reeling with the need to punish me.

I could see it.

Feel it.

"Take them off," he growled, peering slowly at my feet.

Hot fear blazed down my spine at the cold automatic voice that came from his lips, but I did as I was told – my brain deciding to obey before my heart had a chance to argue.

I became smaller, nothing underneath his height and power.

My heart raced against my ribcage, trying to get out, to escape from what was about to happen. It was no use, even if I tried to run, he would get to me before my hand even touched the door handle.

"The dress," he said. "Take it off."

Arctic was the only word I could use to describe his tone.

My mouth began to open, but he grabbed my jaw, pulling me up to him so that I would have to stretch on my tiptoes. Luca's grip on my face didn't hurt my body, but it split my pride into two, smashing around my feet as a tear slid down my right eye onto his fingers.

"Take the dress off. You're not wearing some whore's dress in my house."

Letting go of my face, he took a step back and waited.

My hands trembled by my side at the thought of undressing for him. I would be entirely and utterly at his mercy once the dress was off my body, but I could see I was running out of time.

Before he could grab me again, I lifted my hand to the back of the dress where the zip sat halfway down my spine and kept my head low. My chest was heaving with panic now as the zip slid effortlessly down.

Survive.

Survive this.

The waterfall beads shimmering side by side were the only sound in the room as I slipped the dress down my frigid body. A shaky breath left my mouth when it hit the floor, leaving me with only my underwear and hair to cover myself with.

Luca's sharp intake of air made my soul flinch.

Peering up through my hair, I watched as he slipped his suit jacket off and threw it down on the floor, his eyes regarding me with barely restrained energy as we both remembered my refusal for his jacket earlier on in the evening.

A blush burned my cheeks before I could stop it.

"You just had to fight this. Just had to make it more difficult," he seethed breathlessly, as he stepped further away from me, allowing my eyes to travel around his room.

Unlike mine, this was a modern room with clean, crisp furniture, with all straight lines and no fuss. Behind the bed was a slate paneled wall so that the white leather headboard of the bed contrasted, catching your eye instantly. The room was a mix of greys, white, and black, offering nothing but the perception it wasn't used often.

Would I be used in that very bed?

"Do you know the trouble you've caused?" he snapped, as he returned to me, his shoes now discarded by the bed.

My mouth wired itself shut in fear as our eyes met. Not pleased by my sudden muteness, he crossed the space he had put between us.

"I'll tell you." He grabbed my chin once again, tilting my face up to his. "Do you want the secrets you've desperately been waiting for?"

"Yes."

I balked at my sudden bravery and cursed myself for not having control of my mouth. It only ever got me in trouble with him.

"I wished you had said no, Olivia," he said. His fingers slipped from my jaw to chase away a lone tear that had fallen from my right eye before slipping his hand to the back of my neck, angling me so that I couldn't do anything but stare into his eyes.

"Tell me. I can handle it."

Yes, tell me because at least I will know why this is happening.

Luca's eye's trailed slowly down my face until they rested on my lips. I could feel his urge to kiss me, to touch me, to smother me as it burned through his hands that still held me close to him. Lust seeped from him as we stood inches apart and my heart began to hammer painfully.

Panic and fear swelled as my half-naked body pressed against his, knowing that at any moment, he could ruin me completely, take away the one ounce of control I had left – my body.

"It's your eyes...it's always been your eyes," he began to falter, his anger fading to a simmer as he pulled away from me, leaving me cold and desperate for him to open his mouth. Without hesitation, I grabbed at his arm, ignoring the look he gave me when he paused.

My touch was hurting him.

"Tell me why you're doing this. Please just tell me. I can't take another moment of-"

"Me?" he sneered, ripping his arm from my timid grip.

"Of not knowing," I whispered, "you said we met before, where did we meet Luca, please just tell me?"

My voice did not sound like my own, it was frantic and desperate, trying to get him to talk so I wouldn't have to think about my half-naked body on show for him.

Or, the possibility that his fraying restraint would finally give, and I'd be punished beyond repair.

"At an airport," he told me, as he pushed a hand through his hair. "At first, I was hurt that you didn't remember me, but it's been a blessing really, una dannata benedizione."

"When?"

My brain was desperately flicking through the holidays I had taken when I was seventeen, trying to picture him there with me at the airport, but nothing came forward. Surely, my brain would have remembered him. He was beyond the comprehension of beauty, not something that could be forgotten so easily.

"When you were seventeen. You were going to visit your grandparents in France."

One look at his face and I knew he didn't want me to remember our meeting, for the first time since we had met, he looked worried, his eyes pinched and tight. But my brain was already taking me back.

****

Airports. Usually full of excitement as families waited patiently to start their holiday, businesspeople on their phones as they cut deals across the globe, students ready to forget their worries of schoolwork, and then there was me. Full of dread, waiting to board my flight.

My trip wasn't full of excitement nor would there be any exploring. I was going to visit my grandparents in the south of France, pushed by my aunt who was worried about my recent reclusive behavior.

Six weeks I would have to spend, isolated on a farm, with nothing but the older generation who didn't understand what I was going through. It didn't make sense.

"But you don't understand, I need to get on this flight. It's urgent and-"

"Sir, I'm sorry, but it's fully booked up. We can try and book you onto the next flight."

My eyes wandered to the commotion at the small desk across from me to find a young man pleading with the desk to get him on the flight. Looking him over quickly, he looked like your usual rich businessman who was desperate to get on the next flight out to close another deal, but I knew differently.

"I have two hours to get to the hospital, maybe even less now-"

"Sir. There is nothing I can do."

Carefully, he shared shushed words with the woman who in return scowled his way, pointing her finger at him to move away from the desk before she called security. As he turned my way, I realized my perception of him had been wrong.

The man looked like how I felt on the inside.

Rich in belongings but poor in his soul.

The stranger looked hungover, terrified, and angry as he stomped his way over towards me, taking up the free seat at my side.

We both didn't have to feel trapped.

Turning to him, I held out the ticket I had painfully been holding onto and watched as his eyes look up at mine. The stranger looked like he had recently lost weight –I could tell by the way his clothes fit him up close. Even his brown eye's looked dull and withdrawn under the fluorescent lights. Barely holding on.

I knew that feeling.

"I heard your conversation with the airline." I passed him my ticket, pressing it into his hand. "Take this."

At first, he was skeptical by my sudden kindness then his eyes widened with relief.

"No, I can't take your ticket." He tried to push it back into my hand as his scattered English caught my ears.

"You can. You sound like you need it more than me," I offered him a kind smile, hoping that my small, good deed wouldn't get me in too much trouble.

The stranger leaned into his bag and retrieved his wallet, his shaky hands pulling out wads of cash.

"Let me pay you for this."

Shaking my head, I stood up. "Honestly it's fine. You're actually doing me a favor by accepting it."

"I have to repay you for this. Please let me pay for your ticket on the next flight at least."

"Oh, I'm not going," I smiled down at him, hoping that it was enough, and he could just accept my kindness.

He was confused and rightly so.

"It's my padre!" he blurted. "He's in the hospital."

I had thought as much by the way he frantically begged the airline to supply him with a ticket. That type of fear only came when a loved one was involved. I knew, I had felt it a few times in my life.

"Pay it forward." I offered a small smile as I grabbed up my carry-on bag, "or don't, the choice is yours."

Holding up the ticket, he nodded, "Grazie!"

****

When my eye's refocused on him, he had realized that I had remembered him, remembered a younger Luca who had since filled out with muscles, his jaw stronger, his eyes with little to no innocence left in them.

Cautiously he moved, making his way into the closet, disappearing briefly before returning with a white t-shirt.

"Put this on."

Relief spread through my cold body as I accepted the t-shirt without hesitation. Granting me privacy, he turned around so that I could slip the shirt over my head, covering my body. Gone was his need to punish me. I had gotten through by keeping him talking, keeping his mind off my botched escape.

"I got your name from the ticket you gave me."

CHAPTER SIXTEEN

Luca Caruso

B lack dress. Legs. Eyes. Fury. I had drowned and was revived by her as soon as she had walked into that club. My body had seized into being perfectly still as I watched her walk in with Dante in full siren mode. Every straight man in that club had been ensnared by her beauty, but I had been imprisoned to hell, gasping for air.

I had wanted to drag her to hell with me when she had run away. My body had itched for it during her brief disappearance. Never in my life had I felt such wild feelings of regret, fury, and terror when she slipped into the night without a single glance back or care for what she was doing.

Then I had found her and lost control.

My fingers itched to strip her bare.

To hurt her.

To consume her.

Especially, when I saw her sat in that squalid police station, her big doe eyes blinking wildly up at me with fear. It was the fear in her eyes that had triggered the monster wrapped around my soul, forcing him to awaken as I dragged her ruthlessly back to where she belonged.

Now that rage was fading, leaving me weak, leaving me desolate as she stared across my bedroom at me. My eight-year-old secret was bleeding out between us and silencing the hissing monster that was desperate for me to break.

"I don't understand." Her shaky hands came up to push the hair away from her face. "This is all from me giving you a plane ticket?"

Yes. All of this. Eight years of it.

Shame filled my system as I remembered staring at that plane ticket nearly every day since I had first met her. How could I explain this to her? How could I make her understand the depths of my depravity without dooming myself to the pits of hell?

"Yes," the words slipped between my teeth, sounding like a hiss. My legs started to give in, so I moved to the bed, sitting down and placing my head in my hands.

Olivia stayed frozen in the middle of the room – waiting for me to finally open my mouth, but what could I say that wouldn't make her hate me more.

"Do you know why I needed to get to France so quickly? Do you remember?"

"It was your dad." She moved, her feet padding towards me but not close enough that I could reach out to touch her. It was for the best; if I touched her, I would drag her onto this bed and punish us both.

Since the moment she walked into the club with Dante, I had wanted nothing more than to touch her, to take away from all the prying eyes she had on her and hide her away. Olivia was mine, all mine. Nobody on this earth deserved her, knew her, could protect her like I could.

Looking up, I flinched at the softness in her beautiful moss-colored eyes. There were many things in this world that I didn't deserve, and her comfort wasn't one of them. Even after all that I had done Olivia was still soft, warm…still more than I could ever be.

"I arrived at the hospital and ten minutes later he died."

The smell of bleach and antiseptic still haunted me to this day as I remembered the shrill screams of my mother who clung to the love of her life, begging him to come back to her. Over and over, she screamed until she went mute.

"Luca" she whispered, from the seat next to my window, swallowing her small frame as she urged me on. The way she said my name had my control slipping away from me once again.

"I hated him with everything that I had. My Pa only loved money and power but still I rushed to him, to say goodbye. No man should die without his children by his side."

"Luca, it was just a plane ticket" she whispered through the darkness.

"Your ticket gave me the chance to make a change, with his death I would change everything that he had built. That the misery and despair he caused would be rectified through me. It was just a plane ticket to you but to me it was the chance for redemption - your kindness forced me to open my eyes."

The words were tumbling out, free falling from my lips before I could stop them. Relief was filling my chest making the eight years of hell worth it.

"I know how this sounds to you, Olivia. In my grief, I remembered the one person who gave me something without wanting anything in return. Your face, it stuck with me and that's when this started."

Olivia stood carefully and made her way over to me, going to sit next to me on the bed until she stopped – her fear finally kicking in.

"What started?"

My eyes travelled from the bottom of her beautiful, tanned legs, all the way to her face. For the first time since we had officially met, she had the upper hand, and in my heart, I knew this had to happen now.

"My obsession for you."

The gasp was enough to strike me dead.

"You're crazy," she whispered, stumbling away from me in disgust. "What the hell is wrong with you?"

The monster hissed as I lunged at her, pushing her against the wall and pinning her there with my hips. Chest-to-chest, I could feel her nipples pressed tightly against my skin, taunting me to touch her.

Images of stripping her bare and fucking her against the wall whipped me raw.

"I don't expect you to understand, but don't you dare call me *crazy*, Olivia. You don't have any idea what I've gone through to get to this point."

Trying to turn her head so she didn't have to look at me, only made it worse for her. My right hand grabbed her chin, forcing her to see what she had done to me, to the man I had become. How could she stand before me believing she was still so innocent in this?

"I fucking tried," I hissed against her ear, her sweet smell forcing lust to join in the mix of my bloodstream. "I tried to stay away from you, to let you live your life, but the more I looked into you the more I realized you needed someone. You push everyone away that tries."

Olivia swallowed, heat flushing to her chest as she looked from my mouth to my eyes. Even with hatred in her eyes, she still couldn't deny her attraction to me. The same attraction I felt buzz between us when she was just seventeen.

"At first, it started with getting you into the university you wanted, then it was the offer to work in New York, your apartment, your promotions, your safety -"

"Stop!" she cried, as she tried to bow her head, but I would not let her, we both needed to face this.

Olivia would need to see what she had done to me.

"But I made a promise, Olivia, that we would never meet again and that this would stay hidden from you. I was there for you from a far. Can you understand now?"

Piercing me with her glare, she pushed me, but I didn't budge. "Then why am I here Luca?!" she asked, again pushing me, and my hand slipped from her jaw. "Why didn't you just stick to your promise and leave me alone in New York?" She began to unravel within my arms, burning me with her hatred once more.

I grabbed her face in my hands, silently begging her to stay with me even when I didn't deserve it. One look from her and I was reeling again, desperate to get away before my restraint finally snapped. It had been a long time since anyone had pushed me like this, and the monster was trying to take control.

"Because a week ago, someone else started digging into your life, Olivia."

I felt her body freeze against me, and her legs buckled as the night finally wore her down. Quickly, I pinned her up, holding her as gently as I could while letting her collect herself. A decent man would have given her space, maybe even let her go back to her room but not me. This had to happen now, otherwise, she would never stop trying to free herself of me.

"Four years ago, I began changing the way my business operated and that pissed off a lot of people. People who wanted me to carry on with my father's exploits. As a precaution, security was set up to watch over you in case anyone ever found out about..."

Olivia's slap came out of nowhere, preventing me from defending myself, but her wrists that rained down on my chest after were expected. Even as my cheek ached, I grabbed for her wrists and dragged her to me, pulling her down to the floor where I could continue to ruin her life.

"A man called Black; a member of Chen's team sold information about you to a few of my enemies. Black forced my hand, Olivia. It was either I take you myself or someone else would."

A frail sound fell from her lips that were swollen from crying, but I knew my comfort was not what she needed or wanted. Even as my fingertips burned to touch her, to make her understand that my decision did not come lightly, I remained still.

"When you ran away tonight..."

My heart froze and for the first time since I was a little boy, I felt panic explode through my veins. Images of Olivia being snatched away almost suffocated me as Chen and his team pulled me out of the club to start the search.

"I'm going to fix this so your safe, but you have to stay by my side. Olivia, listen to me," I pulled her head up and saw exhaustion was taking over.

"Please, stop talking," she muttered, trying to free herself from my grip.

The secrets she wanted so desperately had all but burned her. As she suffered in my arms, I felt nothing but relief that she would finally understand that my intentions were never to hurt her.

There was no fire left within her as she slumped forward, her head bowing into submission as she cried quietly between us. My hands gently released her to pull her into me, forgoing my weak rule of not touching her and allowing myself this one moment of comfort.

Olivia stiffened briefly at my touch but did not have enough energy to fight me off. I let her cry into me, soaking my shirt while I held her. I focused on the heartbreaking sounds of her sobs and let them dash cold water onto the unspent lust roaming wildly in my body.

Every part of her warm body was curled within my legs, her head tucked under my chin as she clutched to my chest. The tears had stopped, her breathing had mellowed, and then she was perfectly still with me.

"Olivia?" I whispered.

Slowly, I leaned back and froze as I looked down to her sleeping face. Shutting myself off from the feelings her sleeping face had conjured within me, I picked her up, shifting her gently in my arms, and walked her to my bed.

CHAPTER SEVENTEEN

Luca Caruso

In one week, my days went from being buried in business to worrying about the woman in my bed. It had been nine hours since she had cried in my arms, nine hours since she had sent me a hateful scowl from across the room, and now nothing. Absolutely nothing.

Pacing at the foot of my bed, I spent hours looking over at her at first, willing her to wake up so we could talk, but she refused me once again. Normally, I had restraint and could sit with my thoughts, but this was different. There was so much that needed to be said, to be cleared away but my own needs would have to wait on her now.

We were both at her mercy.

Ignoring the agitation building in my body, I called a meeting with Chen and his team, ignoring my urges to stay by her side.

I found them waiting for me in my office. Only Chen had the nerve to look me in the eye. The rest stood still; arms crossed over their chests as they stared straight ahead. Accusations and animosity tainted the air as I moved across the room towards my desk. Taking my seat, I motioned for Chen to start speaking.

"Sir, we want to apologize for last night, for-"

"Allowing Olivia to slip away?" I snapped, as I looked up from the computer that had emails streaming in every few seconds. Business would have to take a back seat for the next few days.

Chen took in a deep breath before straightening his pitch-black tie as I carefully noted this was one of the first times, I had ever seen him nervous. Last night, they had been witness to my unravelling and today they were now under my scrutiny.

Good.

"Given that there's four of you to the one of her, last night shouldn't have happened. Do you understand how much it has cost me to clean up your mess?"

Rum, in the back, wanted to say something. I could sense it rolling off his tense shoulders, but he remained mute as he stared over at me. Nobody would speak to me unless I permitted it. Especially, if I was paying them.

"You're right and it won't happen again." Chen nodded. "But I wouldn't be doing my job if I didn't highlight the main issue of last night sir."

"And that was?"

"We advised Dante that Miss Heart was a risk last night, but our concerns were not taken seriously," Rum finally piped up, his eyes accusing me of many other things than a relapse in judgement.

It was a good thing there was enough mutual respect between Chen and I, that his staff's comments did not bother me so much. Dante loved to push and had rushed the situation last night, so it was only fair that we all shared the blame.

"I'll deal with Dante."

"Moving forward, I suggest we-"

Waving my hand to silence Chen, I leaned back into my chair and surveyed the room. The group of men had done a good job, an excellent job in maintaining her safety in New York. The common dominator was Dante and his meddling. Ever since he had been involved, he had caused me nothing but headaches.

"Olivia is aware of the situation," I revealed. My careful eyes surveyed their reactions, only to find blank stares looking back at me. "Answer whatever questions she has but do not emit any information on Black, understood?"

"Yes, sir."

Getting up, I moved around my desk to the safe that was built into the structure of the house, hiding in plain sight as a front for a mirror. The only sound in the room was the buttons being pressed before it unlocked.

Grabbing neat stacks of Euros, I turned and placed them on my desk in front of Chen. A hundred thousand to ensure another person kept quiet on the woman that was sleeping in my bed.

"This needs to go to Detective Russe to ensure he keeps his silence. Make sure any files they have on Olivia from admission are destroyed."

One nod from Chen and our conversation was over. All four of them left my office with their unsaid opinions and left me to a room full of silence. Usually, silence soothed me, allowed me to work without distraction, but now it only gave me time to think about her. Just as I allowed my brain a few moments to go over last night's events, an email from my IT consultant Jack

Veen popped up on red alert. Olivia was up and using the phone I had given her to talk to her aunt in England.

Dread washed through me while I fought the urge to go find her and snatch away the damn phone. Instead, I sat perfectly still and stared at my computer screen, my memories of last night coming up as fast as my secrets had spilled out.

Was she okay? Did she remember everything that I had said? Would she let me explain?

Last night, my restraint had barely clung on as the monster sneered and roared to destroy the only person in my life that could force the light back into my darkness. Olivia was still innocent. Having lost her virginity at 18 she never ventured into another sexual experience. For years, I had assumed the worst until she spilled to her cousin Alice, admitting it had made he feel emotionally raw to be connected that way. Olivia denied herself any form of emotional connection. It was her protection.

If I took that from her last night I might as well have died there and then.

Now she was upstairs, seeking out comfort from all the pain I had caused.

An hour had agonizingly slipped by, and there was no patience left as I stormed out of my office in search of her. Making my way through the house, I noted the sun was coming in strong through the windows on every floor, pouring in to cast away any shadows.

Rum was positioned at the bottom of the hallway that led to Olivia's room where I knew she was now. The maids had already been in mine and removed any trace that she had been there, including the t-shirt of mine that she had worn.

Just as I was about to knock on the door, it flew open, forcing me to step back as Olivia looked up at me, her hair loose and free around her face and the fresh scent of her recent shower wafting to my nose. Then the pink chiffon dress with a split hem caught my eye.

Olivia looked perfect, far too perfect for someone who had been told their life had been stolen. Then I saw the phone in her hand, she was clutching it so tightly that her hand was shaking.

"You're bruised." I balked at the bruises around her wrist and tried to grab her hand to look at them closely.

I'd done that. Shit.

Olivia flinched away and stepped back into the room, her eyes cautiously assessing my every move. Choosing to ignore the fear in her eyes, I stepped into the room and closed the door, closing it on our audience of one down the hallway.

As I tried to find a way to get what I needed, Olivia began to step back, her bare feet slowly moving away from me, her chest rising and falling with anxiety from my presence alone.

Sickness rolled heavy in my stomach at the sight of her right wrist when the light from the window caught her skin. The light green bruises glittered in the sunlight from where I had gripped her far too tightly.

"I'm sorry," I told her honestly, and planted my feet in the middle of her room, trying to show her that I wasn't going to hurt her by staying in the one place she could see me at all times.

"For which part?" she replied nervously, her voice dropping as her eyes slipped over my shoulder to the door. Of course, she would want to run from me, the monster that continued to imprison her.

My brain wouldn't allow me to further our conversation from last night, afraid that tempers would unfurl, and I would do something that would fill me with more shame and regret, so I kept my mouth shut.

"What you said last night, was all of that true?" She interrupted my thoughts and took a step closer to me, nervously biting down on her lip.

Fuck. Stop biting your lip.

Olivia moved towards me. Without fail, she would always move closer to me when she sought information, she didn't know she was doing it, but it made me feel slightly better – better that she wasn't completely afraid of me.

There was at least a part of her subconscious that didn't find me so abhorrent but that same part of her kept her away from me, hiding her true feelings for our situation.

"Yes," I told her, as I held out my hand. "Let me look at your wrist."

Olivia's eyes narrowed at my hand, not wanting me to touch her but even her glare couldn't stop me.

Sighing, I moved across the room so that we were only a few inches apart and ignored the fear present in her eyes while she took a non-subtle step backwards. The fear was completely justified, but it still bothered me. There hadn't been a single moment of trust between us both and it was my fault, so why did I expect more?

"Please," I hissed through gritted teeth as I begged with my eyes to allow me this one moment to check her over.

"It's fine-"

Ignoring her, I gently reached for her wrist and brought it forward, her breath hitching in her throat as I inspected the fingertip-shaped bruises around her wrist.

"It's not fine," I told her, as I dropped her wrist, ignoring the electric snap I felt up my wrist when we touched. "That won't ever happen again. I won't ever touch you unless I have your permission."

Olivia tried to mask her surprise, her expression changing from confusion to a cold ice wall that left me on the outskirts of her true feelings once again. Even as we faced the consequences of the previous night, my body yearned and twisted to kiss her, to feel her lips against mine, going against everything that my brain had set in place.

Why should I feel her comfort now that we were both facing the morality of my actions? My need for her had been manageable from afar. It was masked in my duty to 'pay it forward,' but as soon as her life was threatened, I turned from monster to 'want to be' Hero. I was far from that old notion of heroism and chivalry – instead, I was Lucifer trying to get his wings back.

"How do I know you'll stick to that?" she asked me gently, her tone cocooning me in its warmth, transporting me briefly to the first day I had met her.

"Because I'll give those men out their permission to take me out if I so much as lay a finger on you," I told her honestly. "Without your permission."

Olivia's eyes widened as she took a step back, but I kept going, ignoring the pull I felt between us.

"We'll talk more about this when you're ready, but I want you to be able to trust me. If you can trust me, even a little of this will be much easier for you."

A scoff fell from her lips and she shook her head, refusing to acknowledge the olive branch that had been extended.

"Don't you mean easier on you? After all, I'm only here because of your unhinged obsession-"

"Olivia" I warned, before shaking my head, shaking away my impatience. "What more can I do to make this easier for you?"

There was still much more to discuss, and from the look on her face, there were a lot more answers than she needed but today wasn't going to be the day. Even though I wanted to finally rid myself of this burden, I couldn't. I wasn't strong enough to face her judgement for the life that I had condemned her to.

My head was burying further and further into the sand.

"I need to be able to make my own decisions, have control over my life," she told me as she moved towards the vanity where her laptop was open. "I'm not stupid, I know what happens when I use this phone or this laptop. I feel suffocated. I can't even think straight."

Running a hand through my hair, I realized that the longer she was locked in this house, the more she would try to find a way out.

Hope bloomed in my chest. Maybe now that she knew the truth, we could find new common ground where we could learn to trust each other.

"I'll give you as much freedom as possible given the current circumstance," I told her, "but it comes with a condition."

My eyes drank her in as she took a seat in the cream chair, the split hem of the dress shifting higher, distracting me before she pulled me back to the conversation.

"What condition?" I could hear the worry in her voice, but it didn't matter. If Olivia didn't agree to this condition, we would fail before we had even started. Worry would be the last thing on her mind.

"That you won't run away again."

Olivia opened her mouth to contest, but I held up my hand, not allowing this to fail. The beautiful woman in front of me

154

could try with all her might to think of a way out of this but I wouldn't let it happen.

"If you try to leave me again, there won't be any second chances. Your security will be tighter with zero options. The choice is yours."

Moving away, I walked across the room to take a seat on her bed, keeping my eyes on her the whole time. Olivia's eyes were wild with possibilities, her breathing slowing, her shoulders loosening now that I was away from her.

Olivia leaned her head back giving me the perfect view of her beautiful neck, her long hair falling down her back as she rolled her shoulders. My fingers itched to touch her like I had by the side of the pool, to feel her soft skin under my fingertips.

Instead, I clasped them in front of me, knowing that she wouldn't ever want my touch.

"I won't run," she told me, breathlessly. Those three words were music to my ears as I felt my spine become iron rod straight at the small mercy she was offering. Relief spread down my body as a flicker of hope ignited between us until she asked the next question.

"But I need to know, is this situation permanent?"

Ignoring the sinking feeling in my chest, I stood up, ignoring her confusion as I began to make my way out of her room, away from the one question I didn't want to answer.

I had control.

Not her.

We had a deal.

There was no reason to spoil it so soon.

My arrogance came to the rescue as I smirked over at her. "You have so many questions Olivia. Can't you just be happy with the answers you have for now?"

My expectations of her anger were not met as she crossed her arms and raised an eyebrow at me. How did she manage to get anything done when she worked at her job? Just being under her firm stare had my body alive with anticipation, wanting to see more of her strength.

"No, but I'll wait and play this stupid game."

"Good," was all I could manage.

CHAPTER EIGHTEEN

Olivia Heart

My brain was in overdrive, forcing me to relive every second since the fatal moment of my kidnapping. When I had left Luca's room this morning, my body was sore, my thoughts erratic, and my heartbeat spluttering with anxiety. Even as I washed away his scent on my body, from being wrapped in his sheets, I couldn't shake him off.

Luca had all but told me that my life as I knew it was over. Begged me with his eyes to blindly trust him as he led me down his darkened path. My body had caved and fallen into his arms, his power wrapping around my limbs, pulling me into him before snuffing out my last shred of strength.

Even as I stood in the shower with scalding hot water splashing my back, nothing could bring me back up to the surface, not even the torturous droplets. I was drowning in fear and regret, panic unfurling in my chest as I slipped to the floor and cried.

Once my tears dried up and my skin became prune-like, I had somehow managed to crawl my way out of the shower and to the phone that sat on the desk. Clinging to a fluffy towel, I sat on the bedroom floor and called the only number I knew from heart.

My Aunt Sarah was a breeze of calm as she lured me into a false sense of security. The conversation, even without much of my input, was infectious and full of her stories of normality. It all seemed so far away.

Normal and happy, that is what my forced voice sounded like while we spoke, but looking down at my body, I saw that my legs were still shaking. As soon as I recognized the signs, I forced the conversation to an abrupt close, allowing a lie to slip from my lips about work, and promised I would send her my address for Alice's wedding, for the dress I wasn't going to wear.

Now, frozen in the moment, I found myself staring at the spot Luca had just resided in, only minutes ago had he left to go speak to Dante, and yet I hadn't moved.

Paralyzed.

Suddenly finding myself torn between locking myself in this room forever and following Luca, I slowly began to realize that something was deeply wrong with me. My feelings for the situation were changing, the hard edges of my temper softening to him now that he had told me part truths.

Luca was completely unhinged, his obsession for me had spanned nearly a decade, but he hadn't made a single move on me physically. Yes, he had been close last night, but he chose my safety over the devil lurking inside of him, taunting him to get what he had waited so patiently for.

I felt dizzy, so I forced my eyes on the beautiful landscape outside of my window. Feeling the sun heat my face brought me calm and managed to push away some of the fears present in my overworked mind.

****

Maria had tended to me later in the day and bought me lunch while I suspect chiding me in Italian for the breakfast I hadn't touched. This time, she pretended to busy herself in my room while keeping an eye on me as I ate at the vanity table.

The food tasted like ash in my mouth but still, I ate. Even I wasn't blind to the sudden weight loss, so on survival alone, I forced the red sauce pasta into my mouth. Maria sent me a motherly smile when she took my tray with her and I silently thanked her for her kindness.

After lunch, the need to get out of my room was stronger than wanting to wallow in pity, so I left only to be faced with Rum and Bones. Their initial expressions told me they were worried for me, especially after last night, but I brushed by them and headed down the stairs.

The air was cold and crisp as the air conditioning blasted each room that I walked through, but as soon as I stepped outside, the heat took over, warming my skin and lifting my mood. This place was rich with endorphins as I walked through the perfectly manicured gardens, forcing my eyes to enjoy the blue and yellow wildflowers that were growing.

"Do you have to follow me?" I called back over my shoulder.

"Yes, Miss Heart, but we can pull back if you like?" Bones called and without looking, I knew he was smirking.

"Please," I called back. I needed at least one moment where I could pretend my privacy still existed.

As I rounded the back of the house, my eyes landed on four black SUVs sitting in front of two triple garages with Dante and Luca stood in front of them, animated in an argument as their over-the-top Italian drifted to my ears.

Luca was waving his hands in front of Dante, forcing Dante's attention on him as he yelled in his native tongue. From where I stood, I could see Dante's frustration as he took the brunt of his cousin's anger but stood firmly whilst he listened.

Before I could read more into their argument there was a slight tap on my shoulder, forcing me to flinch away from the unwanted touch.

"Miss Heart, you should keep moving," Bones said, with a small impish smile as my face flushed with embarrassment from being caught snooping. It's not like I could understand a word they were saying.

"Fine," I hissed, before turning back around until I saw Luca crossing the lawn, straight towards us. Dante in the background sent me a simple nod before disappearing behind the vehicles.

My breath caught in my throat as he stood in front of me, his black shirt open enough that I could see his tattoo, but I pulled my eyes away and looked up at him.

"Olivia," he greeted me coolly.

"Are they the armored vehicles Dante told me about?" I spluttered, desperate to think about anything but him and his dark eyes on me.

"They are." He nodded at me before motioning for Rum and Bones to disappear. Suddenly, I wanted them to stay, knowing that they were now under new orders.

"Would you like to see them?" he asked me, with a small smirk on his face.

"No, thank you," I told him, as I began to move away.

"They're just for protection," he told me, as he fell into step, slipping his hands into his trouser pockets "Mainly for your protection."

"From Black or the people he sold my information to?"

Luca had hoped that my memory wouldn't remember the exact name of the man that knew of my existence thanks to his delusion, but it did. It would forever.

"In a worst-case scenario yes, but as of now, Mr. Black would be a fool to pursue this. I have eyes watching every move he makes and so far, he's kept to himself. As for everyone else – they wouldn't dare."

I stopped and found that we were at the back of the house facing out to thick trees that hid us from the only road that led to the property. There was a gentle breeze here that was pushing my hair over my shoulders as I looked at him.

"Do you feel any shame in what you've done to me?" I asked him, without anger in my voice, but still full of judgment.

That I couldn't control.

Luca's eyes flashed red-hot before settling on me, his hands slipping out of his pockets to grip a tendril of my hair that was loose in the wind. Gently, he tucked it behind my ear, careful not to touch my skin so that he didn't break our deal.

"I feel shame for disrupting your life but not for protecting you," he mumbled, as his eyes travelled from my face down to rest on my lips.

"I won't apologize for that so don't expect one."

My temper flared once again but I allowed the breeze around me to temper it.

"I didn't ask for an apology Luca. I asked if you felt shame for what you've done to me and it's clear you're incapable of it."

Luca rubbed his forehead before reaching out his hand to me, wanting me to touch him, giving me the choice to hold his hand.

"I've been as honest as I can with you, Olivia. Take my hand."

I did not move. The thought of our skin touching made the hairs on the back of my arms stand up.

"Please."

Against the screaming voice in my head, I lifted my hand and placed it within his. As soon as my hand was in his, I felt his fingers slip between mine as our fingers fit perfectly together. Too preoccupied with our hands connecting, I nearly missed the satisfied smile on his lips as he pulled us away.

As we walked further around the expansive house, he matched his usually long strides with mine while stealing sly glances over at me. I didn't want his touch because every time my body felt him, it reacted incorrectly. Betrayal stung as I realized I liked holding his hand, liked the comfort he had shown me last night when he wrapped his arms around me.

Then I realized he was the reason I needed comfort in the first place. Luca Caruso was obsessed, beyond reproachable in his desire to steal me away, forcing me to need him against my will.

A prisoner in body and soul.

I knew what was happening.

I'd read journals on this illness when my head used to be stuck in law books, psychological assessments of kidnapped victims, and their statements as they tried to protect their kidnapper. That wouldn't be me, no, I would fight tooth and nail to keep him out of my head.

Exhausted by my thoughts, I didn't notice that we had stopped by a large building, at the side of the house that stood alone. The large grey garage door had two state-of-the-art security pads that beeped as we approached.

"If I show you something, will you try to keep an open mind?" he asked, dropping my hand, only to try and touch my face. I moved quickly out of his reach and crossed my arms over my chest.

Luca's face remained frozen, but I could feel that he was hurt by my rejection. It was clear by the way he sighed that he thought we were getting somewhere now that his dirty truths were out.

"I'll try."

Luca nodded before stepping to the first pad on the left of him and hovering his thumb over the scanner. After three seconds, it beeped three times before we heard a loud click. Stepping back, Luca kept his eyes firmly on me as I watched the garage doors pull up.

Sat inside the garage that was big enough to fit a house inside were two cars covered with black dust sheets. They looked lost in the vast space as Luca headed in and flicked on the lights. Unlike the garages that held his armored vehicles and fancy sports cars, this felt empty, almost forgotten.

"You want to show me a car?" I asked, as he moved to the smaller one of the two, his eye's still firmly on me, waiting for me to run.

I could feel his apprehension rolling off of him.

It was easier to deal with Luca when he was abrasive and cold, but this was new territory that I had yet to understand.

"Not just a car," he told me and bent down to grab at the black cover. "It's your car."

Before I could question him, he pulled the black sheet from the back of the car to the front before letting it fall at my feet. The air in my lungs completely evaporated as I looked down at the cherry red vintage Porsche Speedster that had been restored to its original glory. The car had been my father's when I was a child, his pride and glory.

My eyes took in the beautiful curves of the front with its large frozen headlights staring back at me. Memories flooded of me as a child running around the car with a skipping rope while he worked tirelessly on the engine at the back of the car.

I could still hear him humming to the radio while he worked.

"What are you doing with this?" I whispered, as I drifted forward to stare into the car, to see if the original cream leather seats were still there but were buffed to perfection, gone were the scratches on the seats. It was beautiful.

"My contact found it a few years ago at an auction. I had the restoration finished and was going to gift it to you for your thirtieth birthday..." he trailed off when he saw the look of confusion on my face.

"In secret of course," he confirmed, sticking to his story. "I saw the picture of you and your father in this car from his obituary when I started looking into you. I thought this would be-"

We both looked at one another before I looked away, afraid that the towering emotions of grief were going to explode, forcing me to unattractively sob. This was the sweetest gift I had ever received, wrapped up in a messy situation but I could still feel appreciation for the piece of my childhood that had been happy.

The car had been sold by my grandparents when they cleared out my parents' house. For years, I assumed it had been kept in storage until my aunt confirmed it was no longer in the family.

"It was too soon," he interrupted, leaning forward to grab the black sheet, but I stepped forward and held out my hand to stop him, careful not to touch him.

"Thank you," I told him honestly. "It's beautiful."

A small smile graced his beautiful face, lifting his sharp cheekbones slightly. "Do you want to test drive it?"

A laugh fell from my lips before I could stop it. "No, I can't drive."

"What!?" he yelled suddenly, forcing me to jump back as his voice echoed into the empty space. "But your record says you can."

"Legally yes, but I'm not a very good driver."

A dreaded blush crept up my cheeks as I remembered the last time I drove a car, stupidly in the busy streets of New York. In a blind panic, the car was left at the side of the road as I waited for my colleague Simon to collect it.

At least Luca didn't know about that embarrassing moment.

Luca smirked before covering the car over with the sheet, protecting its pristine condition from my terrible skills as a driver.

"We'll keep it in here until you're ready to drive it."

Shaking my head, I watched as he finished up and came to stand in front of me, holding out his hand once again. Even under fluorescent lighting, he looked like a sun-kissed Grecian, impossibly attractive with strong shoulders, firm chest, and taut abdomen under his fitted black shirt. My eyes travelled to his tattoos across his chest, wrist, and hand, wanting to know what they meant.

I took his hand and followed him out of the garage, peeking over my shoulder at the piece of my past that had lifted my mood from the depths of desperation to curiosity.

I was dizzy, but the fear was easing slightly, allowing me to move quietly at his side.

"Olivia, given our new arrangement, is there something you would like to ask me?"

Ask him what? To let me go? To allow me to breathe without monitoring every breath I took, without guards watching me around the house, what did he want now?

Looking at him as we walked, I realized he was softer with me now, his guard halfway down as he waited for me to answer him.

"I'm not sure what you mean."

We stopped at the side of a pool, protected by the side of the house so that the sun didn't blind us here. Luca stared down at me with curiosity, trying to work out if I had an angle but I did not. Frankly, I had no idea what he wanted from me anymore. My mind was still in the garage looking at the beautiful piece of my past.

"Always in your head," he muttered, as he let go of my hand and shoved his hands into his pockets. "It's your cousin's wedding in a few days. Don't you want to go?"

A sarcastic laugh fell from my lips before I rolled my eyes. "Of course, I want to go, but it's not like it's my decision Luca."

Luca's eyes flared with frustration, so he grabbed my hand, pulling me past the pool and into the house. It reminded me of the way he dragged me into the house last night, full of purpose and anger as we slipped into a small office where Chen was busy typing at his desk.

Chen stood up quickly to greet us until he saw Luca's hand in mine. I noted the reserved shock he held in his eyes before masking it once again with nothingness.

"Sir is everything okay?"

"Everything's fine," Luca bristled, as he opened up a chair for me and motioned for me to sit. The last thing I wanted was to sit in this tight space with them both, but I automatically sat down, curious to see where this was going.

"We need to organize a trip to London for Friday. Olivia here needs to attend a wedding Saturday morning."

Chen's face turned from shock to incredulous, matching my expression when we both looked at Luca who was calmly turning over a paperweight from Chen's neat desk.

"Sir I don't think that's a viable option right now," he said. Chen's nervous eye's darted from me to Luca. "A trip like this would take weeks to plan and right now-"

"Make it work Chen," Luca interrupted, "Olivia and I have an agreement that her safety is everyone's priority, so there will be no issues. Plan the trip and have it on my desk by tomorrow morning."

My stomach fluttered at the possibility of freedom. I could almost taste the freedom until I quickly realized that I wouldn't be alone. Luca and my guards would be with me the whole time, watching over me.

It didn't matter. All that mattered was getting home. I would deal with the other issues at the time. As the two men stared across the small room at one another, victory spread through my veins.

"Yes, sir." Chen nodded before sitting back down at his desk, his jaw tight with disapproval.

Luca held out his hand to me and I took it without a single thought. Gripping my hand tightly, he nodded to Chen before pulling us back into the corridor.

"Olivia," he started, breaking me away from the flicker of happiness that had reignited in my chest. We stopped just outside of the dining room where days ago, he had lost his temper with me and sent me away.

"Please don't make me regret this."

Luca was carefully reminding me what trying to break away would mean for me. Zero freedom under his careful watch and he knew I couldn't survive that. How could I hate him and be grateful all at the same time?

"I won't run," I promised. I fought the urge to drop his hand, too scared to upset him. "I'll follow all of Chen's rules. I just want to see my family."

CHAPTER NINETEEN

Olivia Heart

After Luca had informed Chen of our trip, he had all but disappeared. Instead of his dark presence in the house, all I had was the maids and my guards who tightened up their watch, refusing to answer any questions about his disappearance.

After the second day alone, I had wished for Dante to turn up to take me away from my thoughts of my ruined life, but he never came. So, I focused on the one person who could keep me occupied – my Aunt Sarah.

My aunt was more than relieved that I had finally confirmed my attendance for the weekend but wasn't pleased that I was leaving the dress fitting to the night before. Then came the awkward conversation of a plus one, after Chen had all but refused me attending alone, Luca was to be my date.

My date.

I'd held my breath throughout the whole phone conversation as she squealed with girlish excitement, demanding answers to her questions. Is he good-looking? What does he do? Does he treat me well? How did we meet? Is this why I had suddenly moved to Sicily?

My tongue was heavy in my mouth as I numbly answered her questions, creating a vague story, knowing that my conversations were being monitored. Was Luca pleased that we had met at work, he had wooed me, that I found him sweet and charming, enough to persuade me to move to his home country?

It was a blessing that he had disappeared because, after the incredibly hard phone call with my Aunt Sarah, my hatred for him resurfaced and spilled out. My anger after hours of pacing soon fizzled out and I'd found myself crying on the shower floor once again.

The following morning, Marie and Laurel entered my room and began packing my things, getting me ready for my trip. They were small tornados as they raced around the room, talking quickly in their native tongue – isolating me to their girlish conversations.

Dante was the one to finally save me as he swooped into my room wearing tight black gym clothes, his hair damp from sweat.

"Ciao bella." He grinned as he wiped his face with a small hand towel.

"Why are you so sweaty?"

Dante smiled, showing me his perfectly white teeth. "I've just finished kicking Luca's ass." He winked at me. "You're welcome by the way."

No matter the situation, Dante could bring a little light into the darkness.

"I haven't spoken to you since..." My throat closed as we both remembered the night I had tried to escape, remembering the moment that Dante was held back from protecting me.

"Ah yes," he sighed, "I'm sorry for putting you in that situation, I should have realized the temptation and-"

"It's okay," I interrupted him, not wanting to relive that night any longer than I had to. Truthfully, I needed a friend more than I needed vindication.

"Well, at least one thing good came from it," he smiled before leaning against the side of the door.

"And that is?"

"The deal that you and Luca made." He leaned over and playfully nudged my shoulder. "You get to see your family; a little bit of normality will do you good."

Looking over my shoulder, Laurel and Marie were finishing up which meant that we would be leaving soon, and I was desperate to speak to Dante. There were questions I knew he could answer now that Luca had opened the flood gates.

"Are you not coming?"

Dante looked away before carefully composing his face. "Luca thinks it's best that I don't. After all, I am the bad influence here."

Bad influence or a sign of freedom?

"Miss Heart, it's time to get going," Red announced, at the bottom of the corridor.

Dante leaned forward and placed a chaste kiss on my cheek, careful not to cover me in his post-workout sweat before whispering into my ear.

"Stai attento, bello."

As he pulled back, he had a smile on his face, but it didn't reach his eyes, before my hand could reach out to stop him from moving away, Luca joined Red at the bottom of the corridor, summoning me with his dark eyes. Fresh from the shower himself, he watched Dante and I as we moved towards them.

"I'll see you when you get back." Dante nodded to Luca before disappearing down the stairs without a glance back.

Luca barely acknowledged his cousin kept his eyes firmly on me, holding out his hand which I hesitantly took. The tense urge to demand where had he been the past few days came and went as we walked down the stairs, his silence deafening and forcing me into submission.

Was he regretting his choice?

"What did Dante say to you?" he whispered in my ear, as we slipped outside together, his scent stunning me for a second.

"He came to apologize," I whispered back; my nerves highly strung as he dropped my hand, only to place it on the bottom of my back.

Why was he so interested in what Dante had to say to me? Maybe it was their recent argument or maybe it was Luca's intention to keep us separate?

I wanted to know.

The first car parked in front of the gates opened and Chen stepped out, holding the door open for us with his usual blank stare. Luca stood back and allowed me to go in first, muttering something to Chen once my back was turned.

Smoothing down my dress, I watched as Luca took off his jacket before getting in the car. It gave me a better view of his tense shoulders as he leaned back to get comfortable. Everyone around me was worried, stressed even, at the fresh possibility I would run again.

"Where have you been the past few days?" I demanded suddenly, the question burning at the forefront of my head since I saw him in the corridor.

Luca smirked, instantly relaxing. "Missed me?"

Turning away, I rolled my eyes and wished for the car to move faster. The quicker we arrived in England the better, at least I would have some time to spend with my family.

"I've been busy with...business," he told me, as he lightly touched the back of my shoulder. "There's been a lot of jobs that have been put off since your arrival. I wanted to catch up before our trip."

Our trip.

When Chen pulled away, I noticed Red in front, typing quickly on a tablet, but my attention was diverted by Luca's fingers trailing across my shoulder, up to my ear before he tugged gently on my ear lobe.

"Are you nervous about the wedding?" he asked me, his voice dropping low so that only we could hear.

"Yes," I answered honestly, through gritted teeth.

No matter how hard I tried, I couldn't desensitize myself to his touch.

"Relax," he said. His hands pushed a strand of my hair over my shoulder while he openly admired me. "If it gets too much, I'll help you."

****

We sat in silence as we headed to a private airstrip that Luca's family had owned before it had been handed to him. It was on the outskirts of Sicily with only three airplane hangars on the large plot of land. It was forgotten and unimpressive to the naked eye.

That was until my eyes landed on the private plane that was waiting for us. The captain stood firm at the top of the stairs while the air hostesses waited at the bottom of the small plane traditionally used for short-haul flights. On the fuselage, there was a black emblem near the tail end, a large LC with a thick circle around it.

Everything Luca owned was extravagant but as I peeked at him from the corner of my eye, he seemed unfazed by the lifestyle he lived. As we drew closer, I began to wonder if this was the lifestyle his father had accustomed him to, desensitizing him to the wealth and power he possessed.

Then my thoughts slipped into a dark pool, wondering if this was the same plane that bought me here from New York.

I forced the dark thoughts away, deciding to focus on the positive. In three hours, I would be closer to my loved ones, closer to those that would give me a sense of identity.

"Olivia," I heard Luca say; he held out his hand for me. We had come to a stop just at the bottom of the stairs, leading up to the plane.

Blindly taking his hand, we slipped out of the car together and were greeted by two overly excited women wearing bright red lipstick and their blonde hair pulled tightly away from their faces. Their voices were a rush of high pitch noise as they welcomed us onto the flight, shaking both of our hands before gesturing for us to go up and enjoy our flight.

Bitterness bit at me.

"Are you okay?" Luca demanded halfway up, the wind blowing his short hair away from his face.

"I'm fine," I breathed, wanting nothing more than to drop his hand, but I would play nice and force away the dread that was coating my skin.

Chen and my guards took their seats as Luca shook the pilot's hand, who by the sounds of things had been flying Luca around the world for years. Luca was kind as he asked about his children and wife before freeing my hand so I could take a seat.

The only seats open were in the middle of the plane, facing the back with more privacy than the rest. In between them sat a table where I suspected Luca would work while flying. Before I could let my eyes wander the luxurious new setting, Luca slid into the seat across from me.

"We'll arrive at the airport at five-thirty. After that, we're staying in The Blooms Hotel where a seamstress will fit you for tomorrow."

"I'll need to pick up my dress," I told him tightly, aware that I would be trapped in a small space with him for the next three hours.

Luca smirked. "It's already at the hotel. I had your aunt send it over."

My body froze into place. "You've spoke to her? When?"

"Last night," he told me smugly. "You've already told her I'm your date, so I thought why not introduce myself and save you a trip. It will make it easier for you tomorrow when I'm there."

My head spun at the possibility of them talking without me being there to divert any unwelcome questions, but Luca, as always, was one step ahead of me. This was his way of preventing me from slipping out of his grasp.

"What else did you say?"

Luca looked out of the window, his body relaxing into the seat as we slowly began to pull away.

"Nothing you need worry about Olivia. Your Aunt Sarah is just pleased that you've found someone."

Before I could curse him to hell, a hand reached over in front of me and placed a glass of champagne on the small table that separated us. My anger was erupting in my chest, forcing me to glare across at him as the air hostess tried to catch his attention.

Sorry, he is too busy trying to ruin my life. Try again later.

Ignoring my better instincts, I snatched up the champagne and sipped, forcing my hands to do something other than shake with anger. Luca kept his dark gaze pinned on me as the hostess moved away, on to serve Chen and my guards soft drinks.

"Relax Olivia," he told me, leaning forward, dropping his voice so that only I could hear him. "You'll thank me tomorrow when we all meet, you'll see."

I scoffed, ignoring the little voice in my head that was telling me to bite my tongue. "So much for giving me an ounce of control," I returned, placing the glass down; I fixed him with a pointed look, willing him to argue with me.

Instead, he shrugged. "I didn't do this to take control from you. I did it to make it easier for you."

The plane was moving faster now, picking up speed as we raced down the runway but neither of us looked out of the small circular windows. As I stared into his dark eyes, many aggressive retorts presented themselves, but I bit my tongue. There was too much at stake to let him get under my skin so easily.

"You're so beautiful when you're angry," he breathed before pulling back, sliding his hands down his trousers before reaching up and undoing the button on his collar.

My body stupidly reacted to his compliment by flushing my cheeks and forcing my heart to splutter, the opposite of what my brain felt. My brain and my heart were splitting apart, wanting different things from the man that sat across from them.

My body reacted to him in ways it had not to a man before. When he touched me, it craved more. When he whispered in my ear, it wondered what his mouth would feel like on my neck, trailing up the arch of my throat before reaching my lips. Then there were his hands, those hands that I wanted to touch me until I was barely on the edge of self-control.

My brain was restrained, locked behind a foggy glass cage as it tried to fight off my body's weaknesses. Every move or word that came from Luca my brain would calculate the risks, weighing up the next best option. Always on edge. Always waiting.

I decided that it was best if I didn't open my mouth for the rest of the flight. Afraid, so afraid of what I would ask from him.

CHAPTER TWENTY

Luca Caruso

Olivia had left me to my own thoughts when she ended our conversation by turning her head and looking out the window, into nothingness. Giving her time to calm down, I opened my laptop and sunk myself into work, every now and then, I would check on her, trying to decipher what she was thinking.

Olivia was not an easy woman to read. Just as you would see a flicker of who she really was a wall would fall, leaving you cold and on the outside. Even with my vast knowledge of her, I still felt no closer to knowing what thoughts possessed her mind.

There had been a few women in my life that I had read easily, knew their intentions before they did and none of them had excited me the way she did. Granted they were used as distractions, not something I was proud of, but still, none of them could offer what she had.

The very first moment we had met at that airport, for a brief second, I saw the black hole of grief that swallowed her happiness, forcing me to see my own future ahead. It had taken me weeks after my father had died to understand but I did. Olivia had given me a gift knowing that the grief she had would be shared with me, all from a single plane ticket.

As I finished up the last email, the seatbelt sign came on, notifying us all that we were due to land soon. Nerves prickled my scalp as we both returned to the same airport that we had first met. If this went badly, it meant that I would lose Olivia.

If she couldn't find it in herself to stick with our deal, all hell would break loose and the woman returning with me would never give me another chance.

I wasn't ready.

I needed her to trust me.

****

As soon as we landed, we were whisked to a private exit, forgoing the usual security lines as our passports were checked by private security. Olivia paid no attention to me as passport control checked her passport which Chen had passed over to him. The air was palpable, and he scrutinized Olivia, forcing me to grit my teeth as he took his time checking that she matched her passport.

Keep quiet Olivia.

A simple nod later he gave her the passport back and pointed at the next exit. Relief flooded my system and before I could help myself, I took her hand and began pulling her ahead.

"Nervous?" she whispered to me, while Chen and Red moved in front, barricading us in as Rum and Bones took the back. The small smirk on her beautiful full lips told me she had enjoyed seeing me sweat.

More than you will ever know.

"No," I lied, "I would have bought him off if I had to."

That wiped the smirk off her face as we slipped through the back entrance of the airport, slipping by several coffee shops to two black Range Rovers waiting for us. The air was thick with humidity as London suffered a heat wave that I didn't like. There was no breeze to soothe me today.

Rum and Bones placed our bags in the back as I helped Olivia into the car, appreciating the fine sight of her ass as she moved. Following her, I sighed as the air conditioning breezed over my face, cooling me down.

I didn't know whether it was nerves or the close heat but being in a small space with Olivia made my fingers twitch to touch her. Images of my hand slipping up her naked thigh flooded my system, forcing me to react.

"Did you go to school here?" she asked me, while we waited for Chen.

My body instantly calmed down as her soft voice floated to my ears.

"Why do you ask?"

"Well, we met at this airport and you would have been twenty-four. I remember The Brunel University logo on your sweatshirt. I'm assuming masters?"

Olivia had remembered after all.

"Yes," I breathed, as the car pulled away. "In business, but I never finished."

The new bit of information pleased her as all the pieces she had collected about me clicked together. Before our agreement, this would have made me feel uncomfortable, but her happiness pushed away any dark thoughts to the side.

A sigh of satisfaction fell from her lips and I wondered if her sigh would sound the same if I ever got the chance to pleasure-

The door slammed in front forcing me to focus, to push away my dirty thoughts, and focus on getting through the next twenty-four hours.

****

Olivia stood in the middle of the hotel suite in the heart of Surrey countryside staring at the door that joined our two suites together. With a look that can only be described as bewilderment. As I moved further into the room, she shifted, turning to face me completely, to always see me coming.

"It's just for insurance, in case you try to break our deal," I told her softly, before throwing my jacket down on her golden bed, the beautiful dark wooden headboard standing proudly against the light walls.

"Like I could try to run from here when Chen and his pack are just outside," she smarted while kicking off her heels.

No amount of security keeping her by my side could make me feel comfortable now that we were here in her birthplace. Greed itched at me, wanting me to keep her all for myself, to take her back to Sicily where I could feel sane.

"The seamstress will be here soon," my voice sounded sullen. "I'll leave you be until you're finished. We'll have dinner downstairs after if you like?"

"Sure," she told me, as her eyes found the dress bag that was hanging over the wardrobe door. Already, I was forgotten, so I quietly left to deal with the emotions raging through my veins.

****

Chen was the first to greet me as I left her room. Running over tomorrow's agenda, he confirmed that the venue where Olivia's cousin's wedding was being held would be secure with extra guys hired. Replacing waiters, we would have another four men keeping watch.

It stemmed my agitation a little but moving to the hotel gym helped ease the new tension I found myself struggling with. Briefly keeping my mind off the woman upstairs, I forced myself into a cruel routine of cardio until my lungs burned for relief.

All my hard work to reinforce my self-discipline went out the window when I slipped into her room to find her in just a towel, her wet hair dripping down her recently tanned shoulders as she looked through her suitcase. My greedy eyes scanned her long perfectly shaped legs before resting on the bottom of the towel that barely covered her ass.

"Shit," she hissed, when she felt me behind her, her towel nearly slipping, which I am certain would have killed me there and then.

What a way to die.

"I thought you would be ready by now," I mumbled before clearing my throat, trying to simmer my building urges to lick the water droplets across her collar bone.

The blush across Olivia's cheeks was lovely and I found myself drawn to her, closing the distance between us. The only sound between us now was her sharp intake of breath when I stopped inches away.

"Luca, I need to get dressed," she warned me, as she clutched the towel tighter, her knuckles white against her pink fluffy shield.

The urges that I had desperately been fighting off were back in full force, allowing the monster to hiss from my subconscious. My days of avoiding her for this trip had been for nothing now that she was stood in front of me, half-naked and wet.

My hands reached out to touch her face and she shuddered, but to my surprise, it wasn't with disgust. That was all I needed before I closed the gap between us, allowing my shirt to be soaked by her recent shower. Olivia eyed me with confusion and fear as I ran my index finger across her bottom lip.

The monster began to whisper in my ear of Olivia's possible plans of deception now that she was suddenly accepting my affection, forcing me to slowly push her back against the wall.

"Luca," her voice was merely a whispered warning.

Olivia wasn't well-rehearsed in the world of pleasure and sex that I could tell by her blushes. There was the loss of her virginity and then nothing – she had ceased all requirements from men. Pushing them away at every chance.

This only made it harder for me to leave her alone. My body burned to show her, to devour her until it was all she could think about.

"Promise me something," I whispered as I dipped my head, running my nose up her neck, taking in the soft smell of her vanilla shampoo. This was heaven and hell as I fought against the urge to rip away her towel and fuck her.

Olivia shivered at the invasion of my touch and her breathing began to pick up, giving her away.

"Promise you what?" she whispered back, her voice cracking as my right hand trailed on the inside of her wrist, going up to her elbow. Gently I bit her earlobe, tugging it between my teeth before I answered.

"That you won't leave. Just give me your word."

My voice was all but demanding that she agree to my terms, to not leave no matter what.

It's all that I needed to silence the monster who was betting against her and she would remain untouched.

"I can't leave," she sucked in a sharp breath when I placed a soft kiss just below her ear. Even with the towel separating me I could feel her nipples hardening against my chest. "You can trust me."

Those four words were enough to undo me as I pressed harder against her body before crashing my mouth to hers. Euphoria exploded in my head as soon as our lips met. I was lost, drowning in her when she kissed me back, her lips working with me while we both fought for our self-control.

Olivia's soft moan that slipped by my lips went straight to my crotch. My hands became buried in her wet hair as I pulled her as close as possible, afraid that any moment she would pull away from me.

I needed more.

Wanted more.

My erection straining in my trousers, pressed against her stomach which was becoming all but painful until she allowed me to slip my tongue into her mouth. The open invitation to taste her had me free-falling into lust, bloodthirsty lust, and I soon forgot the pain. I felt firepower race down my spine, forcing my muscles to ripple under the intensity of our kiss.

"Luca," she whispered, trying to pull away from me, filling me with brief panic now that I could not feel her lips on mine.

"It's okay," I whispered against her mouth, before taking her again, gently biting down on her bottom lip. Olivia's soft whimper made it nearly impossible to concentrate, but I pulled myself together, forcing my brain to remember all of her.

The monster inside agreed that this could not end on her terms. We both needed the reassurance that she would stay, that she wouldn't try to leave now, so I pulled away.

Breathless, I waited for her eyes to open.

Lust-filled eyes.

Pink swollen lips.

The towel slowly slipping from her grasp.

With my left hand, I grabbed her face, forcing her to look at me, to see that she wanted me just as I did her. This connection zinged and sparked more now than ever as our eyes reconnected.

My right hand rested on her hip, my thumb circling her hip bone through the damp towel as I tried to catch my breath. I wanted to kiss her again, to feed my addiction, but her hand on my chest forced me to stay put.

I should let her go.

This was too much.

Olivia asked me a few days ago if this situation was permanent. The monster and I decided it was.

"I should get dressed," she told me, her voice almost inaudible as she gently shifted out of my grip, her eyes dropping from mine, forcing me back into the cold.

My heart began to slow, resuming its usual pace as she moved gracefully across the room, picking up her clothes and locking herself away in the bathroom.

"Shit," I hissed to myself, before slipping through the joining door to get changed. My restraint had broken and shattered at her feet, but before I could punish myself for breaking, my conscience reminded me that she had kissed me back.

Kissed me back.

Looking back into her empty room at the spot we had both stood in, elation spread through my chest. Maybe we were not doomed after all.

****

All I seemed to do these days was fucking pace. Ten minutes had gone by and still no Olivia. Why the hell did it take women so long to get bloody dressed? My impatience was running thin ever since our kiss, but it didn't go any further as she stepped out of the bathroom.

"Dannazione," I hissed under my breath, my eyes taking in the black form-fitting dress that she was wearing. It was sophisticated with its square neckline, fitted bodice highlighting her tiny waist perfectly, and stopped just above her knees. I was in perpetual hell, as the material hugged her body when she bent down to slip on a simple pair of matching black heels.

In ten minutes, she had turned from siren to goddess.

Damn you Marie for packing this dress.

"Are you hungry?" I asked her, holding out my hand for her to take.

Olivia flushed which intrigued me, but she quickly composed herself and hesitantly took my hand. "A little."

We both needed a distraction, me more than her as we left the suite and headed down the stairs towards the restaurant where our security was. It was not lost on me as we're led to a private table, facing out onto the gardens of the hotel that this would be the first meal we'd had together.

I needed to do better.

Olivia noted with surprise the bottle of wine that was cooling at the side of our table – it was her favorite. As the waiter quietly poured our drinks, I kept my eyes on her, she seemed much more relaxed now as she drank in our lush surroundings, her eyes slipping to the gardens around us until they landed back on me.

"Can I ask you a question?" she asked me, as I began to sip my drink, hoping the alcohol would soothe some of the tension between us.

"Yes."

"The day we first met…you looked exhausted and-"

"High?" I offered before nodding at Chen over her shoulder who was sat with Rum.

Olivia bit her lip. "Yes, you seemed pretty out of it."

I rubbed my chin, contemplating whether I was up for discussing this with her, and decided I would. We were both trying here.

"I was a spoilt ass who had the means to do as he pleased. I spent most of my time in this country high and getting into trouble. There was never a dependency problem, more of lack of direction."

Olivia nodded thoughtfully before sipping from her own glass, giving me the perfect view of her neck. High on my recent win, I hoped to kiss her neck again.

"Have you ever taken drugs, Olivia?" I asked her, as a waiter approached, gently placing down our starters of Scallops and Chorizo with hazelnut picada. The preordering of the wine and meals didn't go unnoticed by Olivia, but she chose to ignore it, for now, biding her time or she was possibly pleased with my control.

"Wait, you don't know if I have or if I haven't?" she asked me, a small smirk across her lips.

"Up until the age of seventeen, no I don't."

I picked up my fork with a sense of resentment as I thought about the years where my information was lacking.

"Well, I haven't before or after. My aunt kept me pretty close to her side growing up, ensuring that I didn't stray with the wrong crowd."

Olivia started to eat now that she had given me a small token of information, pleasing me. If she hadn't eaten tonight, I was certain in my plan to tie her up and force feed her so she wouldn't lose any more weight.

The image of Olivia tied up sent blood pumping to my head.

"I know you haven't," I blustered, looking for a new distraction, ignoring my food.

Olivia's eyes widened for a brief second. "How would you know that? Surely Chen hasn't been running around doing blood tests on me."

Sipping the wine, the cool liquid to burned in my throat as my silence allowed her to find an answer.

"No..." she whispered, as she dropped her fork, the clang causing Red's head to shoot up. Fixing him with a glare, he backed down and I turned my attention back to Olivia whose brows were knitted in distaste. Gone was her relaxed posture and now she was wound tight, her shoulders tense.

"When you arrived, we ran a blood panel to make sure you were healthy. Just a routine test, that's all."

I'm not a monster. I wanted to know that you were okay.

"Wow, not even my blood is safe from you," she hissed with disgust, before pushing her plate away, her appetite gone as soon as it came.

Of course, my inability to control myself around her made my tongue loose and free with my secrets, but she would have to deal with this. If this evening was to survive my stupidity, we would both have to come to terms with my depravity.

"It was just a precaution," my tone was full of warning. "You weren't well after you arrived."

Olivia fixed me with a scowl, her beautiful green eyes shining under the warm light as we both remembered her second sedation. "Were you ever taught the definition of consent Luca?"

I smirked; she was baiting me now to snap in front of all these people, but I was smarter than that. Well-rehearsed in power games.

"I have required your consent for many things over the past few days which you have willingly gave me. Does that answer your question?"

Taking in a deep breath, she decided that I'm either not worth the retort or she's saving her anger for later. Both options are worrying. Olivia was turning out to be a mastermind in keeping me out, forcing me to try harder which often left me reeling for more of her.

Before I could speak, the waiter returned and took away our half-eaten plates, his eyes on Olivia as he asked if everything was okay. Just a young teenager, he blushed bright red when she told him everything was perfect and then asked him for a glass of water.

Nobody was safe from her lure.

"Tomorrow," I cleared my throat, "you'll be alone with your family in the morning."

"Define alone?"

"I'll drop you off in the morning so you can be with them. Red, Rum, and Bones will be around, but they won't be in your way nor will they step in unless you decide to break our agreement."

Even now with her freedom within reach, she barely reacted to the news that she would be alone without me for the first time in a week.

"I don't know how I'm going to explain this all," she said, and ran a hand through her hair before biting her lip. Only an hour ago was I doing the same and now it was all I could think about.

I needed a cold shower.

"Stick to the story you've already told her and if you start to struggle, I'm happy to step in," I offered, as the waiter returned with her water and our mains, ignoring me completely.

Olivia seemed to relax now that she knew she wouldn't be alone in explaining our strange predicament to her expectant family. We could pretend for one day that we were a normal couple and maybe get through it unscathed.

"I hope you're happy to deal with my crazy family and their intrusive questions," she mused, with smug satisfaction while running her finger around the lip of her wine glass.

Happy to deal with intrusive questions? No, but if it meant keeping Olivia by my side while I navigated through our situation, I would.

"I'll be fine," I told her honestly.

Olivia scoffed. "You haven't met my grandparents," she sneered, and shook her head before finding my eyes, worry present in hers. "I might as well apologize to you now because as soon as they get their claws into you, that's it."

I was aware of these 'grandparents' and their fraught relationship with Olivia. Since the death of her parents, they had tried several times to move her to the south of France to live with them. A flash of emails from her Aunt Sarah refusing this move sprung to mind.

"I've dealt with many difficult people in my life Olivia," I replied, and leaned forward so that only she would hear the next bit, watching as she looked to my mouth. "They will be nothing in comparison. Whatever questions they have I'll answer."

"They'll have a lot of questions for you, especially Jack."

Ah, the grandfather.

"Good. I have a lot for him, too," I mentioned. I'd never met the man, but already I felt a distaste for him. Jack Heart had sold off Olivia's parents' house a week after their death, barely allowing their death to settle.

One of the main reasons for allowing Olivia to attend this wedding was to fill the gaps I desperately needed from her younger years. What better way to do that than to speak to the family she was close with at the time? Maybe it would keep the nerves at bay?

CHAPTER TWENTY-ONE

Olivia Heart

L uca Caruso was a triton. The devil with impossible beauty and manipulative charm. I had lost myself in him only hours ago, allowing my body to receive his pleasures as he kissed me senseless. As he worked my body into a frenzy, my brain began to demand more as its pleasure receptors zinged back to life.

I should have stopped, pushed him away in disgust, but I didn't. I was on the precipice of dangerous territory, and every time he stood in front of me, he nudged me closer and closer to the edge.

As I sat on the edge of the bath, the only noise from the tap, my feet dangling in cold water from wearing ridiculously high heels, I contemplated my ever-changing situation. Only an hour ago had Luca walked me to my room, placed a kiss on my cheek before leaving me bereft and lonely. A day ago, I would have flinched if he came too close.

Nothing made sense anymore.

Even my emotions were skewed.

Looking out to the bedroom, more specifically at the door that joined our suites, I wondered what he was plotting next and if I would ever be free of him. As if my dark thoughts had summoned him, the door opened and I panicked, my wrist slipped on the edge of the bath and with a small squeak, I half fell in. My lap was completely soaked alongside my pride.

"I think you're supposed to get undressed before you take a bath," he mused, as he strode through the room, stopping in the bathroom doorway. Even with the cold water soaking through my dress, his gaze heated my skin.

Alive and zinging with pleasure now he was in the vicinity.

My cheeks flushed with embarrassment as I slowly stood up. "Thanks for the advice," I replied, and tried to reach over towards the twin sinks to grab a towel, but Luca stepped in and grabbed it for me.

"Twice today, you've been wet in front of me Olivia. I'm starting to see a pattern," he said, as he held out the towel for me, an arrogant smirk dancing across his lips.

Grabbing up the towel, I hastily wrapped it around my waist, ignoring the amusement twinkling in his dark eyes and the blush burnishing my cheeks.

"The only pattern being that you like to come into my room unannounced. Can you step outside so I can get undressed?"

"I can help with that if you like?" he offered with a smirk, as I tried to move through the bathroom, ignoring his dressed-down look. Gone was the dark suit jacket and shoes, leaving him looking slightly less intimidating. Luca was always so put together, smart, and powerful looking with his perfectly tailored designer suits – this was a surprise.

Sighing, I stood still as he blocked me from leaving. I was tired and stressed, the last thing I needed was him pushing my buttons.

"Keep your hands to yourself," I hissed, as I tried to slip by, only to throw him a dirty look when he didn't move.

"I could," he told me, as he grabbed my hips, spinning me around into the double sinks. "But we both know that's not what you want," he teased, pinning me with his hips; I was stuck between him and the sink. Heat flushed my skin, giving me away as he rubbed his hands up and over my ass until he rested them on my hips.

My pulse began to throb when I looked up into the mirror, his dark eyes hidden from me as he buried his face in my neck. Licking and nipping the delicate skin until his teeth tugged on my earlobe.

I couldn't breathe.

Air was nonexistent as heat and lust began to build in my lower stomach. A sigh fell from my lips, pleasing him so much that I felt his cock press against my back. I could feel his darkness chipping at my crumbling wall while his hands slipped from my waist to the hem of my dress.

"I'm right, aren't I?" he whispered, his eye's finding me in the mirror. I tried to concentrate, to force my frozen limbs to move, but he was one step ahead. Dipping his head, his nose traced my neck before nuzzling against my ear.

Lust pumped in my ears as terror began to spindle painfully in my stomach. My body was stretching to two extremes, not being able to meet in the middle as he pressed against me.

"Answer me," he demanded, as his hand captured the back of my neck, arching me back into him. I was forced into his submissive hold while watching him kiss my neck.

I was free-falling from heaven with a one-way ticket to hell.

"Yes," my lips moved in the mirror, betraying me.

Luca sank his teeth gently into me, claiming me with hooded eyes. A gasp of sweet pleasure ripped away from my throat and I forced myself into the darkness behind my lids.

Gone was his usually fraying restraint – replaced with his need to touch me. Desperate, burning hands ripped at my dress, grabbing at the hem and pulling it up over my waist.

My eyes snapped open when the cool air bit at my naked skin.

Luca growled, "Perfetto, semplicemente perfetto," as he surveyed me, appreciating his new view.

Luca's fingers made quick work as they slipped underneath the flimsy material of my thong, and before I could protest, he slipped the black lace down my body and away with his foot.

Panic blurred into my vision, blinding me from his intensity as I weakly tried to push back. My tummy twisted and tangled in horror as I stood naked, open, and vulnerable.

"Olivia, do you know just how perfect you are?" He tugged gently on my hair, bringing my head back where he kissed the side of my mouth. It was all it took for me to be pushed back over the edge.

My body was alive and alert with a need for more from him, completely at his mercy.

"Just look at you," he said, and let go of my hair which tumbled in front of the left side of my face. My lips were swollen, cheeks and neck pink from his lips and teeth. Even my eyes were full of blind lust for him.

Everything about me was for him.

"I've waited eight years to see you like this and I have to say, you've surpassed all expectations."

Luca's voice was like honey, thick and smooth as he ran a finger down the side of my right breast, my nipple hardening against the tight material of my dress. I needed a release. Needed out of this intoxication before my thumping heart gave up under the strain.

My lungs burned desperately for oxygen I'd deprived them of, and as I tried to suck in a deep breath, my eyes caught his in the mirror and I froze.

"I don't want to take any more from you, Olivia," he whispered, his fingers delicately cupping my ass, "unless I have your permission of course. Give it to me now."

Luca's voice was strong and husky as he demanded my consent. Gone was my fear because my new inner goddess demanded I open my mouth and give him exactly what he needed to help me.

Closing my eyes to us standing in the mirror, I simply nodded.

It was enough for him because he hissed through his teeth, his fingers slipping from my ass to my core in one quick movement.

"Fuck," he murmured, as my wetness coated his index finger, my inhibitions lost when he slipped stealthily into me.

A cry slipped from my lips when the sweet sensations exploded across my skin, while he slowly moved within me, teasing me as he introduced himself to my body. Using his free hand, he clamped down on my waist so that I couldn't move from his delicious assault. My moans were the only sounds that echoed within this beautiful bathroom until he picked up the pace.

All I could do was grip the granite surface as pleasure exploded across my body. My body betrayed me, pushing back against his hand, greedily wanting more.

Luca let go of my hip to grab my face, forcing me to look at him in the mirror as he worked me speechless. I almost exploded when our eyes met in the steamed mirror.

"You're mine," his husky voice infiltrated my ears, as he slipped his finger out before slowly, sliding back into me. Dropping his hand from my face, he reached around me, circling my clit with his thumb while keeping his dark hooded eyes on me.

I cried out only for him to silence me with his mouth. I could taste wine and power as his tongue slid into my mouth, taking more from me.

Pulling away from my mouth he slowed his hands, allowing my eyes to flutter open while my body cried out from the lack of release.

"I'll give you everything, do you understand?" he whispered against my ear, as our eyes connected again in the mirror.

Tears seeped into my eyes as my inner goddess scratched at my walls, crying out for more.

"Luca, please- I don't understand-"

I was desperate now. My breathing had turned to short pants as I wiggled against him, trying to find comfort in his slow torture. I needed him to finish this.

"You won't try and run again will you Olivia?" his voice was low, rumbling in his chest that was pushed up against my back. Luca moved my hair to the side of my face, kissing the newly exposed skin that was weeping for more.

"No," I replied. The words that came from my mouth sounded like a promise, an extravagant agreement my brain hadn't had time to register.

I won't run. Just please do something.

"Good girl," he whispered, before slipping another finger into my dripping wet core, stretching me. A low moan fell from my lips as I fell forward – this was killing me and breathing life back into me all at the same time. Picking up speed, he became relentless as he rubbed my spot, taunting it to succumb to his forceful persuasion.

"I want something from you now," he breathed, as his palm slapped into me, forcing me to moan with surprise. My wetness was dripping between my thighs, coating his fingers as he pulled me closer to the edge.

"Come for me, Olivia."

I was lost and then bursting through as an orgasm rippled through my core, squeezing down on his hand while I came in shuddery bursts. Blinded by the sheer relief, my hand swiped across the granite sink, pushing off a bottle of perfume that smashed against the floor.

Completely sated with relief, I felt my body sink down into him while my brain tried to recover. Luca removed himself from me gently as he held me firm against him, not willing to let me go yet.

"You're perfect," he whispered into my hair, moving me backwards, away from the shards of glass and liquid pooling near our feet.

"You're everything," he uttered, breathless.

My brain was too deep in fog to understand the magnitude of what had just happened until he turned me around, his hands making quick work to push my dress back down. My eyes were on him, his face is soft, but his eyes still full of unspent lust.

I was confused but too tired to open my mouth.

In the twenty-five years of my life, nobody had worked my body the way he had or commanded my mind to submit so easily. Luca Caruso had so easily seduced me that, slighting me once again as the power tipped further to his side.

Gripping my chin, he lifted my face up to him, checking me over. I could see worry etched on his face; an emotion I had very rarely seen him wear. An unknown feeling in my chest moved but I ignored it as he sank his hands into my hair.

"You should rest now," he told me. "Are you okay?"

Why wouldn't I be okay?

"I'm f-fine," the words stammered from my swollen lips, while I swayed in his grip.

Luca gave me a small smile, his high cheekbones moving as he leaned in and gently pressed a kiss to my lips. Gentle and chaste, unlike what had just happened, he comforted me after taking from me once again.

"Get ready for bed, Olivia. You have a big day tomorrow."

I didn't want him to leave, but there was nothing I could do to stop him because he let me go with a satisfied smile, left the bathroom and disappeared into his own room. The sound of the door clicking shut bought me out of my fog all too quickly.

For five minutes, I stood staring at the bathroom sinks, trying desperately to remember how we had gotten to this position. At first, I thought it was his lack of control coming out, but my naivety wouldn't blind me today.

Luca was worried that I would break our deal.

For the first time since we had met, he had opened a vein of weakness to me—he was desperate for control and he wanted that in my body.

CHAPTER TWENTY-TWO

Luca Caruso

Four hours of sleep was all that I had managed, before I threw myself out of bed and punished myself in the hotel's gym while everyone but me slept. After my grueling workout, my body was still humming with electricity. My urges to see Olivia were growing stronger minute by minute as I looked out of my window into the gardens of our hotel.

The clock at the side of the bed said 5:00 am. I was frustrated with myself for being so worked up, but this is what I deserved after pushing the boundaries with Olivia the night before. In the spur of the moment, my rules lay broken as I touched her, desperate for control, knowing that once she was with her family, she could leave me.

I was selfish.

Desperate as I forced her to trust me quicker than she naturally should but still holding on to a strand of restraint as I gave instead of taking more than I should.

It nearly killed me.

All I wanted more on this earth was to sink myself into her so that I could lose myself in her body. Instead, I would settle for the sounds of her moans that still echoed in my ear, giving me comfort – Olivia's body wanted me, and it wouldn't be long until her mind would.

My mood stirred and I suddenly felt a little lighter.

****

Four hours later while on the phone with my accountant, my attention was pulled away by the most unusual noise, the sweetest laugh – girlish and free. I paused, holding the phone away when I realized it was coming from Olivia's room.

How had I never heard such a beautiful sound before?

I felt the urge to stand up and go see what was causing her to relax enough but my accountant, Marino, was spouting numbers down the phone, bringing me back to our conversation about my recent expenditures.

Quickly wrapping up my call, I moved from my chair to the door that joined our rooms. Slowly opening the door, I found Olivia sat on the edge of her bed, dressed, fresh-faced from her shower, and her hair still damp as she spoke into the hotel phone.

"It will be fine, Aunty Sarah, you just need to take a deep breath." She laughed, as she twirled her finger around the phone wire.

Leaning against the door, I crossed my arms and decided to watch her, reveling in this new side of her.

"I'll be there soon, and we can both calm her down, okay? Don't worry it's just nerves."

Olivia sensed me and slowly turned to look at me before dropping her eyes, forcing her attention back to her aunt who seemed to be dealing with a wedding crisis.

Don't get shy on me now, Miss Heart.

"Okay," she laughed again, "I'll see you soon. I love you, too." Shaking her head, she placed the phone down and turned to face me. There was happiness in her eyes that made her brighter, seem lighter when she spoke to her family and I suddenly felt jealous.

I wanted to give her that.

"Hello," she greeted me, as she stood up.

Did *everything* have to look good on her? Dressed in a white and pink floral dress she looked angelic until I saw the split hem that stopped three inches above her knee. A flash of last night's memory gleefully presented itself to me – me pushing her dress up and removing her black lace thong from her perfect body.

More acceptance.

"Good morning, Miss Heart," I greeted. I kept to my spot in between our rooms; trying not to push her good mood, knowing that my fingers itched to touch her, and my lips craved to kiss her.

Instead, I offered her my hand. "Come, you have a wedding to attend."

"Wait, I need to grab my dress and bag-"

"Leave it, Chen will bring your stuff," I told her, while grabbing her hand, relishing in the contact of our skin. Just as we slipped out of the door, Chen and Bones greeted us with a simple nod before entering Olivia's room.

Once we left the corridor, coming out onto the double staircase, Red and Rum were stood waiting for us, dressed casually, ready to blend in. They moved us down the stairs and out of the building to the waiting car with efficiency.

The heat was building this morning as the sun shone brightly over us, highlighting all the warm tones in Olivia's hair-

"Do they ever have a day off?" Olivia asked, as I quietly helped her into the car, trying to ignore the urge to pull her back out.

"They're paid well not to need one," I told her, as I slipped in next to her, grateful for the air conditioning. The humidity in England was really starting to get on my nerves.

"Are you any closer to sorting your...er issues with Black?" she asked, dropping her voice as if she was sharing a secret with me before she clicked her seat belt around her tiny waist.

The question threw me and Red who was getting into the passenger seat. Ignoring his eyes in the mirror, I turned to face her and her expectant expression.

"It's all being taken care of – don't worry about it, focus on today and let me deal with that," I responded. I fixed her with a 'don't argue with me stare' before nodding to Chen who had slipped into the car at the perfect time.

Never one to back down, she opened her sweet mouth. "How can I focus on today when I've-"

"Don't," I snapped. "Don't push me Olivia or we'll be on a flight to Sicily before you can finish that sentence."

Olivia flinched away from my anger as it seared her. Even now, she was still desperate for answers that I refused to give her. Nothing good would come from my loose tongue today when this should be a happy occasion for her. My mess did not need to bring her down any further than it already had.

"Sir we'll be there in twenty," Chen announced, as he clicked his earpiece.

****

It was interesting how attuned I was becoming to Olivia's moods in such a short time. During the drive, she went from cautious, to nervous and settled on agitated.

My new task of learning everything about her settled my nerves as we grew closer to the venue, where for a few hours she would be without me. I should relax given that there would be security to keep her boxed in but that's not what helped me. It was last night when she had allowed me, wanted me to touch her, and made a promise that she wouldn't betray my trust. It was everything.

There was a high price for betraying me and she wasn't willing to pay it.

I watched her as we drove down a lonely road that was covered by trees overlapping us overhead, every now and then, the car being shone on with bright summer light. I watched as her eyes caught sight of the hotel up ahead, causing her to freeze at my side.

"I can't do this." She shook her head. "No, I can't see them. Stop. Stop the car!"

Chen automatically slammed the breaks on the car and before I could grab her, she unclipped her belt and flung open the door.

"Olivia," I called, my heart dropping into my stomach. "Fuck."

"Sir?" Red asked me, watching as Olivia began pacing outside of the car.

"Stay here," I snapped, rushing out of the car to her.

Olivia was working herself up as she paced across the grass verge. Grabbing her quickly, I pulled her in, shielding her from Chen and Red as I squeezed her tight. It was all instinct as I let my body lead the way, giving her something to hold onto.

It had worked on her before.

"What is it?" I asked her. "Tell me, now."

"I can't do this," she cried against my chest, her tears soaking through to my shirt "I can't see them, Luca. They will know – they'll see it on me and what if I cave? You'll just drag me back to Sicily and then I'll never see them again."

Gritting my teeth, I fought against my instincts to put her in the car and take her home, but then another choice of hers would be stolen. We had a mutual agreement, and I wouldn't break it, no matter how much it was upsetting her.

"They won't suspect a thing. You just need to pull yourself together. Enjoy the time you have with them, and I promise you it won't be the last time. All you have to do is get through the day, Olivia."

Olivia sniffled before pulling herself away, wiping her eyes before looking out across the field next to us. It was beautiful and quiet here, with the only sounds being birds chirping above us and the soft purr of the car.

"This is insane," she whispered and looked up at me, stunning me with her all-seeing stare. "You realize that, don't you?"

"I do."

I realized it all too much a long time ago.

Stepping away from me, she quickly wiped her eyes. "I just need a minute, please."

So, I gave her a few.

"Come, let's get back in the car," I said, once I saw that her breathing had steadied. As she slowly returned to me, I held out my hand which she took without hesitation. Just as our fingers weaved together, she paused, pulling my much larger hand up to her face.

"Why do you have a circle tattooed on your finger?"

Ice cold shivers flew down my spine when she looked down at the tattoo on my ring finger. Olivia had spotted this tattoo a while back but never asked me about it and now was the worst time to divulge.

"It's not a circle," I told her, while gently tugging her back to the car.

"A zero?" she asked me with a raised eyebrow, her face still blotchy from crying. Hopefully, her skin would return to normal before we dropped her off with her family; that would only evoke more questions she wasn't prepared for.

"It's an O," I told her as I opened the car door.

"Why would you get an O tattooed on your ring finger?" The question tumbled from her lips; she received her answer before I could even open my own.

"It's not-" she stopped mid-sentence as I opened the car door.

Oh yes, it is.

Eyes wide she cautiously stared back down at my hand. I resisted the urge to pull away, knowing that it was no use, the truth was out. Letting go of my hand, she got into the car and waited until I had shut the door before asking me.

"Why?" she demanded, flipping her long hair over her shoulder as she fixed me with a fierce disapproving gaze.

Chen pulled the car away and I knew our time to talk about this would be up shortly.

"This is a conversation for when we're in private," I told her, as I slipped my eyes to those in the front of the car, doing their best not to listen.

Picking up on my hesitation to answer the question, she slowly nodded while biting her lip, desperate for another one of my secrets to slip out between us.

"But you promise to tell me why?" she asked, breaking me away from my dark thoughts as she lightly touched my hand.

Grabbing her hand, pleased with her touch, I placed it on my lap.

"I'll tell you once today's done with – that's a promise, Miss Heart."

I was rewarded with a small smile of relief.

CHAPTER TWENTY-THREE

Olivia Heart

Cotsworld House was an extravagant 16th-century country house that was surrounded by Saxon-moated gardens, topiary sculptures, and vast manicured land that spanned acres around the house. The house itself was two stories of magnificent original design with a deep brown brick that was mostly covered with large amounts of honeysuckle.

It was stunning as the sun shone down upon the house where my cousin Alice would marry Harry Timpson, a marketing executive for a large production studio in London. They had met at sixteen years old, childhood sweethearts who had not left each other's side since.

We were getting closer as Chen pulled us onto the gravel drive that led to the front of the house. There was a glass sign, stood on a silver easel that was welcoming Alice and Harry's wedding guests with its ornate silver scrawl.

"Olivia?"

Forgetting where I was, I jumped at the sound of my own name. Luca was looking at me, his eyes scanning rapidly over my face for any signs of another breakdown.

"I'm fine," I whispered.

I wasn't. This was all too real now.

In a few moments, I would see my family that I had been avoiding for the past two years who would no doubt had some very in-depth questions for the man sat by my side.

I felt sick.

Before I could focus on my building anxiety, my door was opened by Luca while Chen darted around the back of the car to retrieve my things.

"Your phone is in your bag. I've put my number in there in case you need me," Luca voice was terse and strained, as I slowly stepped out into the burning sun.

"I'm sure I'll be fine for a few hours," I breathed, trying to bring some lightness into the sudden mood change that was wrapping its way around us.

I could feel his nerves and frustration building. Luca did not want me out of his sight, much apparent to the way he gripped my hand when we stood outside the car.

"A lot can happen in a few hours," he mumbled once his eyes caught mine.

Before I could open my mouth to ask what he meant by that, the voice of my aunt travelled quickly to my ears as she raced across the gravel driveway to me.

Luca tensed at my side as we both turned to face her.

"Oh my God, Olivia!" she grinned, rushing into my arms, forcing me to drop Luca's hand. "You're so tanned! Let me look at you – well, I never thought I would see the day." She pulled me back, her blonde hair wrapped in curlers with her half-done make-up. My aunt was a beautiful woman who had held on to her youth with soft-looking skin, plump cheekbones, and perfectly manicured brows – at forty-seven, she was simply stunning.

Eyes full of happiness beamed at me as the beacon of my home held me close and steady.

"Have you lost weight? You look like you've lost weight."

"Hello to you, too," I laughed while squeezing her arms, instantly relaxing into her motherly warmth.

A small cough from my side bought my attention back to our surroundings and I was soon forgotten as my Aunt Sarah dropped my arms to greet Luca. Ocean blue eyes regarded him with surprise as she looked from him to me.

Oh God. This was embarrassing already.

"I mean, I assumed you were handsome Luca being Italian and all, but this is a nice surprise."

I blushed at her young laugh as she leaned in and kissed him on the cheek, welcoming him with open arms. Luca was even surprised by the forwardness of her welcome, his mouth turned up into a small smile.

I expected to feel different now that my two worlds had collided, but it was near impossible with my aunt's infectious attitude.

"Nice to meet you Mrs. Miller," he greeted confidently, with a smile that I had very rarely seen on his usually tense face.

"Please – call me Sarah," she told him, as she patted his arm so easily.

Panic bubbled in my chest until Luca placed an arm around my waist, gently pulling me into him, possibly warning me not to lose it.

"I'm so glad both of you could make it. Alice is so pleased." She smiled at me before turning to Luca. "And it will be nice for you to meet the family Luca. It's not everyday Olivia here lets us in on her busy life."

I nearly didn't.

I wanted to tell her. The urge to relinquish all my secrets were on the tip of my tongue until Luca placed a kiss on the side of my head.

A warning.

"I look forward to meeting them all," Luca replied effortlessly. "Olivia has spoken very fondly about your family Mrs. Miller."

Liar.

"We should go," I interrupted quickly. "We need to make sure Alice hasn't climbed out of the window."

My aunt could not keep her eyes off Luca, especially his protective arm around me and I knew instantly then that she liked him, a lot. I knew that she would pin him down later in the day to ask him a million questions – an image that turned my stomach.

Chen stepped forward and held out my dress bag and a small cream bag that I had packed earlier while keeping his true feelings hidden, but I could feel that he disagreed with today. Before I could take it, Luca pulled me close once more, his mouth by my ear-

"If you need me, I'm here."

****

The deafening squeal that hit my ears was enough to shatter my eardrums. I hadn't even set my foot in Alice's suite when I was attacked by the loud banshee-like screams of her bridal party.

Even my Aunt Sarah clasped her chest when we were barricaded by lithe bodies in silk purple robes as they pulled us into the room. Alice, the one wearing a white robe was the first to pull me into a bone-crushing hug.

"Bloody hell, Liv, its feels like forever since I last saw you," she grinned as she pulled back. Alice was three years older than me with dirty blonde hair, oval-shaped face with a cute button nose. Unlike her parents, she was short but what she lacked in height, she made up for her in curves and attitude.

"Oh Alice, you look amazing," I told her, once I pulled back. There was something about her that was different. She was glowing with happiness as she twirled, showing off her lovely intricate updo and make-up. Maybe it was the pre-wedding glow or maybe she embodied genuine happiness.

"Thank you." She grinned at me, before grabbing my hand and pulling me over towards the window where a makeup artist and hairdresser stood waiting for me.

"Now sit here and let these lovely ladies get you ready while Lilly gets you a glass of champagne – we have a lot of questions for you!"

As soon as my butt hit the chair, my hair was pulled over my shoulders and the makeup artist began wiping at my face. They didn't hold back as they began preparing their canvas. My eyes barely adjusted to the room before a spray was spritzed on my face, making me cough.

Lilly, Alice's maid of honor, a fiery redhead was quick to pass me a glass of ice-cold champagne, but rather than leave, she stood with Alice in front of the dressing table. They shared a secretive glance before turning their attention back to me.

Cold dread filled me up.

Here goes.

"So, Liv, when were you going to tell us that you had bagged yourself a *lovely* Italian man?" Alice started, which earned her a giggle from Hayley who was steaming Katie's dress in the corner of the suite.

Groaning, I closed my eyes. "Alice, this is your day. Can't we talk about that instead?"

"Nope! I need a distraction, so you're going to answer all my questions – it's my day after all, so I get to call the shots."

It was just like being a kid all over again. Alice getting her own way while I silently sulked, hoping she would eventually get bored and leave me alone.

I took a large gulp of the champagne, welcoming the burn as the bubbles slid across my tongue. It was far too early to be drinking on an empty stomach, but needs must when you were facing an ambush.

"Mum said he owns the company you work for."

"He does," I answered quickly, too quickly.

"Did you really move to Sicily to be with him?"

"Ow!" I cried, as my hair was tugged a little too roughly. "No, I didn't. A position came up at the company's head office and I took it."

Alice raised an eyebrow before placing her glass down. Did she not believe my pathetic lies? Who could blame her really-

"I can see why. If I was you, I would follow him to the end of the earth. I mean the man is just gorgeous!"

"Alice!" Aunt Sarah hissed, from somewhere in the room.

"Oh, come on, Sarah you know he is. We saw you fawning all over him outside," Lilly teased, as she began topping up everyone's glasses.

I wanted the earth to swallow me whole as my hair was pulled into curling brushes and my face wafted with a powder that smelled strongly of chemicals and peaches.

"We did some research on Luca last night, Liv. Did you know he's stinking rich?" it was Hayley who spoke up this time, as she joined Alice and Lilly who were expecting me to dish all.

I suspected given that he had the means to control my life undetected for the past eight years that his wealth was vast, but finances had never been spoken about between us.

"He has a lot of businesses," I agreed.

In property, banking, security, law, stalking, kidnapping…the list is endless.

"But now you're this man business, eh?" Alice asked wiggling her eyebrows suggestively, making me groan out loud.

"Alice, get your mind out of the gutter, will you?" her mother snapped, as she picked up my dress bag that sat on the bed.

Alice rolled her river blue eyes before waving her off.

"No, seriously, I'm happy that you've bought someone to meet us all." She bent down and grabbed my hand, her eyes sparkling with happiness. An overwhelming sense of home came over me and I felt my shoulders relax slightly.

"Are you happy?" she asked me.

Happy? The loaded question took my breath away and it took all my strength to push away the warm feeling in my eyes. My heart throbbed in my chest as she looked happily into my eyes, wanting nothing more than for me to share her happiness.

This was Alice's day, and I wouldn't spoil it for her or this family. They had done so much for me and no way would I betray them by dragging them into this terrifying mess.

"I am," I lied.

The lie felt easy.

"I can tell." She grinned at me. "We were watching you from the window. I've never seen a couple look so perfectly matched for each other."

****

Three glasses of champagne and four chocolate strawberries later, I was ready to get into my dress and start this charade. The questions about Luca eased eventually which helped me to relax and enjoy their company as they caught me up with all the comings and goings of our busy family.

My Aunt Sarah was faffing with wedding flowers, triple-checking that there was enough for the bridal party. Hayley and Lilly were helping Alice into her dress, their hands expertly slipping the off the shoulder, trumpet-style dress onto her body.

I focused on the floor-length lilac bridesmaid dress made with layers of chiffon with a V shape neckline that I stood in. The dress was simple with a romantic full skirt that glided across the floor as you moved.

My hair was curled with the top half twisted around my head, pulled loose for an effortless look. In reality, it took a lot of hair-pulling and backcombing which my scalp didn't appreciate, but I didn't complain. Thankfully, the makeup required less pain and was simple and radiant. For the first time in weeks, I felt put together and at ease as I helped Alice place her veil into her updo.

Normal. I felt normal.

Grinning at Alice, I fought back tears as we all stared into the ivory floor-length mirror in the bathroom. My Aunt Sarah had to leave the room, excusing herself to check on the flowers for the fifth time but no doubt to go sob into a box of tissues.

"She really misses my dad," Alice sighed sadly, as we both looked out into the bedroom.

"We all do," I said, squeezing her hand, silently letting her know that I was here if she needed me.

"She misses yours, too," she whispered, before sucking in a deep breath, fighting off her emotions. "There's a prayer for them in the middle of the ceremony – Mum wanted something to honor everyone that we've lost."

I turned away and pretended to smooth down my dress, trying not to think about my parents or my wobbling bottom lip.

"Olivia, there's a man at the door for you!" Hayley called, ducking her head into the bathroom.

"Me?" I squeaked, before clearing my throat.

Entering the bedroom, I saw an elderly gentleman dressed in a dark navy suit with the whitest moustache I had ever seen smiling at me, holding a large velvet black box.

"Miss Heart?" he asked me, as he stepped forward.

Everyone in the room paused, waiting for me to respond.

"Erm yes, that's me."

"A gift from Luca Caruso to the Alice Miller wedding party."

Opening the box delicately, I was the first to see the Cartier logo on the inside of the box. Inside the large velvet box sat five individual red boxes with our names engraved in silver.

"Ah shit," Alice mumbled breathlessly, when she saw her name inside the box.

"Alice, language!" Aunt Sarah snapped, as she dabbed her eyes.

Before I knew it, the box was pressed into my hands and he bid us goodbye with a short wave. Without thinking, I thrust the box into Alice's hands, making my way over to the dressing table where my glass of champagne sat.

"Olivia, you need to see this," Alice called with excitement, but I couldn't turn around just yet. My anger was simmering on the surface and I needed to keep it there before anyone noticed. Luca's gifts were a reminder of his presence in my life, letting me know that he was always there, and I hated him for it.

Expensive cuffs, that's all they were.

A low whistle fell from Lilly's lips when Alice opened her box. I couldn't help myself as I turned to find that inside was a tennis bracelet with individual cut diamonds, perfect and delicate as it sat on a plush red pillow.

"There's one for us all," Alice said, turning to me, her face falling when she saw mine. "Liv, don't look so scared. The man just wants to spoil you."

Oh, he was spoiling me alright. A bad apple in a barrel of good came to mind.

"It's a lot," I replied, trying to smile but my face barely moved.

My Aunt came to my rescue as she stepped to me, grabbing my hand and giving it a squeeze. "Cartier and 'a lot' go hand in hand love. Now don't be rude and make sure you wear your bracelet so he can see," she reached up to move a strand of hair from my face.

I didn't need reminders that he had trapped me, nor did I need his gifts sitting on my family's wrists, but what could I do?

I laughed, to her it was with relief, but I laughed at myself. They had no idea of the 'gifts' bestowed to me from Luca Caruso.

"Thank God!" Alice squealed. "For a second, I thought we wouldn't be able to wear them."

****

Alice was trying desperately not to vomit as we all fussed around her, fixing her dress, her hair and making sure everything was in place. In five minutes, we would move through the champagne lounge to the ballroom where she would be made a wife by a man who would walk over hot coals for her.

I have that.

I should have been focusing on her, but instead, my mind was on Luca who would be sat, with Alice's guests – my family, waiting for us. My brain tried to picture him there, dressed in his dark designer suit with brooding eyes as he waited while someone would try to talk his ears off, demanding to know more about him.

I prayed he wasn't sat near my grandparents.

Looking across the room, I saw two men dressed in black and white stood by the ballroom doors, ready to open them for us. Usually, my eyes would have slid by them, but the familiar earpiece flashing at the side of their heads caught my attention.

"Mum, make sure I don't fall, okay?" Alice whispered, as she grabbed her mother's arm tight.

"I've got you love."

Soft music began to play, and I knew our time alone in this room was up. Hayley would walk first, then Lilly followed by me before Alice would follow with her mum. Alice wanted us to walk alone, without Harry's groomsmen because she thought it would be less traditional, but now all I wanted was someone's arm to hold on to.

The doors slowly opened, and the sounds of soft violins reached my ears. Hayley moved delicately forward, clutching her bouquet of white wildflowers, a relaxed smile on her face as she left us behind and walked down the petaled covered aisle.

Lilly did the same, but she was quicker to move which meant I didn't have time to mentally prepare myself because I followed. The room felt warm as sunlight hit me from the right side through large windows. Eyes followed me the whole way down, but I kept a smile on my face, focusing on reassuring Harry who was sweating profusely.

Turning around to face the room, my eyes quickly found Luca who was sat near the back, dressed in a navy-blue suit, his hair perfectly styled with a freshly shaven face. My shoulders relaxed a touch when our eyes met across the ballroom.

I expected to feel fear at seeing him so close to the people I loved, but it never came. Instead, all I felt were my feelings towards him morphing, stretching thin before snapping back into a place that didn't make sense.

Alice was suddenly stood at Harry's side and passing her bouquet of flowers to me, brimming with excitement as she turned to him and took his hand. The love she had for Harry had spanned across the test of time with both still mad for one another.

My heart ached as I thought about the man whose unhealthy obsession for me had got me to this point. Luca loved me, unhealthily so, but he did, and I didn't know what to do with that. The moment my eyes found his in that darkened bedroom, he wrapped me up in his web of desire, slowly, inch by inch, pulling me in until I wanted nothing more than him.

I had also felt in the night he had touched me. Telling me that I was his, forcing my submission in the forms of his burning touch. My mouth had betrayed me and easily given him what he needed and now I craved it all over again.

Purgatory. That is where I was.

****

I waited in the champagne lounge, carefully dodging relatives who tried to catch me as they left the ballroom. I was desperate to get to Luca before it was too late, so I made my excuses.

"Is that my sweet Olivia?"

My heart dropped at the sound of my grandfather Jack Heart's gruff voice calling my name. Our eyes met as he walked out of the ballroom with my grandma and Luca in tow.

My heart froze at Luca talking to my grandmother, who was holding on to his arm while she dished information that I couldn't hear. Time seemed to pause as his eyes lifted to mine.

"Look at you! Don't you scrub up well?" Jack greeted, as he pulled me into a bone-crushing hug, his scent of old spice and mint overpowering my nose.

"Hello, Jack," I greeted gently, keeping my eyes on Luca who barely gave anything away – his secret conversations with my grandmother hidden.

"Doesn't she look good with a tan, Mary?" Jack said, as he turned to his wife – forcing my attention on him. My grandfather was a short man that still had a full head of dark chocolatey hair with mixed flexes of grey. Oddly, the trimmed beard on his face was white as paper, standing off his own tanned skin from living in the south of France.

"That she does – although she could do with some meat on her bones!"

Mary was wearing a cream fitted suit and heels, the family pearls sitting pretty on her neck. If I didn't know her, I would have said she looked ten years younger than her actual age with beautiful blonde hair and youthful skin.

It took all my restraint not to roll my eyes to the back of my head, but instead, I politely smiled at her throwaway comment. My weight really wasn't anyone's concern right now.

"Are you not feeding her that good Italian food Luca?" Jack grinned, turning back to Luca with a raised eyebrow.

"Oh my God," I hissed under my breath, which caught Luca's attention. This was worse than expected. It would have been easier if they hated him, cast him out as a pompous outsider, but instead, they flocked to him like a god he was not.

"Your nipotina looks perfect the way she is," he breezily replied, heavily emphasizing his Italian accent, which in turn made my grandmother swoon.

"Luca here tells us that you're living in Sicily at the moment, with him?" Jacks' voice was tinged with hurt, but he kept his smile rigidly fixed. Sharing my life with my family had always been difficult – especially with my grandparents who had a history of meddling.

Like Luca. No wonder they were getting on so well.

"For work." I nodded, keeping emotion off my face. "It was a spur-of-the-moment decision."

My eye's flickered to Luca's who didn't seem pleased with my answer.

Mary's attention was pulled away by my Aunt Sarah who had called her from the other side of the lounge, excusing herself, she let go of Luca's arm, but my grandfather stayed.

Great.

"Are you enjoying it?"

"Yes," I ground out, as Luca took to my side, slipping his arm around my waist and anchoring me to him. "It's keeping me on my toes."

Heat spread across my chest.

"Olivia's very amenable," Luca said, addressing my grandfather. "She's an important asset to what I'm trying to build."

Jack grinned as he stuffed his hands into his trouser suit pockets, but I only tensed at the conversation, my frustration for Luca's wooing of my family starting to boil to the top.

"Will you excuse us, Jack? I need to introduce Luca to a few people." I gripped Luca's arm before sliding my hand down to meet his.

"Of course, we're sat together for the dinner so we can catch up then."

"Perfect," I lied, with an effortless smile before tugging Luca across the champagne lounge and out into the gardens. The sun was sat high over the hotel as I walked us towards the moat that ran down the side of the building, away from any distractions.

I stopped and turned, ready to snap at him, but was rudely interrupted by his hands in my hair and his lips crushing mine. My thoughts quickly evaporated as his tongue slipped into my mouth, tasting of champagne. Blood pumped thickly in my ears as I held onto his suit jacket, my body desperate to be as close as possible.

Breathless, he pulled away before I could become lost. "You look so beautiful in that dress."

His soft lips pressed against mine once again while he fought his own control.

"Olivia, it's rude to outshine the bride on her own wedding day," he admonished me with a sultry smirk, his hands now cupping my face as he bought me forward once more.

"So, very rude," he whispered.

I closed my eyes as he gently pressed his mouth on the corner of mine, teasing me, burning me until my nerves were zinging across my body once again.

"You're purposely trying to distract me, aren't you?" I mumbled, finally finding my voice after his ambush.

Luca's small laugh against my jawline was enough of an answer but my anger stayed at bay, deciding it wasn't worth losing his touch over.

"Always in your head, Miss Heart."

Pulling away, he let go of my face and took my hand instead, admiring the bracelet that he had so sneakily sent to Alice's suite. I watched carefully as his eyes scanned the piece of jewelry, watched as he seemed genuinely pleased with my acceptance of his gift, and saw how his body language changed to this new information.

"It's beautiful," I told him honestly, watching to see his reaction. "Thank you."

Luca didn't disappoint because he smiled for the first time around me, showing me his perfect white teeth, pleased with my compliment. A rush of emotions mixed in my chest at the unusual sight, forcing me to take a deep breath.

"I'm glad you like it. If you would let me, I'd dress you in diamonds for the rest of your life."

I shook my head, trying to ignore his sultry voice.

"I don't need diamonds, Luca. The only thing I'd ever want from you are honest answers."

He frowned, a small crease forming on his forehead.

"I'll give you all the answers you want, Olivia. You just need to get through today as planned. I made you a promise which I plan on keeping, just please be patient."

"I know but-"

"Trust works both ways. I'm trusting you here. You need to trust that when we return to Sicily, I'll give you all the answers you need."

"Why when we're back in Sicily? Why can't you tell me tonight?"

"Because I want one day with you that won't be ruined."

My stomach clenched painfully at the worry lacing his words. Luca had always been so strong and firm with me, but this was different, this scared me to the point I felt desperate.

"Ruined by what, Luca? You're scaring me."

"Olivia! Come on we've got photographs to take," came the voice of Hayley who was waving her bouquet of flowers like a madwoman at the hotel doors.

"Come on, Olivia, you need to be with your family today," he began, tugging me over the grass slowly, careful to let me step without my heels sticking in the ground.

"What do you know about what I need?" I mumbled harshly under my breath.

Growling to himself, he stopped midway across the grass, still out of reach from Hayley who now had her hands on her hips.

"The tattoo on my hand," he snarled at me, baring his teeth as he ran his hand through his hair. "Do you really want to know why?"

No!

"Yes," I whispered, as my eyes sought out his ring finger.

"It's a permanent reminder of the only person I'll ever want to marry."

"I don't understand…"

"It's you, Olivia. It's to remind me that if it is not you by my side then it will never be right. Never be enough. It's to stop me from making a mistake with someone else."

My mouth opened but words refused to come, instead, they retreated and hid. Fear and confusion hindered my thought process while I stared up at him, focusing on his eyes that were pleading with me to understand his madness.

"You're scared," he told me, as he took a step closer.

I flinched and took one back, needing space.

"Shit," he hissed looking up at the sky, allowing the sun to bathe his face in all its glory.

"I need a minute," was all that came out of my mouth.

"Bloody hell, Liv, come on, will you? Loverboy will still be here when we're done." It was Lilly this time that was shouting at me from the doorway, her smirk as bold as her attitude.

"You should go," he told me, as he reached into his suit jacket and pulled out a pair of sunglasses.

"We'll finish this discussion tonight?" I whispered, afraid now that I couldn't see his eyes.

Luca gritted his teeth before nodding, but I wasn't sure I believed him. My reaction to his honesty had hurt him but what did he expect springing that on me? Permanently marking your body was something entirely different.

As I walked away, my thoughts remained on my initials tattooed on his finger. Even as Lily pulled me into the champagne lounge where our family was grouped together, grinning from ear to ear, he was the only person I wanted to stand by right now.

I wanted to pick his brain until he couldn't take it anymore.

I deserved answers.

I deserved the truth.

CHAPTER TWENTY-FOUR

Luca Caruso

While Olivia was off taking photographs with her family, the groom's over-enthusiastic friends had decided to approach me, their questions spilling out of their mouths before I'd even taken a sip of my drink.

"Harry mentioned that you studied here, what was your subject?" one asked, I think his name was Thomas, but I had forgotten already. My eyes were too focused on Olivia outside smiling for the camera.

"Business," I answered.

Olivia was talking to the photographer as he showed her the picture, he had just taken of her and her Aunt Sarah.

"Is that how you met Olivia?"

"Something like that," I answered him, my eyes sliding back to his expectant face. The two men stood by his side preferred to sip their drinks quietly.

Before he could open his mouth again, I placed my glass down on the bar when I spotted Chen hovering in the doorway. Excusing myself, I moved quickly to a quiet corner.

"What is it?"

"Nothing to worry about sir. I just want to check in with you regarding tomorrow's flight. Do you still want to proceed for the evening?"

I wanted to fly out tonight, but tomorrow was decided so that Olivia didn't feel put out by the abruptness of us leaving her home so quickly.

"Yes, that's fine. Any updates on our little problem?"

"No, sir," he answered. Chen took a step back before nodding and leaving me to it.

Running a hand through my hair, I settled my frustrations and headed back into the champagne lounge where Olivia was just entering from the gardens, her cheeks flushed when she saw me.

"There you are." She grabbed two glasses of champagne off the bar and thrust one into my hands. It didn't go unnoticed by me that she seemed pleased to see me, almost relieved.

"What's wrong?" I asked, as I picked up her shift in mood, she was anxious again.

Olivia let out a small laugh while she sipped from her glass, "If it's not taking a million pictures, it's answering a million questions about you."

Imagining Olivia awkwardly answering questions made the corners of my lips turn up, which she noticed, she always noticed. It was worth the glare.

"I hope you were nice about me," I whispered, as I inched closer, placing my hand around her hip so I could pull her closer to me. Even with the layers of chiffon between us, I could feel her body's anticipation.

"At this point, I could have told them everything and they wouldn't believe me. They like you."

A. L. Hartwell

Of course, they liked me. I had spent most of the morning being the perfect guest; I answered their questions, met relative after relative who was so surprised at Olivia bringing a 'boyfriend' to meet her family.

"Can you stop smirking, Luca?" she whispered, as she looked up at me with those stunning emerald green eyes.

"I'll try, Miss Heart, but no promises," leaned down and placed a kiss to the side of her head, enjoying her sweet perfume.

Turning to me, our faces inches apart, she fixed me with a cautious stare before smirking, her pretty eyes glinting mischievously at me.

"Well seeing as you're in a 'trying' mood, I have a proposition for you," she told me proudly, before gently pulling us away from the bar so that we wouldn't garner anyone else's attention.

"Oh?"

"Yes." She pulled me away from the bar, no fear present in her body as we stood by a table decorated with gifts for the happy couple. Gone were her shaky hands and lack of eye contact, stood before me, was Olivia Heart, lawyer to be.

"Well, what is it?"

"You want one normal day and I want answers…so, my proposition is that if you answer three of my questions, I'll give you one normal day with no questions and no push back."

My imagination ran wild with me, spinning and stretching to these possible 'three' questions, but then I forced myself to imagine the reward I would get for agreeing to this deal. I would get her.

"Deal."

Olivia laughed, catching herself off guard. "Just like that?"

230

"You've presented a good deal." I shrugged, grabbing her by the elbow and helping her out into the lush gardens. There were a few guests milling about, but luckily none of her immediate family to distract me from closing this deal.

"All I ask is that you play fair, Miss Heart. I don't have to tell you that this proposition is fragile at best."

"I know," she sighed, as we began walking down the side of the building, moving towards the front. Once again, my urges to touch her won, and I grabbed her hand and intertwined my fingers with hers.

Olivia was too busy preparing her first question to notice how easily her body accepted me now.

"My first question, do you have any other family other than Dante?"

I wasn't expecting it or the relief that breezed through my body.

"I do. I have a sister called Aida who has a little boy called Mateo."

Olivia wanted to ask more, but she knew that with only two questions left, she had to choose wisely. I would be a liar if I didn't admit to being a little smug.

"We'll come back to that. Okay, question two, have you had any relationships since the first time we met at the airport?"

This wasn't a question I expected nor had prepared for. Olivia's distaste for our situation had me assuming we wouldn't get to this point for a very long time.

Stay focused. Two questions to answer.

"Once. There was a woman I had tried to be in a relationship with," I answered, my urge to bite my tongue was fierce, the monster inside was furious that we were weakening our control to let her in, but I was in charge now.

"It was at the beginning, after meeting you. I thought of the relationship only as a distraction, being in a normal situation would force me to forget you, but she saw right through it. After it ended, I got this tattoo, so I wouldn't hurt anyone else."

We had come to a natural stop in front of the large water fountain at the front of the house. Olivia was pensive, reserved but still holding my hand as we stood staring at one another.

All I wanted was for her to understand.

Olivia groaned before dropping my hand and lifting her face to the sun, sucking in deep breaths. "I have even more questions now," she told me.

"Just one more, Olivia," I whispered, enjoying the freedom of purging a few of my secrets and knowing my reward was close.

"Fine," she mumbled, as she turned to me, her dress swishing across my legs. "You said that you were never going to interfere with my life, that you only did because of…well, what's happening with Black. Is that true?"

What was with this woman's senses? So much for easy questions. My response could open a jar of worms that would make her want to ask more, to leave our deal in shambles. I could not have that. Not now that my subconscious was running wild, planning our day of 'normality' together.

"Yes, it's true."

****

Olivia was polite and kind to those that sat around our table. Like a beacon of light, she attracted everyone's eye and their curiosity. A queen in deflection, she always managed to turn the conversation back on the person she was speaking to, feigning interest in their lives.

Under the table, my hand rested on her thigh, gently stroking her through the layers of chiffon that separated our skin. Since our little deal, I was finding it extremely difficult not to touch her especially given that she was more comfortable with me now.

Watching her sip her drink, I thought about last night when she was pinned in front of the mirror, remembered the gasp that escaped her beautiful full lips as she came around my fingers. Olivia gave me everything in that moment but left me physically reeling for more of her.

"Luca, please you're distracting me," she leaned into my ear and whispered but under the table, her hand had covered mine, preventing me from sliding further up her thigh. My senses were overwhelmed once again by her perfume drifting to my nostrils.

"I don't know what you mean," I replied coyly, while taking her hand under the table.

"So, Olivia, are you and Luca staying around after the wedding?" Mary, her grandmother, asked from across the table as she pushed away her dessert.

Before Olivia could answer, I butted in, politely with a warm smile. "Afraid not, Mrs. Heart, I'm taking Olivia to Paris tomorrow morning."

Olivia's head snapped to me, her long hair hitting me across the shoulder while her big doe eyes blinked at me with confusion.

My reward Olivia.

"Oh! How lovely," Mary cooed, as she and Jack shared a look. "What are your plans while you're there?"

Olivia tried to slip her hand from mine, but I squeezed hers, hopefully giving her enough reassurance to keep us together.

"I'd love to tell you, but I don't want to ruin the surprise."

Jack seemed pleased with my answer because he smiled lovingly at his wife while filling her water glass. If I didn't know Jack as well as I did, I may have liked him, but unfortunately, that wasn't a possibility.

My loyalty lay with Olivia.

Olivia leaned into me once again. "Are we really going to Paris? I thought trips like this would take time for Chen-"

"I have one normal day with you, Miss Heart. I don't plan on wasting it and Chen will cope, he always does."

I heard her breath hitch, delighting my ears with the sweet sound, but she turned away from me, hiding her face.

"You must go to the Le Mur Des Je T'aime Olivia. It's must hot spot for all you young ones" Mary smiled before her eyes slid to me, a blush creeping up on her cheeks.

"What's that?" Olivia asked, still hiding her face from me as she picked up her wine glass. I hated it when she hid her face, forcing me to return to my own thoughts and possessive tendencies.

Under the table, I pulled her hand over to my lap and she turned to look at me, finally. I didn't like what I saw, she was back in her head, hiding her true feelings away from me with her usual blanketed look.

"It's the wall of love. It has 'I Love You' written across it in two hundred and fifty languages. Isn't that lovely? It would make the perfect picture."

Olivia was quick to reply. "Sounds great, Grandma."

What a polite liar.

The day was wearing thin on Olivia and she was reaching her point – I could feel it as she squeezed my hand, not knowing that she was using it to vent her frustration until I rubbed my thumb across hers.

Did she believe in love? Did she have it in her to love someone? I had never seen proof in her few past relationships. All I saw was three stages in her love life.

Acceptance of a date.

Date.

Nothing.

Olivia became the perfect ghost when she worked out the intentions of her suitors and it irked me not knowing why. Maybe once she worked out my intentions, she would try again to disappear. I'd have control over her body, but she could always shut me out of her mind. The one place I wanted to possess more than anything.

I looked to her and found her mid-conversation with one of Harry's groomsmen who was leaning over her shoulder, his mouth far too close to her ear for my liking as she smiled at something he said. Gritting my teeth, I sucked in a deep breath and kept my simmering jealousy at bay, and focused my thoughts on tomorrow.

CHAPTER TWENTY-FIVE

Olivia Heart

My brain had been hacked. It was the only reason I could come up with as we left Cotswold house later that evening. At the start of the day, I had panicked, cried in desperation, but now I was leaving hand in hand with the man that would go to extreme lengths to make me his.

I looked at him, with his jacket draped over my shoulders, and wondered if he understood how far in the deep end he really was. Luca's intentions were clear; he wanted to own me and to love me, smothering my independence until all I needed was him.

No one could survive that.

"I've forgot my bags," I mumbled, as he helped me into the car.

"Chen's taken care of it. They're already back at the hotel."

As soon as he got into the car, Luca surprised me by leaning down and lifting up the bottom of my dress, where he took extra care in slipping off my heels. My tongue froze in my mouth at his searing touch, but he wasn't done with me.

"Turn around," he demanded softly; his usually harsh stare replaced with softness.

"Why?" my voice was a slight whisper, barely audible against the car's engine but he heard me.

"Just trust me."

So, I did. I gently turned as much as I could because the skirt of my dress took up a lot of the room between us.

I was holding my breath when I heard him move across the seat to get closer to me, only to be surprised by his hands in my hair.

"How many of these things did they put in?" he mumbled, while he picked at the bobby pins in my hair. Luca's hands in my hair did things to my body that I had never felt before. My scalp was tingling with anticipation and sighing with relief.

"You don't have to do that," I laughed, trying to pull away from him so I could pull myself together, but he wouldn't have it.

"I've counted ten so far," he mumbled. "Cosa fanno le donne."

My scalp cried out for his touch, begging for more as he pulled pin after pin. My hair began to release bit by bit, more curls dropping down the front of my chest as he worked quickly, affectionately as he made sure not to tug at my hair.

"You know, Olivia, you have the sweetest laugh I think I've ever heard."

"Mhm," was all I managed, I was too lost in his touch.

"I'd like to hear it more often," he told me, as he pulled another pin out.

"Luca," I turned to face him. Even in the darkness of the car, I could see him clear as day, his dark broody eyes following every move that I made.

"Why are you doing this?"

Luca didn't understand my question, it was obvious by the way he squinted at me and his jaw flexed with tension.

"Why are you doing all this?" I clarified, while I looked down at his hands.

"Ah," he held up his hand. "Not today, Olivia, you've had your fill of questions."

I opened my mouth to protest, but he placed his index finger on my lips with a small smirk that silenced me immediately. Usually, this wouldn't have stopped me but the promise I made to him earlier did.

"Now turn back around so I can finish what I started."

****

My last bit of energy all but evaporated once we entered my hotel room. The day had been full of variables that Luca and I had tackled together, side by side. As I moved into the room, I felt him lingering in the doorway, unsure.

This was new. Luca's uncertainty was pulling me towards him, the curiosity in me wanting to know why there was a sudden shift between us. My eyes still on him, I slipped off my heels and his jacket and waited for him to speak.

Instead, the room remained deadly silent.

Sighing, he crossed the room and stopped in front of me, the soft light from the lamps bathing his face, reminding me of the first moment we spoke in his house. A lot had happened since then.

"We'll be leaving for Paris in the morning," he told me, his softness disappearing as he slipped into powerful Luca Caruso, businessman.

238

My body reeled for the man that had spent the car ride here with me.

A rush of bravery made me forgetful as I opened my mouth. "Why couldn't you have just come to me years ago, Luca?"

A different life presented itself to me. Luca coming to find me while I lived in New York, asking me on a date like a normal person and we would have gone from there.

Instead of getting an answer, he stared down at me with blunt force, angry that I was asking questions.

"No more questions."

"Okay." I shut down my sadness before it could open. "Can you unzip me out of my dress before you leave, please?"

I turned my back to him and waited for him to touch me. Gently, his hands found the hidden zipper, but he was careful when he pulled the zip down, his hands refusing to touch me.

Touch me.

And he did, his finger gently started its caress at the top of my spine before moving down my back, massaging away my tense muscles. My eyes closed while I shut off my loud thoughts, ignoring them so I could enjoy this moment of pleasure without consequence.

"Did you enjoy today?" he mumbled, as his finger paused on the middle of my spine.

My day? Did I enjoy it? Yes, in parts. Did I enjoy having to lie to everyone? No. What I did enjoy was getting to know Luca, getting to know the way he weakened his control when I needed something from him. The power was tipping between us and my fear of him was fading as it leveled back towards me.

"Yes, thank you," I mumbled, while he stepped closer, dipping his head to my neck that I was already arching, expecting his mouth.

Instead, he spun me around so quickly that my hair hit his chest and gripped the bottom of my back, forcing me to look up at him.

"Damn it," he hissed, before smashing his lips against mine, forcing me backwards slightly. I remained tight in his grasp while his tongue slipped into my mouth without invitation, tasting me, devouring me as he burned in urgency.

A gasp slipped by my mouth when he picked me up, forcing my legs around his waist, he moved me towards the desk to his left. Everything was happening so quickly, his hands cupping my face, then in my hair until they were ripping at my dress, pulling the material up and over my hips.

I could feel him through his trousers, pressed against my core as a grunt of primal satisfaction hissed against my lips.

I pulled away gasping for air and saw Luca was blinded by lust which sent waves of heat to the center of my legs. Lifting my chin with his finger, he forced me to look back at him, to watch as he unraveled his meager control.

Watching him like this, panting, wanting, made my head spin. I was weak as my body accepted him.

If I was stronger, I would have pushed him away and slipped my dress back down, forcing him to heel back to his control but I was desperate to relive the sweet sensations only he could give me. My experience in the world of sex had been insignificant until now, there was no chance I could go back to that.

I needed to see what could happen next.

"Tell me what you want, Olivia," he hissed through gritted teeth.

My heart thumped at the sound of his husky, sex-starved voice.

You.

Now.

Here.

"You have to tell me. I can't take anymore from you," he breathed. With his grip still on my jaw, he moved my face to the side so he could have full access to my neck, paying careful attention to singe me with his chaste kisses and sharp nips.

My brain was chaotic and desperate for my mouth to answer him.

"Tell me. Now."

My eyes closed as he smothered me and still my tongue remained frozen.

"If you don't open that pretty mouth of yours, I'll have to leave, and you won't get what you want from me, you'll suffer."

I would suffer. I knew it. The bed behind him would hold my wanting body with nothing to relieve the warmth between my legs.

"You," I snapped my eyes open. "That's what I want." Breathless, I surprised myself as the words slipped between us.

A shuddery breath slipped by his tight lips as he dropped his hold on my face. Moving his hands down the back of my dress, he placed on gentle kiss on my mouth.

A kiss that signified an end to his softness.

"Do you like this dress?" he demanded from me, as his fingers rested on either side of the material at the bottom of the zip. The temperature in the room peaked when I realized his intentions.

"It's not a favorite." I bit my lip, stopping myself from saying any more.

It was enough of a confirmation for him to tear at it, splitting it from the back, leaving me in nothing but my underwear.

"Black lace," he muttered appreciatively, as he lifted my chin, taking my eyes away from the piles of material floating to his feet.

I was on the edge between lust and desperation when he fixed me with his all-seeing stare. Under his gaze, I was confident, enjoying the emotion on his face while he slipped from my face to my naked breasts.

"Se muoio oggi morirò felice," he murmured. His hands were on me once again as he picked me up, our chests pressing together and walked us towards the bed.

A spark of excitement flew down my spine when we fell onto the sheets, his lips bruising mine once again. My hands pulled his shirt away from his trousers, desperate to touch him, desperate to get this moving.

A groan slipped by his lips when my hands trailed down his stomach, to the firm muscles designed by God Himself. Pushing me onto my back, he began his assault of kisses but didn't start at my neck this time. This time, he went straight for my right breasts, with his hand tweaking my nipple, forcing me headfirst into bliss.

My back arched off the bed as his left hand slid to the band of my underwear, teasing me with the possibility of where I needed him desperately.

Moving quickly, my hands gripped back at his shirt, trying to get the damn thing off so I could see more of him.

"You want this off?" he asked, when he came back to me, his perfect smirk hovering over me.

Shyness painted my cheeks.

"Please."

The groan from his mouth sent waves of pleasure washing over my body but nothing compared to seeing him doing what

I asked, carefully undoing his buttons with deft fingers, bit by bit, revealing his perfectly toned body. In seconds, the shirt was tossed to the bottom of the bed.

We both paused at the same time, our eyes meeting in the dim lighting with the only sounds being that of our shaky breaths. Glorious light glinted from his muscles as he stood before me, waiting for me to make the next move. Luca understood that this had to be on my terms, but I could tell he was struggling to contain himself.

"Do you want these off?" he demanded, gripping the waistband of his suit trousers.

My inner voice taunted me to be brave, to take what I wanted from him, in the same way, he had taken from me.

I nodded.

"Olivia, are you sure?" he whispered, as he hovered over me.

Leaning up, my hair falling over my shoulders, I pressed a hungry kiss to his mouth, gently biting his bottom lip, showing him that this was what I wanted.

"Please."

Pressing his forehead against mine, he dropped his worry like a hot stone and got off the bed, leaving me breathless. There was something so erotic about watching him undress for me, maybe it was the power high or the way his intense eyes followed me, but all I knew was that I wanted more.

Once his trousers dropped, I felt my heart shoot for the stars. Luca's body was pure perfection as the light glinted across his abs. My eyes couldn't focus, they were too busy drinking in every part of him. Defined pecs with a small island of hair in the middle of his chest, tattoo above his right pec, chiseled abs from punishing control, toned calves…the list was endless. Adonis was barely an equal to the man who stood over me.

My lust was burning so brightly now that I was becoming lightheaded, so I moved quickly, ambling up to my knees and looking up at him from under my eyelashes.

"They need to go, too," I was brave, as I asked him to remove his boxer shorts.

"My siren," he whispered, and kissed me, pressing hard against my lips while taking my hands and placing them on the elasticated band of his navy boxers.

Luca's eyes remained firmly on me as I pulled away, watching with anticipation while we slid the material away.

Nerves shot up my spine and panic seized my chest as I took him in. I didn't realize I had frozen until his hand came up to my face, forcing me to look at him.

"You'll stretch don't worry."

Don't worry? Impossible. It was beyond comprehension as nerves began to stifle my lust, trying to smother out the fire, to protect me from his size.

Luca could sense my apprehension but knew what I needed by taking me back into his arms and placing me back onto the bed while slipping his hand quickly into my underwear until his finger reached his prize, my clit. I had dived straight back into pleasure as his touch rocked away my fear. Eyes squeezed shut, my hands gripping onto his forearms, I tried desperately not to lose it.

"Is this for me?" he murmured, as my wetness coated his fingers, dripping down into his hands as my muscles clenched pleasurably, reeling for more.

Everything is.

My breath evaporated into my lungs when he slipped a finger inside of me, forcing me to stretch to him, preparing me. Luca began to move inside of me, placing kisses across my naked chest.

My moans matched the rhythm of his hands until he silenced me with his hungry mouth. Our tongues fought for control, until he ripped away my underwear in one swift pull and my tongue lost. Moving over me, he gently pushed open my legs with his knee, and I let him.

My inhibitions lost.

Around him I was free.

Luca worshipped my body, leaving me with only blind confidence.

"You're covered, aren't you?" he asked, as he pulled away, sweat glistening down his chest.

"Yes," I whispered, but we both knew that he already knew that. After all, he had my medical file. Before my brain could scramble away, to lose itself, he pressed his cock against my entrance, bringing me back to him.

"Fuck, eight years I've wanted you," he whispered, as he took my mouth and bit my bottom lip, sinking his teeth into me.

The pain stung but I didn't care.

"Keep your eyes on me," he growled, as he pulled his mouth away.

Luca moved his hips forward and pressed the tip of his cock further into me, only a touch, but the gasp of pain and ecstasy rolled in one, sent me to dizzying heights.

I moaned and gripped at his forearms as our foreheads met. As breathless as I was, he closed his eyes first, his jaw tense while he moved again.

My fingers itched to grab him, to pull him into me, but my bravery was not there yet. This was going to hurt.

"Stay with me," he whispered, his warning before he thrust into me, pushing through tight muscles as a deep pinching sensation took over. I cried out in pain, my eyes stinging with tears, but he stopped, allowing me to acclimatize to him and to catch my breath.

Breathless, his voice is tight, he asked, "You okay?"

I think he's close. I can see it in his eyes. I did that to him, me.

I whispered my 'yes' before kissing him, begging with my tongue for him to start moving again. Slowly, with deliberation, he pulled back before sliding back into me.

It stung.

I'm in heaven.

This was pure bliss as the pain was forced away by him.

"Shit, you're so tight, Olivia," he groaned in my ear, as I lift my hips to meet him.

All I could hear were my moans and our bodies joining, over and over again. Heat building at an immense rate and I was desperate for release. My hands dug into the bottom of his back, willing him to move faster and he gladly met my demands by slamming into me.

"Luca, please."

Luca froze, his breath shuddering while he stared down at me with his glistening dark eyes.

"Say that again," his voice was raw and husky, as he desperately held on, his orgasm closing in fast. I could feel him building inside of me, moving, and my body stiffened in anticipation.

"Luca, please."

It happened so quickly as he pulled out before slamming back into me. My vision blurred as my orgasm rippled and exploded around him, forcing searing heat from the bottom of my toes up to my chest. My core muscles clenched around him, forcing him to buckle forwards, catching my lips as he groaned out his own release against my swollen mouth.

Shuddering into me, he slipped from my lips to my neck, biting down while he spilled into me. My body hummed delightfully as my muscles began to unfurl, but my breathing struggled to return to normal.

Finally lifting his head from my neck, Luca's forehead was glistening with sweat and he took my head in his hands, pressing tender kisses to my swollen lips. My eyes closed and I felt the exhaustion pull at me, adding weights to my limbs.

"Are you okay?" he whispered, slipping from me, as gentle as he could.

"Yes." I winced, my eyes still closed while he pulled the covers from the bottom of the bed and covered us. The heat of his body lured me into his side before I understood what I was doing.

The last thing I remembered before I slipped into unconsciousness was his hands in my hair as he whispered-

"OL ti amerò sempre, mia rosa, mia spina."

CHAPTER TWENTY-SIX

Luca Caruso

I was bathing in her. My skin was covered in her scent, my hands in her lust, and my heart in her web — she owned me completely now. Olivia's naked body would forever be ingrained into my head. Those beautiful small but perfect-sized breasts with rosebud nipples, her stomach was flat, but she had hips of a woman, her pussy smooth, soft, and perfect — even her long legs turned me on. Everything about her was perfect. If it was not enough to torture myself further, I remembered her moans while she urged us on, blending us together.

I needed her again, but she was sleeping peacefully at my side, her mouth pressed together in the most perfect pout. Even asleep, she was picturesque and elegant, her skin glowing up at me. Closing my eyes to her painful beauty, I focused my attention on the sound of her breathing, slow and even.

Fear was trickling into my system, pushing out my elation at gaining Olivia's trust. My chest felt tight when I looked down at her sleeping face. Olivia was the moon, and I was a mere star ready to burn up and turn to dust.

What would happen if she woke up and realized this had been a mistake? The monster that joined me in my moments of weakness was laughing at me and my fickle plans.

Shit.

I wanted to kiss her, to banish away my dark thoughts, but she needed to sleep. I settled for kissing the top of her head, taking in the scent of her hair. It soothed me for a few seconds, but the tight feeling in my chest returned.

Olivia trusted me.

Did she?

Slowly sitting up to look around the room, I saw the disarray of our clothes that lay scattered, forgotten. Would I be like them once she realized what we had done? The lines that she had blurred when she let me in?

My shaky hands came into focus on my lap, and I froze. This was getting out of hand and I needed to resolve this quickly. Leaning over the side of the bed, I found my phone still in my trouser pockets. The screen lit up, momentarily blinding me until I found the number I needed.

"Sir?" Chen's voice was bright and clear down the line.

Does this man ever sleep?

"We need to leave. How quickly can you get the plane on the runway?" I kept my voice low to not wake Olivia.

"Er, in a few hours sir. Is everything okay?"

No.

"Yes."

"To Paris?" he asked, for clarification from my evasive tone.

"No, change of plans. We'll be returning home."

"Okay, sir. I'll ready the team to move out in two hours."

"Thanks, Chen," I cut off the call and buried my head into my hands.

****

"Olivia," I whispered, gently shaking her. "You need to get up, come on."

Stirring a little, she pulled the covers around her chest and sunk back down into the bed. What I wouldn't give to be able to sleep peacefully by her side right now.

"Come on now," I said a little louder this time, stroking her hair, pushing away curls from her face.

"No," she huffed, "I'm sleeping."

I couldn't help myself as the smirk curled at the edges of my lips. Even half-asleep, she was full of attitude. If I was in the mood, I would have spanked her pert ass before taking her once again, but my urges would have to heel to the building anxiety in my chest.

"We have to go, Olivia. Something's come up. We need to get in the air."

That got her attention as she blinked away her sleep.

"What's wrong?"

Everything.

"Nothing, just some business I need to take care of. We'll have to postpone our trip to Paris," I told her. I moved off away from her before she could realize what had happened only a few hours before, to avoid her telling me that she regretted it all.

"You have time for a shower, but you need to be ready within the hour."

"Okay," her voice was soft and sleepy, as she pulled the sheets around her, pushing away her unruly hair as she tried to force away her exhaustion to look at me.

Moving quickly without a glance back, my feet took me to my room, to the far end where I began stripping off to shower. My chest was tight and unruly anger was lighting up my blood so I did the only thing that I knew would help. I turned the shower to freezing and stood under the cold spray.

In this shower I was safe, frozen in time while the woman I loved realized that she had made a mistake and would try to leave me again. Grief stripped me of my skin, leaving me with nothing but a body of exposed nerves.

Shivering under the powerful spray, I remembered the one time I had tried to visit her in New York. It was the week after I had taken over Slater Law, merging it into my business portfolio. Under the guise of a business meeting with Jackson, Bells, and Dante, I had used the time in hopes of a glimpse of her outside of his office.

Olivia had not disappointed me when she walked in with a female colleague, her demeanor full of authority as she listed her requirements for their first-morning case. Everyone in their shared office space turned to look at her, greeting her with polite hellos and complimenting her outfit choice.

A coffee was thrust into her hands by a man whose suit was ill fitted as he walked her towards her desk, demanding to know if she got his text message the night before.

Olivia was not impressed as she stopped, only four feet away from me while I watched through the ridiculous glass cube of Mr. Bell's office. Mr. Bell was desperately trying to pull my attention back to his proposal, his voice grating on me. I held up my hand, silencing him immediately.

Dante cleared his throat and began to distract Mr. Bells from the real reason I was there.

"Simon, I told you the other night that I'm not interested in-"

Olivia's voice was muffled through the glass, but I could hear her perfectly.

"Just one date, Olivia, come on?"

I didn't like this 'Simon' with his dirty blonde hair, blue eyes, and charming smile. Even with his ill-fitting suit, he was still a threat.

"I don't think it's a good idea. We work together and I'm really not looking to get involved in any messy drama," she replied, then sipped her drink, leaving a faint pink lipstick stain on the white lid.

Simon leaned forward, licking the corner of his lips and my body froze.

Fucker.

"There's no drama here." He held out his hands. "Come on, one date isn't going to hurt and if you're not feeling it, we can just go back to being friends."

Olivia had the good sense to roll her eyes at him before she checked her watch. Eyes wide, she thrust the drink back into his hands as she mumbled about being late.

Simon was left dumbfounded as he watched her leave the room, slowly looking around the office to see if anyone else had witnessed the crash and burn.

It only took him a year to get her on that date and even then, it ended with her brushing him off after a meager thirty minutes.

I am different. I can offer her what they never could.

Coming back to the now, my teeth were chattering in my head as the cold water had completed its job. I was frozen and calm.

****

It was still dark outside while I waited in the hotel foyer for Olivia. The only people occupying the small space were myself, a sleepy hotel receptionist, and Chen. Olivia and her team were on their way down. I had wanted to go to her after my shower but decided it was better for me to pull myself back together before we spoke.

I would apologize for leaving her. Make her understand I needed some space to gather my thoughts.

The elevator pinged and its doors opened. Olivia was barricaded in by Red, Bones, and Rum who nodded at Chen as they moved around her. Even with a few hours' sleep, she was completely breathtaking with stunning brightly lit eyes and glowing skin.

Heat trickled across my skin once again until Red sidestepped, and I saw what she was wearing. Tight black skinny jeans, heels, and somebody else's sweatshirt that dwarfed her frame. It was grey with a small undiscernible white logo on the right breast.

Scolding anger snapped at me.

"Whose is that?" I demanded, as soon as she stopped in front of me.

Olivia blinked before looking down at the sweatshirt she was wearing, confused by my outburst.

"It's mine, sir," Bones announced, as he stopped just behind her right shoulder, protecting her.

Olivia raised an eyebrow my way, fixing me with her observant stare, and waited to see what I would do – testing me.

"I was cold," she told me carefully, her eyes slipping from mine to Chen's who was waiting patiently to move.

Taking a deep breath through my nose, I took her hand and decided that arguing would get us nowhere. After all, we had come so far in a short space of time, and losing it over another man's sweatshirt wasn't worth it.

Even if I had a burning urge to fire Bones for even overstepping this way.

Everyone moved quickly around, and we slipped into the waiting cars outside, but my attention was still purely on her. Without realizing it, my hand had found hers, but she didn't look at me, instead, she focused on staring out of the window.

My eyes focused on her hands, her slender fingers as they were snug against my much larger ones, especially those fingernails that had dug into my back only hours ago. A wave of heat shot down my body as I replayed the event over and over in my head.

Would I ever get another chance? I had to. My body knew hers now and without her, I would be lost, stranded in a sea of lust.

We were moving quickly towards the airport and soon we would be back where I would be more comfortable. My environment would give me the opportunity to claw back some control before she would demand her half of the deal, the whole truth.

Twenty minutes later, I was helping her out of the car into the overly lit airport. The whole time, even when a security officer checked us all over before boarding, she remained pensive at my side. The only time her demeanor changed was when we began boarding.

I watched her shoulders tense when she was greeted by the overly eager air hostess for four in the morning. Sweeping her away, we moved towards the back of the plane where she could rest.

"Do you always fly this way?" she asked me, when she took her seat across from me.

"I do. It's the best way to get around plus I'm too impatient to queue." Even a smile couldn't tempt her from her shell.

Panic flurried in my chest. Maybe she did regret us after all.

Pushing up her long sleeves, she moved a piece of hair from her face and watched as Chen and his team began boarding, taking their usual spots around us.

"And nobody to give you their ticket," she added, as her eyes slid back to me.

I didn't understand why she would bring that up now but there was something in her eyes that told me she was thinking back to that exact moment. The moment that I saw her.

My phone in my jacket pocket rang, pulling us away from one another. Dante flashed up on my phone and I knew I had to answer it before liftoff.

"Dante."

"Luca, have you checked your email?" he was breathless, his voice tight as he tried to suck in air while he spoke. Ice cold shivers shot down my spine – Dante was never worried, never flustered. I gripped my phone tighter.

My eyes slid to Olivia who had accepted a water from the air hostess, still unaware to the panic building in my chest.

"No, I haven't had time. What is it?"

"Ah shit," he hissed. "Black was spotted near your location a few minutes ago."

My body tensed when I looked over to Chen who was checking over his emails, his eyes widening only a fraction as he no doubt read the email that I had missed.

"Spotted by who?"

Olivia was slowly taking the lid off her bottle of water as she watched me. Shit, I should have switched to Italian so she wouldn't worry.

"Airport CCTV. How long until you're in the air?"

"Two minutes."

Dante sighed down the phone, but I didn't share his relief. Getting up from my seat, I moved down the plane and stood by the side of Chen who was waiting for me to finish.

"I'll come to the house when you land. Luca, have you told her yet?"

"No. I'll see you in a few hours," I said. Before Dante could reply, I ended the call and motioned for Chen to move towards the front of the plane.

Chapter Twenty-Seven

Olivia Heart

Luca returned to his seat two minutes later when the air hostess had interrupted his private meeting with Chen, informing him that we needed to take off. Silently, I observed him, noticing that when he was worried or stressed his shoulders would tense forward as if bracing for impact. What impact was heading his way now?

"What's wrong?" I asked, as soon as he sat back down but his attention on his phone once more.

"Nothing you need to worry about," he dismissed me, as he slid the phone back into his pocket.

I buried down into the sweatshirt Bones had kindly offered me and let the soft material soothe me; I was exhausted and running off a few hours' sleep, but our deal remained. Luca would have to start being honest with me now.

"Are you backing out of our deal, Luca? You promised me answers...."

Luca groaned and pressed his head back into the leather seat.

"I haven't forgotten."

"Well then, answer my question. What's wrong?" I asked. Sitting up straighter in my seat I waited patiently for him to look at me.

Look at me.

When he finally did raise his dark eyes my way, he fixed me with a stare of pure determination that made my chest tighten with worry.

"I'm evoking my reward of one full day without having to answer any of your questions, starting from now."

Damn it!

He was smug as he slipped from my grasp once again and even though he was playing dirty, I had expected this. Luca wasn't as hidden as he thought. The panic in his eyes this morning told me he was very worried about me slipping away again. So, I decided to wait, after all, he had a lot more to lose.

"Very well," I replied, and glared at him. "What's the time?"

Luca, without hesitation, answered, "It's four thirty."

"I can wait."

Twenty-four hours was nothing in the grand scheme of things. Luca knew as well as I did that if he broke his promise, it would only be a matter of time before I tried to leave again.

Luca was glaring back at me now as he shared in my thoughts.

"Well," he cleared his throat. "Now we have cleared up the next twenty-four hours, I think it's fair you answer some of my questions."

I sniggered. "I thought you knew everything about me already?"

Luca sighed before pushing his fingers through his hair. "There's plenty I don't know about you, Olivia. Now, stop being difficult, or you'll breach the terms of our deal."

Crossing my arms over my chest, I motioned for him to continue, deciding this wasn't worth picking a fight over. There was far too much to gain from being on my best behavior.

"Your parents, you don't talk about them. Why is that?"

Ice filled my veins and I faltered; my eyes moving from his to the air hostess at the front of the plane who seemed keen on getting Rum's attention as she giggled while serving his coffee.

How long had he wanted to pry into that part of my life?

"It's not something I'm comfortable talking about. They died when I was thirteen and that's all there is to it."

The pity in his eyes was the reason my parents remained locked away in my head, to never be spoken about.

"You were close to your father, that's what your grandfather told me yesterday."

"I was." I nodded while twisting the cap off my water and taking a drink, my mouth suddenly dry. "My aunt told me a few years after they died that they had wanted another child – hoped for a boy. I'm just glad they didn't because at least I have memories of them. They would have had nothing."

It came from my mouth before I could stop it.

Luca nodded to himself, seemingly pleased with my private thoughts that had escaped my loose lips.

"Your grandfather – you don't like him very much?"

"It's not that I don't like him, he's my family after all. I just don't care for the way he dealt with my parents' death."

Liar.

"Ah," Luca breathed, as he sent me a knowing smile. "The man that sold off your parents' assets within weeks of their death. I can see why that would piss you off."

I took in a deep breath and closed my eyes while I tried not to relive in the anger that had burned through my teenage years.

"That bothered me, yes, but the forcing me into therapy was the worst part of it all," I said. Keeping my eyes shut, I listened to the sounds of the plane's engines rumbling, Bones noisily telling Red a joke about a blonde in a bar, and then Luca's sharp intake of breath.

He really didn't know everything.

Opening my eyes back to him, I could see he was at a loss, trying to work out how this information had bypassed him.

"How old were you when you stopped?"

"Oh, it was a year later."

Luca was internally noting this information down in his head and I realized my mistake.

"I'd prefer it if you didn't go snooping into those files Luca," I hissed quietly. "You don't need to know about my fucked up teenage years."

Luca held up his hands in surrender. "I'm not, you have my word. I'm just surprised it wasn't picked up in our searches."

The air hostess stopped by us, her keen brown eyes on Luca when she asked him whether he wanted tea or coffee. It was interesting how he barely registered her presence, already annoyed that we had been interrupted.

After I declined a drink and she left, Luca straightened up and leaned forward towards me, pinning me to my seat.

"About last night, well early hours of this morning."

"What about it?" I whispered quickly, suddenly flushing at the memory of Luca tearing at my dress, leaving it in slithers across the desk.

"Do you regret it?" his steely tone suddenly catching me off guard.

Regret it? Of course, not!

Confused by it? Yes.

I shook my head. "No, I don't regret it."

Shifting further up his seat, he caught my chin with his fingers and made me look at him. My body burned at his touch alone, desperate to close the gap and press my lips against his.

I knew what was happening. My heart could sense it and was already chipping away at its own wall ready to let him all the way in.

"Always in your head," he mused, and he leaned forward but didn't touch my lips. Luca's relief was coming off him in electrifying bursts, his whole body relaxing in front of me.

I wanted to know if this was why he had left so abruptly this morning or why he spent twenty minutes in the shower muttering to himself in Italian. Had the man who had everything under his control start to see himself slip away....

I bit my tongue as I shut down my bubbling thoughts.

"I'm glad you don't regret it Olivia because I would very much like to do it again."

Luca closed the space and caught my lips with his, his tongue forcing an entrance into my mouth and I gave in to his delicious possession. In seconds, I was consumed, burning, desperate, and taken as my tongue joined in the dance.

Luca pulled away with an unsteady breath. "You'll be the death of me, I'm sure of it."

Only a week ago I had wished that was true.

****

Luca was quiet on the way back from the airport but that was fine with me. Running low on sleep, my energy was all but depleted. I just hoped that he would allow me a few hours before he started his twenty-four hours of his rules.

I was granted the small mercy when we pulled up at Luca's sprawling house to find Dante waiting at the door. While Luca slipped out of the door to greet his cousin, I pulled off my sweatshirt that wasn't appropriate for an Italian summer and tried to hand it back to Bones who told me to keep it.

"Ah, Olivia, you're looking lovely as ever. How was the wedding?" Dante grinned with as much charm as one could handle on an early morning and pulled me in for a hug.

Luca, his eyes firmly on us was carefully watching his cousin's hands on my lower back. Under his scrutiny, I pulled back quickly.

"It was lovely, thank you," I answered, trying to keep my eyes off Luca who was eager for the niceties to wrap up so he could talk to his cousin in private.

"Dante, can you wait for me in my office? I'll be five minutes."

Luca grabbed my elbow, steering me into the house and up the stairs without a backward glance.

"What's the rush?" I asked, as we came to the top of the stairs.

"You need to sleep before we can start our day," he told me absentmindedly as we entered the wing to our shared corridor.

Instead of taking the few extra steps towards my room, we stopped at his and he opened the door.

I paused halfway over the threshold. "My room's down there-"

"It's my day, Olivia," he said, turning to face me with a look that required no argument from me. "I want you to sleep in here."

"I should have bartered for more questions," I mumbled, while I looked down at his bed, too tired to argue with him.

"This deal of yours is working out perfectly," he teased. He was far too pleased about getting his own way. Annoyed and tired, I simply glared his way and crossed my arms over my chest.

"I'll come wake you in a few hours," he told me and with a quick kiss to the side of the head, he left and shut the door behind him.

****

Maria was the one who came to wake me a few hours later with bright eyes and an apologetic smile. Luca was still busy with Dante, but wouldn't be much longer, well I think that's what she told me as she rushed to the bathroom with fresh towels in her arms.

"Miss, do you want breakfast?" she asked me, once she reappeared from Luca's bathroom.

"Can I have a tea please? My stomach isn't quite ready for food yet."

"Of, course, Miss, I'll bring it right up."

It was uncomfortable being waited on, Luca lived his life, full of luxuries and people to take care of everything and this was now being extended to me.

As she left me to ponder my thoughts, I walked across the room into Luca's bathroom which was like mine except the shower sat in a large glass cubicle in the middle. It was an ostentatious glass box with touch screen pads on the inside. As I stripped down, I couldn't help but roll my eyes, this shower was perfect if you were an exhibitionist.

Once I was out of the shower, I found that Maria had picked out a few clothing options and left them over Luca's freshly made bed alongside a pot of tea on his dresser. Shaking my head, wrapped up in a fluffy towel, I looked at the summer dresses and realized I really missed wearing my own clothes.

Missed my own underwear that was not picked by someone else.

Was that all I missed? My material possessions? Not the job that I thought I had loved? Not the sort-of friends I had made in New York? All I missed was my freedom to pick and wear my own clothes?

Picking a navy button-up dress with short sleeves, I snatched the rest of my clothes up and angrily got ready. This was all his fault; he had made me realize that my life before him had been monotonous and lonely with work being my distraction from it all.

My life had been nothing but lonely.

By the time he had found me, an hour later, my anger had gone from boiling to simmering, just below the surface of my subconscious.

I didn't want him to see my weakness, too afraid that he would pick up on it and see it as a victory.

Luca grabbed my hand, pulling me up from one of the sun loungers around the pool, and fixed me with a breathtaking smile. Gone was the tension from this morning, only to be replaced with excitement. Dressed in black jeans and a plain white T-shirt, he had gone from firm businessman to Givenchy model.

"Hello to you, too," I replied, hidden from him under a pair of sunglasses that I had found in my room.

"Did you sleep well?" he asked me as his hands, the one with my initial tattooed on it, clasped my hand.

"I did – why are you so happy?" I asked, trying to hide my amusement at his infectious attitude, failing miserably as a smile curled on my lips.

Was this normal? To feel so comfortable by his side...

Luca began to move, pulling me with him. "You'll see, come on the car's waiting."

"Where's Dante?" I asked, while we walked the length of the pool and down the short steps towards the front of the house.

"Gone to meet his latest conquest for the day," he told me, as he made a face of disapproval.

"Oh, you don't approve of his lothario ways?" I teased, as Bones opened up the new bulletproof car for me. Instead of focusing on the new vehicle, I kept my attention on Luca, allowing his mood to affect mine.

"I don't, especially when he barely remembers their names afterwards."

Slipping off my sunglasses, I watched as Chen and Bones entered the car, this time, Bones' bulky body was the one driving. It did not go unnoticed that we would only be leaving the house with two guards today.

Maybe that was the reason for Luca's change in mood?

"Where's everyone else?" I whispered, not wanting to bring Chen's attention who seemed preoccupied with his phone.

"They're back at the house. Where we're going, we don't need them. Don't worry, you're safe with me."

I was not worried. I was relieved at the stretch in my freedom.

"And where are we going?"

Luca's lips curled up slightly. "You and your questions, Miss Heart. Need I remind you that today is -"

"Your day, yeah, yeah, I know," I interrupted sullenly, "I should have picked better questions."

Luca laughed, deep and throaty as it cracked through the car, catching us both off guard and Chen tensed in front of us.

"I'm sure you'll make up for it," he laughed again, which made me flush with confused embarrassment. Crossing my arms over my chest I waited for him to finish.

"Oh, I will," I replied, flicking my hair and fixing him with a glare, letting him know that I was ready to go. My questions were practically listed in chronological order in my head with his name brightly lit above them.

Luca's smile didn't falter, me and my foul mood could not sour his day no matter how much I wanted to. Playing fair when I was losing was never my strong point. Alice used to say I was a sore loser and truthfully, I was - a trait from my mother.

The car moved down the familiar country road and my mind was allowed the time to begin processing the past twenty-four hours. He must have sensed the change in my mood because he pried away my hands from my chest, bringing my right to rest with his on his thigh.

CHAPTER TWENTY-EIGHT

Luca Caruso

Burning curiosity niggled at me when she turned mute and disappeared on me. Lips pressed tightly together she stared out of the window, building up a wall of distance between us once again.

In under twenty-four hours, that distance would grow, stretching until any remnants of our time together would be destroyed by all my dirty little secrets. Any hope of gaining her forgiveness had disappeared the moment we slept together. Olivia would hate me as soon as she stole the truth away from my lips.

The thought took my breath away.

How would I survive without her now?

In our short time together, I had grown comfortable with her company, seeking her out when usually I would be buried in business matters. Olivia was the light in my otherwise dark life.

"I don't understand," she muttered, her voice pulling me out of my thoughts and back into the car.

We were here.

"La casa delle farfalle," I whispered, as I took her hand. "The butterfly house."

Olivia eyes found mine instantly and I saw the confusion melt away into disbelief. Opening my door, I took her with me, bringing her back into the sun and letting her heels touch the car park before dropping her hand.

I watched as she looked around, the place seemingly deserted, and watched carefully as her eyes landed on the building ahead of us. The gothic arched building was all windows at its sides with vegetation, unruly trees, and wildflowers ready to burst through the glass. It stood in the middle of acres and acres of land like a sore thumb, but I had been assured it would be special for Olivia.

"Your aunt told me that as a child, you and your father had a fascination with butterflies."

Had I got this wrong?

Why isn't she saying anything?

I had been alive with excitement at the prospect of bringing her here, showing her that I was not all evil, that there were redeeming qualities within me, but...her silence was deafening.

I squeezed her hand for comfort.

Chen and Bones stepped out of the car, talking in hushed tones as they began eyeing up our surroundings, but I didn't care. My attention was on her.

Finally, she turned to me and the reaction that I saw gutted me, she looked scared as her emerald eyes scanned my face.

Had her aunt set me up to fail?

"Mr. Caruso?"

I hadn't even spotted Leon Jeritila who had slipped out of the front of the building to greet us until he pulled me away from Olivia. My eyes met his briefly, he was short and bald, his uniform a mismatch of bright colors but he was friendly enough with his bright smile.

I dropped my eyes from Olivia to shake his quickly. "Thank you for setting this up for me Mr. Jeritila."

He grinned as he enthusiastically shook my hand back. "No problem at all," he replied. I detected a French accent but could not be certain as he spoke quickly.

Dropping his hand, I took Olivia's and pulled her into me. "This is-"

"Ah Miss Heart! You're one special lady. We have only ever closed the house down once before and that was for the president!"

"You've closed it down, for us?" she asked him with sweet bewilderment, while he grabbed her hand.

"We have. Your boyfriend here has very kindly donated towards the preservation of one of our rarest species- the Macedonian Grayling, in your honor."

Ah Merda! I hadn't expected him to just throw that out there. And boyfriend? What kind of *pathetic* term was that?

"He has?" she asked, and side-eyed me briefly without giving anything away. Pushing her hair away, she was calmer now, less frightened by whatever was troubling her.

"There will be a silver plaque in the reception as a thank you for your donation."

I didn't have to turn to know that Chen and Bones were just as perplexed by the man as I was or how strange their jobs were becoming. Our tour guide's excitement transferred to Olivia who began asking him questions about how many types they had.

I was trailing behind, scratching my head as this butterfly fanatic stole Olivia's attention away from me. Rolling my eyes, I followed them, allowing her the space she needed to get answers to her questions.

We slipped inside to what felt like a large industrial oven. It was dark and humid with little to no air when we entered the reception area.

"My dad bought me all the books when I was a child. We would spend weekends in parks across England in search of them. I'm not sure how many I found in the end."

Olivia's admission to this stranger had me reeling with confusion and anger. Why had she so willingly given this man-child her thoughts when she could barely open those pretty lips to me?

It was time to step in.

Clearing my throat, I took her hand and glared at Mr. Jeritila, but it went unnoticed, without skipping a beat, he continued his rant about how they currently had two hundred species of butterflies in this sauna.

Olivia looked up at me and smiled, her face relaxed as she reassured me that planning this was worth it-

"This is amazing," she whispered while our third wheel said something about keys. "You must think I'm a nerd."

"I don't think. I know," I smirked, as I touched her face, my possessive fingers desperate for more.

"You didn't have to do all of this. We could have come here when there are people around," she whispered, "I wouldn't have run."

Is this why she looks so scared outside?

My eyes widened at what she was inferring. "It wasn't because of that. I wanted you to be able to experience it without other people getting in the way."

"Oh," she murmured. Her cheeks flushed a delicate rosy pink, shaking her head, she looked back up at me. "This must have cost a fortune to organize Luca and-"

"Worth every penny," I cut in then bent down and kissed her, relishing in the softness of her mouth.

Truthfully, it hadn't cost all that much. Twenty thousand to shut the place down for the day seemed reasonable.

Pulling away, she settled her hands on my chest. "I hope you're ready for the time of your life." She grinned at me, her humor glinting freely in her eyes.

Just that look alone was worth standing in this oven.

"Ready to go?" Mr. Jeritila interrupted with an overly enthusiastic grin.

Olivia was the one to take my hand this time as she pulled me to follow the man in miss-matched colors. If I thought the heat was bad here, I was unprepared as we stepped through two large steel doors, bypassing a white net and forced into the man-made wilderness.

"Wow..." she whispered as she looked up. My eyes followed hers and up the arched ceiling where tree branches twisted above us, reaching for the sunlight.

"Impressive, isn't it? The arch allows the sun to access and heat all points of the sanctuary."

Looking ahead, I saw the middle of the floor was taken up by a large pond that was covered in algae and lily pads. There was a pathway on either side, leading you to behind the pond that held a small seating area.

"Why does it smell so sweet?" Olivia asked our tour guide, her eyes scanning the large space for the source of the overly sweetened scent.

"It's all of the nectar plants Miss Heart. We have over forty inside here alone," he told her proudly while picking at a nearby bush, rubbing his fingers across the leaves.

Olivia nodded thoughtfully at his information. As much as I had appreciated his effort of securing this for Olivia and me, he was starting to get on my nerves. My time with Olivia was limited and I did not want to spend it talking about nectar plants.

Olivia did not share my thoughts as she dropped my hand and stepped forward into the room. The only sound now was her heels as she left us both to go peer over the pond.

"Miss Heart," Mr. Jeritila started, as he left me by the door. "Open up your hand like this."

Olivia watched him while he outstretched his hand, palm facing up but paused, unsure by his unusual request.

Cheerily laughing, he moved forward and grabbed her hand. My body lurched me forward, ready to snap his hand from his body until I saw what was happening.

Olivia caught her gasp before she scared the large aqua butterfly that was trying to land on her index finger, its blacked-edged wings fluttering slowly before stopping on the pad of her fingertip.

In girlish surprise, she looked over at me, her eyes bright and full of happiness as she stood there, glowing like the sun.

I was breathless.

Relieved.

I was desperate for her to be in my arms, but I locked my knees, allowing her happiness to continue for a little longer, without me.

"Looks like you've got yourself a Morpho," Jeritila interrupted, scaring the insect away with the mere sound of his gravelly voice.

Olivia wasn't fazed as it flew away, instead, she followed it along the edge of the wall until it landed on a branch that hovered over the pond.

I should buy this place for her.

Yes, that would be romantic right? It would be a place for her to find true happiness and relive some of the happier times in her childhood. I'd have Dante look into it later tonight.

Lost in my thoughts of buying the place that was slowly cooking me alive, I hadn't noticed she had come back to me until her fingers slipped within mine.

"You have something in your hair," she whispered as she bit down on her bottom lip, forcing my attention to her pretty mouth.

Olivia had bit her lip the same way, in the midst of her orgasm.

"And what's in my hair?" I whispered back softly – savoring the gentle caress of her thumb across my hand.

"Polyommatus," she whispered, while peering up at the small insect that was using my hair as its new home. "This is perfect, thank you for bringing me here."

"You're welcome," I had to squeeze the words from my throat before they got stuck.

Mr. Jeritila, finally sensing that I wanted to be alone with Olivia mumbled about checking on something and left through the steel doors.

Pulling her further into the butterfly's enclosure, I helped her across the small pathway, my hand on her lower back the whole time, so that we could sit on the small bench together.

"Was there anybody at the wedding who didn't have loose lips?"

I laughed, scaring off a few butterflies that had settled on the bench arm next to her. "I don't think so. Your family was very welcoming. In fact, your cousin Alice gave me a list of all the things you love."

Olivia turned, the smell of her sweet perfume wafting to my nose and I turned my head to meet her. A heady mix of grief and happiness collided in my chest when she leaned up to touch my face.

"I can't imagine you would need Alice's lists," she told me while tracing her finger from my temple to the bottom of my jaw.

If I wasn't cooking before, I was now, my skin was on fire.

"I don't really," I told her honestly, ignoring my tightening chest. "But I wanted you to see that not everything with me is...complicated."

"I don't understand what's happening here Luca – between us," her voice was for my ears only as she cupped my face, our faces inches apart. Big green eyes pinned me to my seat. "I should hate you; I know that. I also know I can't ask for any answers right now, but can you show me?"

Show her?

Show her that I had loved her for the past eight years without hesitation?

That every waking moment was centered around her?

That now I had her, I was not strong enough to let her go.

My hands were in her hair as I pulled her to me, pressing my lips softly to hers even though I wanted to be forceful. To show her how deep my love for her ran, to show her that she was etched beneath my skin, her name written over and over again across my bones.

Instead, I controlled my tongue as I begged entrance to her mouth, groaning once she opened up for me. Olivia was sweet and perfect as she cupped my face, her touch had me pouring my love into her, hoping she could see the real me.

Begging for her to trust me.

It was the small gasp from her mouth when my hands gripped within her hair that sent me into a lust-filled black hole. In seconds, without removing my lips from her, she was on my lap, my hands skimming across her naked thighs as I sought more.

My cock was rock hard, straining against my jeans while it sought release from her body. Spellbound and lust-sick, I pushed my lips harder against hers while moving her directly on top of me, wanting to feel her.

"Luca," she breathed and tried to pull away, but I bought her mouth right back to mine. Sweat was dripping down my back as our body heats blended but that wouldn't stop me from showing her.

"Not here," she whispered, panic in her voice as she breathlessly pulled away from me.

"Yes, *here*. Focus on me," I demanded, as my hands slipped under her dress, resting on her underwear that would have to go.

"I need to show you, Olivia."

Olivia froze while her eyes stared back into mine, but I was prepared for her hesitation and fear.

"Undo my zip, Olivia."

Still frozen on me, her eyes searched mine for bravery, luckily for her, I had enough for the both of us. Slipping from under her dress, I grabbed her hands and forced them down between us.

"I've got you, okay? It's just you and me," I comforted. I was desperate for her, only seconds away from doing it myself.

Her shaky hands that slipped between us poured petrol on my lust, forcing it to explode around me. As soon as the zip was undone, I whispered against her mouth for her to touch me.

Olivia, the siren to my lust was back as she slowly reached into my boxers, her hand gripping my cock, forcing me to keel into her.

I almost came at her touch.

Instead, I focused on her, my hands slipped back under her dress, slipping her underwear to the side before I pulled her up and hovering above me. Just as her intense gaze met mine, I pulled her down onto me.

Smothering her cry with my lips, I didn't wait for her body to acclimatize to me – we didn't have the time. I lifted her in my arms, willing her to move atop of me, and without hesitation, she did what we needed.

Delicious muscles clenched around me, making it near impossible to hold on much longer. Olivia moaned when her lips slipped away from mine, arching, allowing her hair to spill down her back while she rode me.

A fucking queen.

That's what she was to me.

My lifeline.

Mine.

Mine.

I'm spiraling, unravelling within her and I can feel my orgasm ready to burst through. Olivia pressed her lips back to mine while I gripped her hips, steadying her a beat before slamming her back down to me.

"Ah!" she cried out, as she clenched deliciously around me, her body letting me know she was seconds away.

"Look at me, keep your eyes on me. I want to see you come," I panted, my body slick with sweat as I wrapped my hand around the base of her throat, pulling her down to me.

"You're mine," I hissed through gritted teeth, triggering her orgasm to explode around me. I gasped as mine shot alongside hers, my chest shuddering as I spilled into her.

Fuck.

Pressing my forehead against hers, my lips placed soft kisses against her swollen mouth, thankful for the woman sat on my lap. Pulling away so I could look at her, desperate to see her, I paused when I saw we weren't alone.

Sat on top of her head were five different butterflies, resting in her mussed hair in the perfect halo shape.

"There's something in my hair isn't there?" she asked me, and I found her eyes once again.

"I can't tell you their names, but yes," I laughed, lifting her up off of me so we could both stand. Olivia winced, forcing panic to hit me across my chest but reassured me she was okay with a small smile. Quickly, I zipped myself away so I could help her get dressed.

I found her blushing with several butterflies in her hair as she smoothed down her dress- picture perfect.

"I hope - oh God, you don't think he heard, do you?" she groaned, as she scrunched her eyes shut in embarrassment.

Even her small friends couldn't save her blushes as they flew away.

Grabbing her hand, I helped her into her heels that had slipped under the bench.

"Oh, he most definitely heard us, Olivia," I teased. I couldn't help but grin as I pulled her into my side, carefully letting her use me as support as we walked the small pathway.

Seeing Olivia blush would never get old.

"Would it be rude if we just slipped away?"

I gasped in fake horror. "I think your new best friend would be offended if you didn't say goodbye Miss Heart."

Olivia shoved me playfully and she rolled her eyes. "You relish in my embarrassment."

"A little," I teased, as I held back the net and pushed open the steel doors, eager to be out of this blinding heat. Especially, after our recent activities, I needed to feel the cool air on my skin.

Mr. Jeritila was not waiting in the small reception area as expected, instead, he was outside talking to Chen who had been keeping watch at the door. Chen's frozen eyes caught mine through the glass and I knew he was in butterfly hell.

Olivia sighed with relief and I was almost saddened that I would not be able to tease her further. Still, I would forever have the memory of fucking her in the middle of mother nature's man-made glass box while butterflies landed in her hair.

No man had gone where I had, with her.

My heart could barely contain itself.

I saved Chen from further talks about butterflies and the perfect habitat for them by thanking Mr. Jeritila for our visit and promised that I would bring Olivia back.

This was quickly becoming the best day of my life and I wasn't ready for it to end. We had two stops to go before my time was up and her questions would spill from her wanting mouth.

Five hours left.

Shit.

****

Chen and Bones reserved their judgment once we made it to our second stop. Amongst the tourists, it was a must-go-to spot but to me, this was a part of my country's history.

Café Sicilia was a small café down a narrow street within the city that sold the county's finest ice cream that had tourists queuing to be seated at one of the small black tables in the sunshine.

As soon as our car pulled up outside, we were greeted by a young male shop assistant who was sent by the owner to greet us. It didn't go unnoticed by Olivia that we were accumulating attention when we entered the busy café, people wondering what was so special about us.

The smell of freshly brewed coffee and sweets overwhelmed both of us while we were bought to a small, reserved table by the window. Normally places like this wouldn't be on my radar. I did not care for sweets or masses of people but for her, it was worth listening to a few tourists and their screaming children.

Before Olivia could take her seat, she excused herself to the restroom and it took all my strength to keep seated. Even with Chen at the front and Bones around the back, I knew I would have to start reigning in my need for control, to allow her to move freely now.

After all, she told me earlier, she wouldn't run.

Even if she didn't run, there were still outside influences that could get in the way. I had to get off this dark path of what if's and I caught the attention of a passing waiter. Ordering for us both, I picked a few selections of ice cream that I knew she would like and two espressos.

"I didn't have you down as a sweets person." She smiled while taking the seat next to me, her soft scent soothing me.

"I'm not." I shook my head. "But apparently they have good coffee here."

Olivia nodded before letting her eyes travel around the busy café, taking in the atmosphere while we sat in comfortable silence. Just in front of us, there was a young couple tending to a small boy who was happily shoving pieces of cake into his small mouth.

"I'm dying to ask a million questions," she blurted with flushed cheeks, as she fiddled with her sunglasses.

"I know," I mused.

I can feel it.

Not ready for this to end, I decided to bring out my last option.

"You know, Olivia, I am open to extending the terms of our deal if you are?"

Olivia's eye's brightened at the possibility of getting what she wanted, but the new deal would weigh further in my favor. Any good businessman worth his salt would gain more than his opponent.

"It depends" She fixed me with her skepticism, her lips pouting as she let her thoughts get the better of her.

"I want another twenty-four hours."

Olivia shook her head, ready to crush my proposal without even hearing what I had to offer. Quickly, I took her sunglasses, forcing her to focus on me.

"Twenty-four hours and you can ask me three more questions, right here and now."

"I want five," she demanded, tilting her chin, willing me to argue.

Five? Shit. A lot could change with five questions. If she came in guns blazing, we wouldn't even get to question two. I would lose my time with her and the void would open again, swallowing me whole.

"Olivia, the rules still apply. You can't ask questions that aren't er, fair to our situation."

Olivia pulled her hand from mine and glared right at me. "I've been playing fair this whole time, it's you who hasn't Luca," she admonished me.

Before I could open my mouth to argue, our waiter returned with our order, paying careful attention to Olivia as he asked in broken English if she would like anything else.

"No thank you," she replied. She was as eager for him to leave as I was. As soon as he left, she peered down at the three bowls of ice cream, hazelnut, black cherry and lemon – her favorites.

"This is a prime example of how unfair this is. You know everything about me, right down to my favorite ice cream. Yet, I know so little about you."

"Well, you'll have five more questions to change that."

Angrily picking up her spoon, she stabbed at the hazelnut ice cream, her slim fingers turning white as they gripped the spoon. The itch in my fingers to stop her was hard to ignore. I wanted to pull the anger from her body, remove her barbed wire shell but I remained perfectly still.

"I want five questions with the option to ask them whenever I want" She cocked her chin in defiance as she waited for me to agree.

Nerves pricked at my scalp, but I was desperate. Another day with her like this meant I had more time to show her that I cared, that I wanted nothing but to break into her, to shatter her walls, and plant my feet. I wanted to make it so she couldn't leave.

My nerves would hold.

"Fine," I growled.

Olivia popped a spoonful of ice cream into her mouth, victorious that she had outsmarted me on this round. "Ready for question one?"

No.

"Go on," I told her, as I picked up my drink in hopes of distracting myself enough not to show signs of weakness.

Licking her lips, she bought my attention right back to her mouth. Damn, everything about her turned me on and lit me alight in mere seconds. Rearranging myself discreetly under the table, I waited for her to start.

"Your mother, does she know about me?"

Ice-cold water rushed through my veins as soon as her question slipped between us. Grief gripped its ruthless hands at my throat and began strangling my vocal cords as images of my ma flashed into my consciousness.

"Luca." She touched me, her hand warming the spot in the middle of my bicep. It was enough to free me, to center me back into the busy café.

I cleared my throat. "My ma died a few years ago."

Olivia's eyes pooled with pity as she squeezed my arm with knowing.

"I'm sorry," she told me sincerely.

"Me, too," I breathed, placing the cup that I had been gripping back down onto the table. "I had told her about you a long time ago and she had been nothing but understanding. My ma was a wise woman when it came to these-"

I stopped myself before I said too much.

"Do you have a picture of her?" she asked me, kind enough to ignore my last sentence.

Olivia wanted to get to know me.

Slipping my hand into my pocket, I pulled out my phone, hastily opening the photo application where I skimmed through for the last picture I had of her.

Olivia peered over my shoulder to look at the picture with me. It was of her and I teasing Mateo who had cut a chunk of hair from his fringe.

"She was so beautiful, Luca. Now I know where you got your good looks from." She smiled at me before giving me my space to collect my thoughts.

Olivia was the only person who knew exactly what to say and the relief I felt was palpable. I had never been so willing when it came to talking about their deaths, never wanted to share that part of me, but with her, I'd tell her everything if she asked.

Picking up the spoon from her melting ice cream she scooped up a small morsel of the black cherry flavor before popping it into her mouth. Surprising both of us, she groaned at the taste, her eye's widening a fraction as she caught herself.

"This is so good," she mumbled, while scooping more and holding the spoon out to me, forcing us back into the light.

Smirking, I leaned over and accepted her offering. It was far too sweet for me, but I had to admit, it was not bad. It would be even better smoothed over her body –

"Always in your head." She threw at me with a playful smile. I could not help myself; it had been far too long since I had last kissed her. Surprising her, I grabbed at the front of her dress and pulled her against me, feeling her breasts against my chest as I ensnared her mouth.

The ice cream tasted a lot better now.

CHAPTER TWENTY-NINE

Olivia Heart

W e were supposed to be going somewhere else after the café, but Chen had interrupted us, his glare passing secret messages to Luca that I wasn't privy to as he stormed the small venue. Taking my hand, Luca promised to make it up to me when we were bundled back into the car and taken home.

Today, I had tasted more than freedom since he eased up on the guards and his control. It was as sweet as the ice cream he had ordered me, as intoxicating as the delivery of a mind-blowing orgasm in the middle of a man-made rain forest. My brain was buzzing, high on him and his darkness as I slipped into my bedroom.

The first moment alone in hours.

There were two of him, the man that had taken me and the man that wanted to keep me. I was inexperienced in the world of relationships and love, always pushing it away but this, was it normal to want to be touched by a man you hated? Want to be kissed breathless by him, to give up complete control while resenting him the whole time?

My stomach clenched.

I needed to bring my feet back onto solid ground.

Reaching into my bag for my phone, my fingers slipped by an envelope.

Had Luca left me another gift? Turning the envelope over, I opened it up, eager to see what was inside.

It was Alice and Harry's wedding invitation...squinting at the strange gift, I turned it over.

Olivia Heart,
You deserve to know the truth. He will not give it to you.
Find me here www.intblack.com
Be safe.
- Black.

A hiss of shock fell from my lips before I could stop it. Panic swirled in my head, descending me into a spin while my eyes glared down at the note left by Martinez Black. The man that had sold information to Luca's enemies.

The man that started this.

I looked over my shoulder to the door that separated me from my guards and resisted the urge to give in to my terror and show them what I had found.

They needed to know he had been close.

But he knew the truths I had so desperately tried to pry from Luca...

My body hunkered down, protecting itself from the onslaught of anxiety as I realized this man had been around my family, having slipped by Luca's team, he got to my bag without anyone realizing. If he could get this close, what else was coming?

All I could hear was my own breathing, as I rushed towards the laptop that sat on my desk. My hands numbly tapped the mouse pad to bring the machine alive. Hovering over the laptop, I inputted the web address and hit enter without a second thought.

A bright blue screen blinded me until my eyes desensitized to the light. It was a one-page website that had one word in the middle.

Chat.

I clicked the button and waited.

My fingers trembled as the screen flickered and a small chat window popped up in the left-hand corner. It was just me in the chat, but my name was already showing in the window.

I had been expected.

I looked back to the door with a stomach knotted with fear and impatience. Luca would be furious if he knew what I was doing, but my impulsive tendencies were winning, whispering in my ear that this was the right thing to do.

A small ping bought me right back to my screen and I saw the name Black appear next to mine.

Black: *Miss Heart?*

Scrambling, I picked up the laptop and rushed towards the walk-in wardrobe where I would have more time if I was caught. Already hope for the truth was blooming in my chest as it forced my chest to accommodate the feeling.

I knew this was my only way to get what I needed.

My fingers returned to the keyboard the second my backside hit the carpet.

Heart: *Yes, it's me.*
Black: *We are on a secure site Miss Heart. Mr. Caruso will not know that you are talking to me.*

How does he know my devices are monitored?

Black: *Are you safe?*
Heart: *Yes*

I stared at the screen as a bubble popped up, he was writing back to me and I found myself wringing my hands in frustration. It wasn't quick enough.

Black: *I have all the answers you need Miss Heart. I am not the bad guy in this situation so whatever he has told you, you must not believe it okay? I'm the one trying to protect you here, not him.*

My heart thumped loudly in my ears while I read his message over and over again.
Protect me?
I don't understand.
A wave of sickness rolled through me as the floor beneath my legs started to crumble away. Somebody was lying.

Heart: *You sold information to Luca's enemies. You're the reason I'm trapped here.*

Black: *We do not have much time. It's not true. If you want the truth and your freedom back, try and get out of the house alone. I'll find you. I'll explain it all.*

"Olivia?"

"Shit," I hissed, slamming the screen shut at the sound of Dante's moving voice.

"What are you doing in here?" He grinned down at me from the doorway, wearing his usual leather jacket and boyish smile.

I swallowed noisily. "Er, I was looking at photos from the wedding…that my aunt had emailed over."

Shit, I was a god damn awful liar under pressure. I could hear the tightness across my vocal cords as I squeaked up at him.

Dante, fortunately, didn't think anything of it as he waltzed into the room and dropped to the floor in front of me. The smell of perfume coming from him told me that he had been interrupted mid-date to come here, to see Luca.

Something was happening.

Fingernails dug into my palms as I tried to calm my inner thoughts. "Why are you here?"

Dante rolled his shoulders and cracked his neck, pushing off his stress. "Luca called me over to sort a few business matters. Ever since you came along, he's taken a back seat – it's great, but it means I have to actually do something."

Dante laughed while pushing his hands through his inky colored hair.

"This includes the illegal side of things?"

Dante looked away quickly before coming back to me. "It does."

"Are you also resolving this problem with Black, is that why you're really here?" I asked.

I couldn't help myself – I needed to find proof that the man across from me was also lying before I blindly followed Black's request and went against all the progress I had made so far with Luca.

For the first time since we had met, Dante's eye's clouded darkly, his loyalty to his cousin weighing heavy between us.

"It's getting there," he told me defensively. "Luca is doing everything to protect you while he pins him down. You don't have to think about him anymore."

Liar. I can see it on your face Dante.

"Say Luca gets a hold of Black, what happens then?"

Dante's jaw flexed as he looked across at my expectant face. "He'll do what needs to be done."

I flushed with fear as my eyes stared at the closed laptop between us. The back of my eyes burned as everything around me began to shift. The first moment my eyes saw Luca, I knew there was darkness within him, it had cast its shadow over me, sucking me in but today – he had shown me another side, a softer, kinder side that I gravitated to.

I didn't want to believe he could hurt somebody.

I refused it.

Instead, I began to clamber back up on my feet, ignoring the wobbling in my knees, and left Dante and the laptop on the floor.

"Olivia, are you okay?" he called after me, once I left the wardrobe space.

"I'm fine. I'm going to take a shower," I answered. I hoped he would take the hint and leave.

****

I had spent the first thirty minutes in complete silence with nothing but my reflection to keep me company. I was a walking time bomb, ready to detonate with the slightest push. I could see the stress rolling off my chest as it rose and fell rapidly, could see the way my hands repeatedly clenched at my sides to de-stress, could see the tears of confusion pooling in my eyes.

I was a mess.

Uncontrollable.

Snapping at myself, I rushed to the shower and moved the dial to the cold position. I didn't wait as I stepped into the high-pressurized waterfall, gasping when it hit my heated skin.

Clarity opened up now that my body began to lose its steam, and I tipped my head up to meet the water. Memories of his hands pulling me close while he slipped inside of me forced me to remember our time in The Butterfly House – where he had shown me his love, bathed me in it until it's all I wanted to feel.

Luca was opening up; he was another twenty-four hours away from telling me everything. So why did a few messages from a stranger affect me so greatly?

It shouldn't.

I was overthinking this.

Black wanted to set a trap and use me as the bait.

My heart thanked me for seeing sense and it slowed back to its usual beat. My lungs ached as I sucked in the final few ragged breaths, but I was safe, my safety net had extended just in time.

When I stepped out of the bathroom, I found Luca waiting for me, sitting on the bottom of my bed with his possessive eyes regarding me carefully.

"Dante seems to think you're upset. What's wrong?" he demanded, standing up, his athletic frame towering over me. His eyes softened on me once he took in my silky attire, unbeknownst to him.

Looking up at him, I could feel the heat coming from his body, calling to my cold skin but resisted the urge to move into him.

Luca would know something was wrong.

"I wasn't upset," I lied easily. "Just a little grouchy," I added. I moved around him and froze when I saw the wedding invitation in the middle of the bed.

Had he seen it?

"Does this mean you're too grouchy for a gift?"

My subconscious breathed a sigh of relief while I turned to face him. Luca walked gracefully over to the vanity by the window and picked up a large black envelope.

"I've been thinking," he started, as he took my hand and walked us over towards the bed, my eyes trying to remain on his beautiful face instead of the ivory pressed card in the middle of my bed. "Maybe it's time to ease up a little, after the past few days we have shown one another that we can follow the rules."

Pressing the envelope into my hand, he waited for me to say something. It reminded me of the file he gave me by the pool, the same file that had bundled the life that he had taken so easily.

Barbed wire began to wrap tightly around my skin, protecting me.

"What is it?" I asked him, my eyes seeking him now that his familiar scent cocooned me into his safety net.

"Open it and you'll see."

How could I tell him I was all out of surprises today? Instead, whilst I bit down on my tongue, I turned the envelope over and ripped at its closing. Out fell a single credit card with my name written across the black piece of plastic.

"I don't understand," I flared. "You're giving me what was mine in the first place?!"

"I'm easing up, Olivia, extending the trust that we've built-"

"Oh well, thank you so much," I sneered. I threw the card on the bed and pushed myself up. "Thank you for returning a slither of my freedom back to me Luca. You have honestly outdone yourself."

"I know that, Olivia, that's why I'm giving it you back. I'm trying to say sorry-"

"Sorry for ruining my life?"

My body froze as he jumped up, standing inches away from me. "What's wrong with you? You didn't feel this way earlier," he snapped, as his eyes locked onto me. In two blistering seconds, I was prisoner once again.

"Well?" His arctic tone transported me back to the night I had tried to escape.

"What's wrong with me?" I whispered the question back to myself.

A lot. Everything was wrong with me and it all started with the man across from me.

"Please leave," I told him and stepped back, dropping my eyes from his so I could wither away. Luca ignored my request as he stalked forward, his right hand roughly grabbing my chin and forcing me to look up at him.

"I'm not going anywhere until you tell me what's wrong. Only a few hours ago everything was fine, and now you can't even look at me."

I winced when his grip tightened on my face, but he didn't remove his hand, he continued to demand an answer with his near-black eyes.

"You know what's wrong with me."

My fickle bravery was showing its naivety once again, not caring that it was going to force me headfirst down a dangerous path that ended with Luca's temper.

"I'm trying here, Olivia. Really fucking trying not to lose it so just tell me, open your fucking mouth and tell me what you're thinking before-"

Fire burned in my veins as I bared my teeth. "Before what?"

I was pushing, urging him to lose his temper, so he could consume me in blistering fire. Hoping, his fire would burn me enough that I'd find it in me to hate him again, to not need him to hold me or make love to me.

I needed to burn.

Luca's shoulders tensed above me while he tried to read my face, and his grip tightened, making it impossible to ignore the pain across the bottom of my face. Our eyes connected once again, and he burst.

"Is this what you want?" He moved quickly, dropping his hand from my face as he pushed me against the nearest wall. My spine cracked against the solid surface, forcing me to cry out from the pain until he smothered my mouth with his hand.

"You want me to hurt you, Olivia. I can see it in your eyes. You want me to ruin all the progress we've made so you don't have to feel what's happening between us."

Scrunching my eyes shut, my heart and I hid away from him and his brutal honesty and begged silently for him to do what needed to be done.

Give me the reason to hate you Luca because if you don't, I won't survive this.

Luca dipped his head forward, his hair tickling the side of my face as he lowered his mouth next to my ear. "Is that what you want? You only want pain from me Olivia?"

He removed his hand from my mouth.

Yes.

Everything else was too much.

"I won't do it," he said, and pressed the softest kiss to my temple, leaving me breathless, reeling, and desperate once again.

I fought the urge to open my eyes, but settled on the darkness instead where everything still made sense.

"I know this is confusing for you," he whispered, while rubbing his nose down my cheek, his hands moving to lock my hips firm, "but understand this, no matter how much you try to run away from this, you'll never be able to make me hurt you, ever. You need to accept what's happening – you're only hurting yourself by fighting this."

A sob rippled up my tight throat and slipped between my lips that I had desperately tried to seal shut.

I was still kidnapped.

I'm still a prisoner.

But this was worse because now I knew that I was falling without wings, without a parachute, and right into the arms of a man who was the devil himself. Tortured by his eyes, his lips, his body, and his words, I had all but broke in his arms.

"It's okay," he soothed, while he held me against his chest, his hands in my hair while sobs wracked my body. "I've got you."

My hands gripped his chest desperately as my legs gave out from underneath me and we descended to the ground. Pulling me in, he wrapped his large arms around me, cocooning me in his body warmth and masculine scent where I felt the slow sedation began once again.

"Ask me a question, Olivia," he uttered, while stroking the hair down my back.

I bowed my head against his chest whilst the tears began to slowly fall onto his lap, leaving dark spots of salty water across his crotch.

"No," I denied him.

"You have to ask me, Olivia, so I know you're okay. Ask me a question so our deal still stands."

My questions laid shredded and abandoned at the back of my brain where they deserved to stay. Shying away, I sat hidden beneath his body where for a few moments I could pretend my heart was safe with him.

Where I could pretend that my short conversation with Black hadn't happened.

"Please," his whisper floated to my ears, as he squeezed me tighter, keeping me together while undoing me all at the same time. Even with my mouth begging to open up to him, keeping my silence was the only bit of control I had left, so I remained mute.

Sighing, he loosened his arms around me and shifted underneath me so he could get comfortable, but I stayed glued to him, to my lifeline. Did he realize we had been here once before? Did he remember that the last time he held me like this, he had told me that he took me to protect me?

Now I was not sure that was true. Black had shown his hand and warned me against the man whose heartbeat I could feel against the side of my face.

Steady.

"Don't shut me out now, Olivia, please. I have so much to tell you, to show you. I'll answer all of your questions."

"I don't want to hear it."

He sucked in a breath at the sound of my broken voice, and I felt his muscles seize around me. Gone was the steady beat of his heart and now it was replaced with a violent pounding.

"Listen to me," he demanded, and tried to move back to see my face, but I followed his chest and pinned myself to him. "The decision made to take you wasn't done lightly. It was a last resort in order to protect you, to keep you out of harm's way. My love for you, my...desire for you started this and that's on me."

Love for me?

His love for me?

My head spun but time to process this information was taken away from me as he continued-

"But you cannot hide how you feel anymore. You're scared, you've never done this before. I can feel it every time I'm with you, see it in your eyes when I take your hand-"

His voice dropped to the softest whisper next to my ear. "And when you come for me, your body recognizes mine. Don't you see it, you've already let me in Olivia."

I was too slow to react as he pulled away from me, using his hands to lift me onto his lap and forcing me to look into his eyes.

My tear-filled eyes could just make out the etchings of worry across his face.

Two large hands slipped into my hair, holding me firmly while the silence stretched between us.

I wanted him to kiss me.

"You love me." It wasn't a question this time when the words fell from my lips.

Without missing a beat, he answered me. "I have for a very long time."

Agony stretched out from within him, twisting around his firm limbs while I stared back, muted and confused.

Nobody had ever told me that they had loved me before. Granted there had been no one significant in my twenty-five years of life, so I had nothing to compare to the overwhelming feeling that was blooming in my chest too.

This couldn't be love between us. What we had was tainted, warped to fit the needs of him. Even as I felt myself falling into his trap, I still had enough courage to fight for reality.

"You need to sleep," he sighed, dropping his tortured gaze. "This has been too much. I shouldn't have told you that."

No, you shouldn't have.

The beautiful man below me who's wild, festering love for me had got us to this point where I could barely function was still in complete control.

I have to do something.

My eyes went to the bed where my last slither of hope lay. An invitation to an event of true love. How ironic that it may be my only way out of this.

"You need to leave now." I scrambled up quickly, ignoring the ache in my knees from being bent for so long and I left him on the floor. In one quick move, I had grabbed the invitation and shoved it back into my bag, all while pretending to look for my phone.

Luca was back on his feet by the time I turned around, his features painted with dark curiosity as he watched me flit from one extreme to another.

"What are you doing?" he demanded coldly, while I began dialing the number for the one person who could center me back to earth.

"I'm calling my aunt-"

He panicked and stepped forward, ready to snatch it away from me but I held up my hand.

"Just to check in, Luca, that's all. I need to talk to somebody who isn't you."

He took a step back, strained before deciding it wasn't worth the argument over, my frailty wasn't worth pushing right now.

"Fine, but we have to talk about this. I'll come see you when you're done on the phone."

I shook my head with fierce determination. "No, Luca. I want to be alone. We can talk about this tomorrow, but right now I want to be alone."

Storming away, I left him standing in the middle of the room, dumbfounded and put out before slamming the bathroom door on him and locking it from the inside.

CHAPTER THIRTY

Luca Caruso

An hour alone and all my hard work had shattered, obliterated, and fucking disappeared into finite dust. Again.

Fuck!

Barely sucking in air, I left her room with enough rage to last me a lifetime. My mood didn't improve as I stepped into my office to find Dante waiting. In all our many years of being blood, we both knew what the other needed before a word was uttered, so once my body was in that room with him, he stood up.

"What is it?" he demanded, his voice dropping low, preparing to fight for me already.

"I don't fucking know," I hissed, as I raced forward to my laptop and ripped open the lid. "I don't know what's happened, she was fine an hour ago and now she can barely look at me."

Dante sighed before moving to the drinks caddy. Alcohol wouldn't touch me now, I was too highly strung, but it would give my hands something to do so I allowed him to continue.

My mouse moved to my emails where I could ask my IT guy to send me over the audio file from Olivia's conversation once she was finished.

"Maybe she's just a bit emotional today. You know what women are like, Luca, she probably just needs some space."

Space? She just put a whole solar system between us.

I shook my head. "No that's not it. Olivia was fine, more than fine earlier," I said. I accepted the glass from Dante and threw back the burning cognac before slamming the tumbler down.

"Maybe it was the credit card? I did tell you she wasn't ready for it."

I passed my glass back to him for another. "That started it, but she was already…upset before."

"You think it's this Black thing?" he asked. Dante had been warning me for the past few days about Black and his meddling, but I had put him at a distance, not wanting to disrupt my hard work with Olivia. But now? It was all I could think about.

"Maybe. I don't know." I pinched the bridge of my nose trying to stave off the headache that was quickly incoming. So far, we had done a good job of keeping him out of the conversation, but now I was second-guessing how much she knew.

"Whatever caused this has already been superseded by my stupidity anyway. We're right back at square one."

If my brain was not already in perpetual hell, it forced me to remember the damning request that came from her emerald stare, as she begged me to hurt her because, in her pain, she couldn't understand what was intertwining us together. Olivia lived with misery every day that she could not separate it from happiness – I knew this about her a very long time ago, but being up close and personal had affected me more than it should have.

Dante handed my glass back to me without hesitation. "What did you do?"

"I told her."

He eyed me suspiciously as he sat back down, bracing himself for more of my bad news. "Told her what exactly?"

Bowing my head into my hands, I felt a second wave of embarrassment and regret ripple through my body.

Snatching up the glass, I downed my drink and wiped my mouth with the back of my hand. "I told her that I loved her."

Dante coughed into his glass, spluttering cognac down his tailored jeans.

"The fuck you do that for?" he hissed, his eyes sending sharp daggers into my already frail skin.

I deserved it.

All I could see was her face when I told her the truth. See the confusion warp into pain before settling on ice-cold nothingness. The Olivia that had opened up to me earlier in the day had disappeared before I even had the chance to explain myself.

Fear pushed me to reveal myself too early.

I'd been an idiot.

"I was just trying to make her understand," I snapped back while avoiding the wide eyes of my cousin who would no doubt be making silent plans to lock me away.

"Don't you think she's got enough to deal with without you piling that on her? Shit, Luca. Olivia isn't you; she hasn't known you for eight years."

"Don't fucking start," I growled, feral and cold, my final and only warning slamming him back into his place. Ice wrapped itself around my shoulders as I leaned forward, ready to expel my rage on him if he as much as pushed an inch.

Dante eyed me carefully, swirling his glass while he weighed up his next words. "I told you I would let you know if this was going too far, and this is your first warning Luca."

Before I could bite back, he continued. "Look, you've seen what happens when you give her space, she opens up and you get what you need from her."

I need more.

Want more.

Want it before it disappears completely.

My heart was selfish and undeserving of anything she could possibly give me, that I knew, but it didn't stop me from wanting it. Even as my frail hopes began to shatter, I remembered the happiness in her eyes at The Butterfly House.

I had given her that.

Me.

"I'll give her space," the words rolled from my mouth, but not without pain. "That's what she needs right now," I added. Nodding with determination, I closed my laptop screen and forced control back into my body.

Dante sighed with relief. "She'll come around, Luca, you just have to be patient."

****

I had spent an hour staring at her bedroom door while trying to find the courage to disobey her orders and go to her. My fingers twitched to touch her face, to trace her lips while I apologized for all that I was putting her through, but instead, I backed away and returned to my room.

The smell of her hit my nose, her natural perfume enveloping me as it clung to the air. A groan slipped by, echoing into the large open space as I thought about her sleeping in here.

Regret filled me to the brim at not being able to see her wrapped in my silk sheets, to not have been able to wake her up by placing soft kisses across her collar bone while my hands slipped into her underwear.

I practically bent over at the image of my fingers taking her, her pussy milking my fingers until her toes curled until she cried out in an explosion of bliss. Then I would taste her, drinking every drop while I worshipped her beautiful body.

My cock strained against my jeans, desperate for friction, desperate for her. Even down the hall, she had full control over my body, leaving me empty and desperate.

Moving to the bathroom, I snatched up my toothbrush and angrily brushed my teeth, trying to ignore the humming in my blood as it whispered for more. If only Olivia could see me now, I thought sarcastically. Would she understand that it wasn't her that was prisoner? That it was me.

My sentence was eight years and running.

Consumed by her wasn't a big enough statement. It didn't offer enough of an explanation for what happened that day in the airport, but right now it's all I had.

Tomorrow I will do better. Tomorrow, I would ease up on her and give her the space that she needed. Olivia would see it for herself, that what we had growing between us was worth opening her eyes to.

While I made plans for a new start, there was a soft knock at my bedroom door. My hand froze, toothbrush dangling from my mouth until I heard the second knock.

Olivia.

Rinsing my mouth, I moved from the bathroom to the bedroom, eager to see her until I yanked open the door to face Chen and Bones.

"What is it?" I hissed, pissed that it wasn't her, pissed that they were bothering me so late at night.

Chen glanced down towards Olivia's door before answering me. "Contact has been made, sir."

CHAPTER THIRTY-ONE

Olivia Heart

The weather was beautiful today. Not a single cloud in the baby blue sky while I stretched beneath the canopy where Maria had served me breakfast. I'd ate alone and used the time to pull myself back together, to forget the words uttered from Luca's mouth last night and to remember that his feelings for me were dangerous and not to be trusted.

Sitting quietly with my thoughts, my eyes lazily searched the property and saw only gardeners pruning the property borders, their pretty Italian accents filling my ears with conversation I didn't understand.

My guards were hanging back, stretched across the expansive property now that I had earned Luca's trust, but this didn't afford me an opportunity to relax – they were always there.

Maria suddenly blocked my view as she slid from the left and began collecting my breakfast plates.

"Thank you, Maria," I told her, with a small smile.

"You're very welcome, Miss. Can I get you anything else?" she asked, while expertly holding all three dishes with her right hand.

"No, thank you."

With a curt nod, she moved away from the table and crossed the patio where Luca and she abruptly met. Maria greeted him in their native language while I froze, statue still against the wrought iron chair. Luca shook his head with a small smile before pressing his hand to her arm.

Maria flushed before ducking her head and leaving him.

At least I wasn't the only one suffering his charm.

I was better prepared now that I had slept and eaten.

"Olivia," he greeted curtly, stopping in front of me, sticking his hands into his suit trouser pockets. Today, he was dressed impeccably in a dark navy custom Versace suit that was perfectly tailored to accommodate his rippling muscles under the expensive threads.

"Luca." I tilted my chin up and turned away, letting my eyes focus back on the gardeners who were trimming back the bushes.

"I have a few business matters to attend to, so I won't be around for most of the day."

"Okay," the words were idle and unbothered, and the opposite of how I felt.

Luca moved closer towards me, his shoes clipping at the ground when he stopped in front with just a foot between us. Turning my head, I looked up through my silver-tinted sunglasses expectantly.

His gaze tightened on me. "Chen and Rum are waiting at the front to take you into the city."

"Why?"

307

Fear exploded into my chest as multiple scenarios appeared. Had he had enough of trying with me that he was going to take me back to the police station? Was this a test of his trust?

"So, you can do whatever you want with your day." He shrugged his tense shoulders, but I saw what it was doing to him.

Luca didn't like what he was offering, not one bit. It was there on his face as his jaw hardened, giving away his displeasure at me being away from him with only two guards.

I leapt up at the opportunity, completely forgetting myself for a moment as we stared across at one another. Luca was tortured while I was victorious; the scales tipping back once again.

"I have one condition," he warned me, and held out his hand for me to take, asking me for my forgiveness in the simplest of gesture.

I won't forgive you, Luca, but I'll take your hand to taste freedom.

I placed my hand in his and ignored his sigh of relief.

"What's the condition?"

"That when you come back to me, we will talk. Forget the deal, forget your allowance of questions. Tonight, you can ask me every question you want. Okay?"

Every question?

Was this a trick?

Would Luca really give in this easily? Had my silence scared him straight? My vision blurred for a second with a mix of relief and anxiety at the thought of him opening up his mouth and giving me everything.

"Okay," my whisper mixed with the gentle breeze, and for a second, I was worried he didn't hear me until he nodded.

Tugging me gently, he began to walk me towards the front of the house but without purpose, his feet deliberately slow and cautious.

Luca was struggling with this already.

"Chen has my card so spend what you like, do what you like and when you're tired, he'll bring you home. They have been warned not to interfere and to be as discreet as possible."

"I have my own money," I told him, while he helped me down the small steps, giving allowances for the ridiculous Louis Vuitton's I was wearing.

My money had been sent to an Italian bank account which included my inheritance money, so I didn't need him. If he was really giving me more freedom, he would give me my own money to spend.

"I know," he bit back. "But I want this day to be on me. It's the least I can do."

You want me to remember you are still there.

"Chen also has your phone in case you need to reach me."

We paused a few feet away from Chen and Rum who were standing by the car, waiting to babysit me for a full day. Just the sour look on Chen's face told me enough, he didn't like this, and he didn't think it was a good idea.

I felt a little smug at his small sufferance.

Welcome to my life.

"Olivia." He tugged at my hand, bringing my attention back to him. The sun was shining down on him, perfectly highlighting his inky hair that was still drying from his recent shower.

A. L. Hartwell

"Yes?" I answered. I was distracted, too busy trying to pull myself away from him.

Calculating eyes fixed me to the spot. One minute, he was nervous and reserved, the next he was firm and demanding now that he had to let me go.

"Your promise not to run still stands," he said. It wasn't a question it was a warning.

I rolled my eyes with great satisfaction "I'm aware. You don't have to remind me every time we're together."

He sucked in a sharp breath in anger, but I didn't care. "Don't worry Luca, I'll be your perfect little prisoner. I'll even send you regular updates of my day if you like?"

Luca sniggered, my anger rolling off his back as he dropped my hand. "You know what that's a good idea. I look forward to your updates, Miss Heart."

I opened my mouth to snap at him, but Chen stepped forward. "Miss Heart, shall we get going?"

"Fine," I growled, as I stalked forward towards the car, ignoring Rum who scrambled to open the door for me. Grabbing at the handle, I snatched the door away and slammed it shut.

Keeping them out.

"Assholes"

****

Once Chen slipped into the car, he reeled off multiple rules that I had to follow in order for me to go about my day of shopping and sightseeing. It was the most I had ever heard him speak.

I was not to stray any further than six foot.

310

No talking to strangers.

To not dwell.

To carry my phone with me, at all times

Speaking of the iPhone that was to anchor me to my babysitters, it started pinging in the door pocket, calling to me. Pulling it out, I grimaced when I saw it had a message waiting for me from Luca.

Already I was being told to behave.

Sliding across the screen, the message popped up and caught me completely off guard. I had expected a warning, but instead, a picture of Luca and I decorated the whole of my screen.

It was us on the day of Alice's wedding where I had dragged him next to the water, surrounded by beautiful white flowers, we looked like a couple from a wedding brochure. Luca's hands were cupping my face as he kissed me, my hands gripping onto his suit jacket while I leaned into him.

We looked completely lost in one another.

It felt as though my heart had stopped while I peered down at the snapshot. I remembered the shock I had felt when he crashed his lips to mine, it was exhilarating and terrifying but completely perfect.

Then, I remembered him stopping me, telling me the reason he had tattooed my initial onto his ring finger. Luca would live his whole life without giving himself to another if it was not me.

My stomach dropped as all the harsh realities began to cave in once again. I wasn't naive, I knew that his love for me was dangerous and complicated. Luca's love, if accepted came with the severity of submission.

A lot for anyone to handle.

Another text message came through, breaking me away from losing myself in the confusing emotions seeping into my head.

Luca: *Your aunt sent them to me.*

Of course, she did. I had called her late last night to catch up, but she heard the stress etched in my voice and I had lied to cover my tracks. My story was simple: Luca and I had a fight.

It was true.

I just lied and said it was about work rather than his suffocating obsession.

Tapping the screen, I typed my reply.

Olivia: *Five minutes after that kiss you told me about your ring tattoo.*

The speech bubble popped up instantly and I did not have to wait long for his reply.

Luca: *Even then, I struggled to contain my secrets from you.*

I leaned back into the leather seat and closed my eyes. Rum was flickering through the radio stations, trying to find a station he liked while Chen hissed at him to pick one.

Secrets. I was sick to death of them. They made me feel like an outsider in my own life, simply stuck in limbo as I waited for him and now Black to put me out of my misery.

Olivia: *Now, it's ironic that your secrets are keeping me from you.*

Not bothering to wait for a reply, I angrily shoved the phone back into the door pocket where I would not have to deal with him anymore.

****

Palermo was probably the most beautiful city I had ever had the pleasure of stepping into. As I stepped away from the car, into its beating heart, my breath stuck in my throat when my eyes drank in every magnificent detail the city offered.

The city was a crossroads between ancient history and the twenty-first century, indulging in the eclectic mix of gothic palaces, byzantine mosaics, and Saracen arches. The narrow streets afforded my eyes with the beauty of modern extensions of the 21st century, with mouthwatering restaurants and high-end boutiques.

Lost in the exciting buzz of the moving city, for a few seconds, my soul had the chance to drink in the luxuries my eyes afforded it and breathe.

"Miss Heart, we should move on," Chen interrupted, he touched my elbow, gently guiding me through a small market with my phone in his hand.

I didn't have a plan, but I felt the urge to explore.

My eyes were greedy as they took in all the details of opus sectile tiles beneath my feet, silently wondering how they had stayed so immaculate after all these years of being walked on.

"We're here," I heard the loud gravelly voice of Rum, who was talking into his headpiece behind me, slamming me right back into my reality.

I pulled away from Chen and stopped. "Who are you talking to?" I demanded while pointing to his ear.

"Mr. Caruso," he told me, his eyes going from mine to Chen in a single beat.

"Of course," I muttered angrily to myself, before leaving them both to walk up ahead.

It was strange, but nobody else seemed to notice the two men dressed in black suits, under the blistering summer heat following behind me. Or maybe, they did not care to notice. Either way, it suited me perfectly to blend in with the people of Palermo where I was no different to them.

Where my life had a shred of normalcy.

"Miss Heart, we will begin our pull back now" Chen came up from behind and joined in my step. Dark, beady eyes scanned the streets ahead of us as he awaited my reply.

"Okay"

"Here's your phone," he said, gritting his teeth while he held out the device. Conversation clearly wasn't his strong suit "If you need us just raise up your hand and we'll get you."

I won't need you.

I took the phone from him "Thanks, Chen."

Chen nodded before falling back and leaving me to continue my walk past a boutique that sold custom-made jewelry. Their specialty: engagement rings if I understood the vinyl sticker of the happy couple on the door.

Rolling my eyes at their wide-open smiles, I pushed on, desperately trying to keep my attention focused on anything other than Luca. I had the urge to cross the busy street full of fast cars and moving so carefully, I teetered across the street where a row of designer boutiques glinted with open doors.

Lazily, my eyes skimmed their windows, my interests had never been in clothes or fashion. I had been too busy studying for the bar exam to keep up to date with who was wearing what and the latest fads. Even now, as I walked around wearing head to toe expensive garments, I could not tell you what designer dress hugged my body.

My interest was pulled away by a boutique up ahead with gold mannequins dressed in beautiful black lace bodysuits and emerald green corsets. Smugly, I moved forward, knowing that the two men tailing me would no doubt feel uncomfortable at my first stop.

Just as I reached the door, I spotted Chen in my peripheral vision with his hand out to stop me.

"Miss Heart, we will be out here while you, er shop," he told me, whilst he eyed the mannequins behind me.

"Perfect. Just try not to hover around the door. We don't want the locals thinking you're a creep," I remarked, and with a smug smile, I opened up the glass door and slipped inside.

The air conditioning was the first to greet me as my heels touched the blood red carpeted floor. The boutique was the gentlest of pinks with accents of gold, forcing me to be enveloped in a soft femineity.

"Good afternoon, miss, and welcome to Rosa Aperta," the shop assistant greeted in English from behind the counter that was a large white floating cloud with pink lights shining brightly underneath.

"Good afternoon," I replied, as I browsed the racks of lingerie, blushing at the deep purple open cut bras that glinted mischievously up at me.

"Is there anything I can help you with, miss?"

I bit my lip as my fingers traced a pair of cotton panties with lace edges.

"I'm looking for…comfortable lingerie."

I was looking for anything that hadn't been picked by somebody else. I would start with my underwear and once the day was over, I would have clothes that were my choice.

Small victories.

The blonde with icy blue eyes and a dainty body floated from behind the counter to help me, her painted pink nails working quickly as she began piling choices into her thin arms.

"Comfortable but sexy!" She smiled while I admired her choices of color and size.

"I'm not too worried about the sexy," I mumbled sullenly.

"You shouldn't be, just look at you. There isn't a piece in this shop that wouldn't suit your body."

A blush burned my cheeks before I could stop it, but she waved me away with a confident smirk.

"You'll see," she told me. "Come on, the dressing rooms are just through here."

We slipped through another glass door to a long corridor that held five changing rooms. Each door was decorated with a pink rose with gold edging. I was placed in the middle one and passed the pile of lingerie before I'd had a chance to blink.

"Just call if you need anything." She grinned before floating away, leaving me to stare at my first task.

Slipping out of my heels, my feet sighed with relief as I fingered through the sets she had picked, looking for the easiest to put on that didn't come with a thousand straps and clips.

Just as my hand reached for a baby blue bustier, the white door behind me opened and I panicked, ready to tell the person that the room was occupied until a hand slapped over my mouth.

I was pushed back, my head cracking against the glass as I faced my attacker. My scream didn't even have a chance to leave my throat because he pinned me against the mirror with wide eyes with sweat covering his forehead.

Dark tousled hair slick with sweat hid his eyes from me until he pushed it away. My attacker was familiar, around the same age as me, his eyes green and dark with stubble across his sharp jaw.

Sweat tickled my palms as he turned and kicked the door behind him while his grip on my face remained.

"Olivia, it's me. It's Black. Please don't scream, okay? We don't have much time."

His eyes darted widely in their sockets as he begged with me silently, but he didn't have to worry. My silence was guaranteed because terror unfoiled from my gut, poisoning any power that I thought I would have.

"I'm sorry I had to do this," he hissed quietly with an English accent, his breath touching my eyelashes now that he was closer. "I saw an opportunity and took it."

My knees wobbled, threatening to buckle, but he didn't notice.

"I'm going to take my hand away, okay? Don't scream," he warned me, before he hesitantly took a step back and removed his hand from my mouth.

My mouth was bruised but I didn't care.

I was scared, silently begging Chen and Rum to decide they had enough of waiting for me.

"Good. I'm not going to hurt you, okay? We have about fifteen minutes before those idiots out there start getting antsy.

Olivia, I don't know what you've been told about me, but I'm not the bad guy."

I flinched away as he held out his hand to me. "Don't touch me!"

Black nodded quickly while swiping his hand across his damp forehead. "I won't. I've been trying to get to you for weeks now, every time I got close, he swept you away. Are you okay? Did he hurt you?"

Black's voice turned to melting liquid in my ears at the strange worry falling from his flushed lips.

"I-I'm fine."

Blank.

My brain started and stalled again.

"Do you know who I am?" he asked, as he pulled off his camo jacket, revealing tattooed sleeves but my brain couldn't focus on the details of his inked skin. Jittery nerves started to take over when I realized I was going to be taken again.

"Black." I flinched at the terror in my own voice, hating myself for not moving – for not fighting.

Black scrunched his eyes in confusion. "Yes, my name's Steven Black. Look-" He reached into his pocket and pulled out a slim brown wallet. Flipping it open, he revealed his English driving license.

Steven Black.

"Olivia, he's concocted this story, painting me as the bad guy, but I'm not. I was a part of your security detail. I was the person that monitored your technologies – I did not sell information to anyone."

My world froze and cracked apart as an old memory flooded forward. I was sat at my desk, pissed at my computer screen because my emails had frozen until IT support was bought up to help me. Unlike the others, he wasn't built like a marine, he was slim and athletic as he drifted over to my desk.

"I worked for Slater Law and monitored you from there. We met a few times."

"Yes, yes. I remember you."

Relief spread across his face and he threw his head back with silent victory. In the short time his eyes were off me, I searched the dressing room for my phone, for a way out.

"The day before you were taken, I had told Caruso that I was going to tell you what he had been doing, what we all had been doing," he dropped his voice, as he focused on me. "I was reckless and naive, it only forced him to speed up the process."

It could have been stopped. I would still be in New York if Black had got to me in time.

"What process?" I squeaked while leaning forward, my fingertips suddenly itching to shake him so all the truth could tumble out.

Running a tattooed hand through his hair, he fixed me with a firm stare. "Of taking you, he was always going to take you."

My chest filled with ragged inhales as the tiny white walls around me began to close in. Brick by brick, my world came tumbling down. Dark spots dotted my vision, making it impossible for me to see as images of myself being taken in the middle of the night slammed into me.

"Olivia!" he hissed. "Shit, it's okay, breathe, just breathe!" His clammy hands were all over me, pulling me into his shirt that smelled of mint and smoke.

"We don't have time for this. Please, keep it together and I promise you I'll get you out of this."

A lifeline was thrown in the murky water, but my fingers barely moved. I was drowning, slipping further underwater.

Black pulled me back and shook me hard. My bones cracked and jolted in their joints bringing sharp zaps of pain.

In the pain, my fingers gripped the lifeline.

I sucked in air and pushed him away, scrambling to the wall and used the cool surface to bring me back down to earth.

"He-he told me he was keeping me safe from you."

"He was covering his tracks. If you had taken my information to the police, it would have ruined his plans. Caruso is a sick bastard, Olivia," he spat harshly, the name distasteful on his tongue. Black reached into his jeans pocket and pulled out his phone while angrily tapping the screen.

"Just listen," he told me, as he held the phone between us.

The phone crackled and then I heard his voice.

Luca: *What?*
Black: *I'm fucking done Caruso. I'm not doing this anymore-*
Luca: *You're not done until I say you are-*

My stomach dropped at his cold voice, full of threats and promises.

Black: *You can't fucking do this to her, she doesn't deserve this sick charade. Leave her alone and I won't tell her-*
Luca: *You know what happens if you open your mouth Black, so you have two options, your family or you get on with it.*
Black: *Don't you fucking dare-*
Luca: *Make a decision.*

The line went dead, and Black pulled the phone away, letting his eyes fall on me as he gauged my reaction.

"He moved you to New York because he wanted to distance you from the people that cared. Luca wanted you to be completely isolated so it would be easier when he took you. For eight years, your life was all about calculated possession."

Possession.

My tormented struggle now came with a reason I couldn't swallow.

No, I was choking, gagging on the evil that Luca had committed against me.

Luca had loved me, used my body, manipulated me into giving him chance after chance, proving himself as an angel when he was Satan himself.

"He was never going to let me go," I whispered, while remembering The Glass Butterfly House.

Was he trying to tell me then?

"He wasn't," Black confirmed. "There's a lot more that you don't know, Olivia, and right now we don't have time. We only have a short window to get you out of this mess."

"I don't understand. How are you going to get me out of this?"

Before he could answer me, my phone buzzed loudly underneath the piles of lingerie on the cloud-like chair. We both stared down at the intrusion, neither of us making a move.

Black sighed. "Answer it, they're checking to see what's taking so long."

He leaned down and with deft fingers, pushed away the silky garments until he found the phone.

"Act natural," he demanded, while holding the phone out to me.

My hands were shaking, but I took it, letting autopilot kick in.

"Hello."

Black glared at me in frustration, my voice was tight and high – the opposite of natural.

"Miss Heart, is everything okay?" it was Rum, his deep voice penetrating my eardrum.

"Yes- sorry! I'll be out in a few"

Black turned around in the small room, no doubt hiding his frustration for my terrible acting which only made me more nervous. Before I could give myself away anymore, I ended the call.

Turning to face me, he swiped his sweaty brow. "Do you have your passport?"

"No, it's back at-"

"Shit - Listen, you're going to have to go back and get it."

A squeak fell from my mouth, but he was there, slapping his hand back over it while begging me with his eyes to be quiet.

"It's over for him now, Olivia. You know the truth. Go back and get your passport. I'll wait for you outside the gates."

I yanked my head away from him, anger burnishing in the mix of my fear. "Just like that? He's not going to let me go. There's only two of us!"

"There's a file with your name on it, Olivia. If he doesn't let you go, it will be sent to the police back in England. It has everything from the start of his stalking to your kidnap - we'll make sure he has no choice just like you didn't."

CHAPTER THIRTY-TWO

Olivia Heart

My brain had been restarted with autopilot now taking over. Chen was the first to greet me as I stepped back into the boutique. Feigning sickness, I demanded to go back, ignoring the strange look of the shop assistant and allowing Rum to guide me away.

Instead of enjoying the beautiful opulence of my walk back to the car, I had focused on walking, ensuring my weakened legs didn't give up on me. The streets were busier now, but my ears only heard my heels touching the ground. I was still stuck in a silent panic attack.

"Miss Heart, do you need me to help you?" Rum asked with a worried smile, as he stepped to my side, holding out his bulky arm.

A spark of anger flared at the back of my skull and I focused on it, gently blowing on the naked flame in hopes it would help me.

"No, thank you," I mumbled, while stepping off the pavement to cross the street.

Chen was a few feet in front, guiding us back to the car while he spoke quickly into his earpiece.

Was Black far behind? Trailing us to make sure I would make my destination? Would he keep his promise?

Forcing away the tears, I lifted my chin and dragged in a deep, shaky breath to my oxygen-starved lungs.

One task.

That is all it would take.

All I had to do was get through the next hour and survive.

CHAPTER THIRTY-THREE

Luca Caruso

D ante had stepped into my third meeting of the day without apology, his hand clutching his phone with enough force that the screen had cracked. My focus was instantly pulled away from the men who wanted to use my shipping company, and on my cousin, who was barely containing himself.

Excusing myself, I told them I would be in touch with merely a glance back.

I had the good sense to ignore my own fear that came from his silence as we slipped out of the warehouse and into the side street.

"Luca, we need to get back to the house," Dante told me, as he ripped off his leather jacket and threw it into the back seat of the car.

"Where's Bones and Rum?"

Dante thrust his phone in front of my face. Suddenly, the collar around my neck felt like a noose as I stared down at the text message from Chen.

"Fuck."

"Exactly," Dante agreed, snatching the phone away from me.

Fear and stress, a heady mix I wasn't used to feeling hit me squarely across the chest and I looked around at his expectant eyes. Even though we had planned and prepared, we hadn't expected it so soon.

"Is she safe?" I asked, as we slipped into the car with Dante taking the driver's seat.

"Chen confirmed five minutes ago that she was, they're taking her back to the house now."

The urge to punch something grew strong but I batted it away. Losing myself in rage wasn't going to help the situation. Dante side eyed me, but didn't say a word, instead, he put his foot down and did what I needed him to do.

I needed to see her.

Desperately.

So much, that it fucking hurt.

But I also wanted to hurt her, to mark her, to push her to the edge of sanity where we could meet, and she would see the consequences of her actions.

The taste of revenge would be sweet for us both.

Addicted, that's what I am.

"Wait until you hear what she has to say, don't go in all hot-headed because you don't know the choice she'll make."

I pinched the bridge of my nose, trying to ignore my urge to snap at him to shut the fuck up and put his foot down. Dante had been there to prop me up when I could barely stand, had been there when nobody else understood the savagery that ran through my veins.

I knew what choice she'd make.

I had seen it in her eyes last night when she shut me out.

"Per favore, dalle un'opportunità, Luca."

"I've given her plenty of chances. I'm all out of patience."

****

What was it about her and time? Why did the minutes tick back painfully slow whenever I needed to see her?

My feet paced down the edge of the pool as I waited for the familiar sound of a car pulling up the drive, to hear tires crunching the ground beneath them. In my hand, I clutched a glass of alcohol that Dante had forced upon me, urging me to calm down but it was no use.

I could not relax.

Too many eyes on me – waiting for the next step.

"How fucking long?" The betrayed part of me snapped at Dante who was sat on the same bench Olivia had this morning.

"A minute, sir," Bones replied, as appeared from the house, wiping down his hands on his trousers.

I bristled. A minute was too long.

A small mercy was thrown my way when the familiar sound of the front gates swinging open caught my attention. Dante stood up and caught me before I could go to her, his hand pushing back against my chest.

Shoving off his hand, I took a step back and nodded, my eyes tight across the pool as I waited for them. My wait didn't last very long because she was the first to climb the small steps that led up to us, her long hair hiding her face as she focused on the steps in her heels.

My knees twitched for my legs to move to her, but I remained perfectly still while I waited for her to see me standing there.

Once her emerald glare landed on me; I would know what I was dealing with and how to defend myself.

Olivia's eyes found me as soon as she stood level to me across the pool.

Our eyes connected and she froze, her face told me everything I needed to know. Olivia didn't have to open her mouth to tell me that she had my secrets, it was written across her sealed lips.

Raw betrayal stripped me of my skin, leaving me nothing but open nerves.

My anger flared.

Dante moved quickly to secure me to my side of the pool. Chen's long fingers snaked around Olivia's wrists while he pinned her back to him, ignoring the thrashing of her arms as cried for him to let go.

"Careful now," he uttered in my ear, his voice of reason slipping by the rational part of my brain and right to the monster that sat lingering in its dark corner.

"Bring her here," I demanded to Chen. "Now."

Chen did as he was told and did it quickly as he yanked her by the top of her arm and dragged her across the side of the pool. Olivia didn't fight him this time, she was too busy looking around, her wild eyes scanning for her way out.

"Olivia, do you have something to tell me?" I growled, once she was placed in front of us.

Olivia ducked her head, hiding from me. My spine locked into attack mode, but I planted my feet, not allowing myself to reach over and grab her until she answered me.

Rum and Chen took a step back from her and waited. Dante kept himself at my side, protecting both of us as he stood carefully watching.

"Open your fucking mouth."

Olivia flinched. "You're all sick," she whispered, before finding her voice, her shoulders straightening when she found her spark of courage. "Especially you – you're the sickest of them all!"

Dragging in a breath, she continued to wage war with her tongue. "You were never going to tell me the truth, you were going to keep me locked away here forever, weren't you, like some prized doll?"

Dante slammed his arm across my chest as I flinched to move. Olivia's hatred was spilling out between us and poisoning the air. My mood, self-sinking into the abyss of poison only spurred me on.

"No." The monster smirked, even with its back against a wall.

"Liar!!" she lunged forward to strike me, but Rum caught her hand and pulled her back.

"Miss Heart, calm down," he tried to soothe her, but she was past the point of resolve, she wanted me to suffer. That I could see in her wild eyes through the curtain of her long hair.

"I won't," she snapped back, trying to wrestle herself free. "Not until you let me go. I'm done with this fucked up game - it's over, okay? I know everything!"

Over?

How could it be over? We'd barely gotten started.

"I know about you all. I know about your families, your real names - everything!"

"What do you plan on doing with that information?" I sneered, while I shoved Dante away, my hands now into my pockets, resisting the urge to grab her.

The look she gave me could melt the ice from the alps. Every soft look she had ever given me, all but disappeared, the first smile she sent my way, the excitement in her eyes at The Butterfly house…. all of it, gone.

I laughed, vicious and cold at her pathetic attempt to get away. "You think Black can get you out of this, don't you?"

The pathetic excuse of a man who could not leave well alone. Oh, she was banking on him to protect her, to save her from me?

It was laughable.

Olivia's eyes widened in fear as soon as his name slipped from my lips and her hand twitched at her side, ready to make a run for it.

The monster inside grinned deviously at her fear, devouring it in large bites.

"If I don't leave here, the file that he has on you goes out to every country's judicial system," she said, her chin tilted as she tried to battle her tears, but she was weak.

Broken.

Thanks to me.

"Interesting."

Moving forward, I closed the gap between Olivia and me, paying extra attention to her chest that was rising and falling as panic began to consume her.

I felt my shoulders relax for a brief second.

I was still in control.

"And what does this file include, Olivia?" I asked. I reached out my hand and softly moved a piece of hair that was in the way of her left eye. Turning her head away from me, she recoiled in disgust.

Gone was the affection she felt for me, and now I was right back to square one as her captor.

"Everything," she whispered, "it has everything."

"I'm not worried," I told her honestly, taking a step back, a smirk across my lips as she whipped her head up to look at me.

"How can you be so cruel?" She moved towards me. "Do you not understand how wrong this is? You were manipulating me this whole time, getting into my head, promising me-"

Her words stopped as she fought back her urge to cry and with a shaky hand, she touched the bottom of her throat. Having witnessed her panic before and knew the signs of when it was becoming unbearable, it would only be fair that she would have to suffer it alone now.

Olivia's eye's slid from mine to the two people joining us, her mouth falling open at our newest guest. Olivia moved forward as she tried to slip through Dante and me to get to Black, but my hand around her arm kept her at my side.

Black was bruised and bloody, the front of his shirt split and covered in his blood from a recent scuffle with Rum who had taken great pleasure in capturing our tyrant.

"No," the barely-there whisper fell from her pretty mouth, as she watched him be marched to us and then forced to bow at our feet.

"Nice of you to join us, Black," I greeted, with great pleasure.

Chapter Thirty-Four

Olivia Heart

My eyes burned with tears as Black was forced to kneel in front of Luca. Agony stretched from my soul when my eyes caught sight of his injuries. There was blood pouring from the side of his head, a finger on his left hand broke and at an odd angle, and then there were his wrists which were bound behind his back so tight his skin had turned white.

"Let him go!" I lurched forward and scrambled to help him, but Dante and Luca pulled me back, forcing me to stand between them.

"I'm sorry, Olivia," he coughed, spluttering blood across the front of my shoes.

"Look what you've done, Olivia," Luca whispered in my ear, his mouth brushing against my skin.

Look what you've done.

My eyes focused on the splatter of blood drying on my heels. All because of me. My heart ached and screamed for it all to stop.

"Please, let him standup," I begged. I was crying, my tears stinging my eyes from the mix with mascara.

No man deserved to kneel like a dog.

"He stays on the floor," he spat. Luca shoved me harshly into Dante's arm who wrapped his arms around me and pulled me in.

I could barely breathe.

"Olivia, please," he whispered in my ear, "Please don't make this any worse for yourself."

My eyes glued themselves to Luca's back as he bent down to face Black.

"The wedding invitation was a nice touch."

"Fuck you, Caruso," Black spat to his side; his disgust evident as he snarled, showing his bloody teeth at Luca.

"The website – not so much. Did you really think we wouldn't know?" he growled. Luca looked over his shoulder to fix me with his glare, punishing me for going against him and promising to make me pay for it.

I shivered into Dante's arms while the bones in my legs began to liquefy.

"You can't do this to her," he coughed, his next words wheezy and tight. "What you're doing is sick. You can't make her love you."

Luca shot up, keeping his back to me, but I knew from the way his shoulders tensed that he was barely containing himself. Rage and darkness lived in him, swallowing us all up in his dark cloud.

"Luca, please don't hurt him," I begged, as Black bowed his head, his eyes scrunched shut from the pain of his injuries.

Luca turned so quickly that my eyes barely registered him as he yanked me forward by the back of my hair. My scalp cried out in pain while my hands desperately tried to pull him away, but it was no use.

None of my guards came to my defense, instead, they all watched on with the blank alert stares I had seen many times before.

"Why shouldn't I hurt him? What makes him so fucking special that you would choose him over me?"

Luca's hand was so tight in the back of my hair that my chin tilted up, forcing me to look at him.

"We were finally getting somewhere, Olivia, but you chose him instead, even when I had promised to tell you everything."

"Luca," Dante hissed from behind.

Luca's eyes were full of demons and fire as he held me to him. Dante no longer existed. "You're sick Luca, you need help," I cried out, as his knuckles squeezed tighter at my roots.

"You can't keep me like this anymore. I won't tell anyone about any of this. Please just let me go," my voice was strained, as I pleaded with him for my life, begged openly with my eyes for him to see sense.

"You don't want that," he snapped back, before letting go of me. My right foot hit the back of my left and I tumbled down, my hands slamming against the hard tile as I fell in front of Black.

Blood and fear hit my nostrils and my pain was soon forgotten.

I outstretched my hand and took his, pleading with him to look at me. If it was the last thing, I would ever do, I'd make sure he knew how grateful I was for him attempting to free me.

Luca's sharp intake of breath at our hands touching did not stop me. Nothing would stop me from doing this.

"They've threatened my family," Black whispered, looking up at me.

"Wellesby Drive," Luca snarled from behind.

Cold shivers touched us both as we slowly realized we were firmly planted in Luca's trap with no way out.

"Olivia, stand up," Luca demanded, but I pushed his ice-cold voice away and focused on Black who was barely conscious.

"I'm so sorry," I whispered, tugging on his blood-soaked hands with desperation.

Black bowed his head. "It's me that should be sorry. This is all my fault -"

"STAND UP NOW!"

I won't.

Ignoring my body's urge to stand, I focused my attention on the floor beneath me, choosing to kneel like a dog rather than submit to a man who was hell-bent on destroying me.

"Pull them up."

Black was the first to be pulled away by Bones and Red, forcing our hands to snap away from one another. Black's weak body was sandwiched between their muscles, holding on to his arms with ease.

Dante and Chen took me, their hands more delicate on my arms but still firm enough to make so I could not move if I wanted to.

Luca stood venomously in the middle, ready to strike at any moment if one of us even spoke out of turn. My fear edged up a nudge when he moved towards me, his dark eyes narrowing in on the blood smears across my hands.

"Do you still want control, Olivia?" he asked me, his voice lower now as it travelled to depths of hell.

I wigged, trying to move away, but Dante hissed in my ear to remain still.

"Please, just-"

"Answer me," he snapped.

"Yes."

Nodding quickly to himself, he moved so that both Black and I could see him, and he could see us. We were pinned and desperate while he stood in full control before us.

"Make a decision. Your freedom or his."

Black lurched forward, spitting blood as he blurted insult after insult towards Luca. Bones reigned him in with disgust, his gnarly scar crinkling as he forced Black back into silence.

Luca was unbothered by him, in fact, he was more interested in gauging my reaction as I swam under a familiar, nauseating panic attack.

The man that had shown me my father's long-lost car, held my hand, reassured me, taking me to the one place I found sanctuary, made love to me when I needed him, he had disappeared.

Instead, I was faced with a monster that saw me as nothing but a possession that he would keep locked away. I was a butterfly and he had taken my wings.

My freedom was never to be redeemed again. I could see it in his eyes as he demanded an answer to his question.

Now I was a believer.

I never had a choice not to be.

"Answer me, Olivia. Your freedom or his?"

EXTRAS

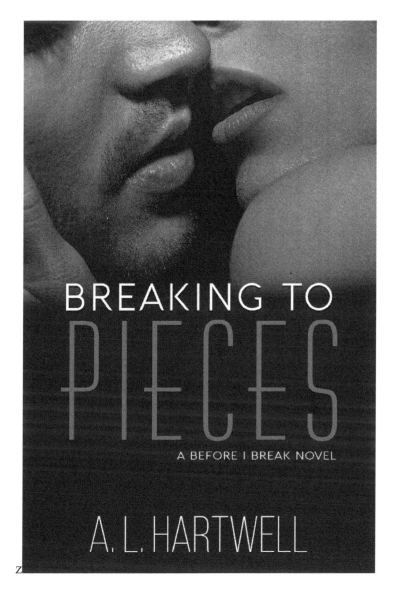

Keep a look out for *Breaking to Pieces*, A Before I Break Novel set to release in Fall 2021.

ABOUT THE AUTHOR

A. L. Hartwell lives in Nottingham, England with her wonderfully patient husband and sassy dog Lyla. From the age of fifteen, as part of an escape, she spent years writing short stories, accumulating them and sharing them online. With a vast taste in genre's, she found herself drawn to the wonderful twisty world of Dark Romance. When she discovered the freedom in writing within this genre, she delved headfirst into writing her first novel, Bending to Break.

When she's not working or spending her time locked away in her writing cave, she's reading, drinking tea or obsessing over her niece and nephew.

A. L. Hartwell

ALSO BY THE AUTHOR

<u>Bending to Break</u>
Breaking to Pieces (Coming Soon!)

ABOUT THE PUBLISHER

Kingston Publishing Company, founded by C.K. Green and Michelle Areaux, is dedicated to providing authors an affordable way to turn their dream into a reality. We publish over 100+ titles annually in multiple formats including print and ebook across all major platforms.

We offer every service you will ever need to take an idea and publish a story. We are here to help authors make it in the industry. We want to provide a positive experience that will keep you coming back to us. Whether you want a traditional publisher who offers all the amenities a publishing company should or an author who prefers to self-publish, but needs additional help – we are here for you.

Now Accepting Manuscripts!

Please send query letter and manuscript to:

submissions@kingstonpublishing.com

Visit our website at

www.kingstonpublishing.com

Printed in Great Britain
by Amazon

67606853R00194